CUTWORK

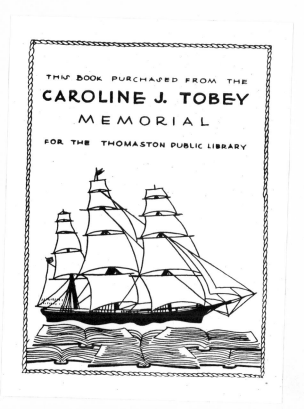

This Large Print Book carries the
Seal of Approval of N.A.V.H.

CUTWORK

Monica Ferris

WHEELER
PUBLISHING

Copyright © 2003 by Mary Monica Kuhfeld.
A Needlecraft Mystery.

Published in 2004 by arrangement with The Berkley Publishing Group, a member of Penguin Group (USA) Inc.

Wheeler Large Print Cozy Mystery.

The text of this Large Print edition is unabridged.
Other aspects of the book may vary from the original edition.

Set in 16 pt. Plantin by Minnie B. Raven.

Printed in the United States on permanent paper.

Library of Congress Cataloging-in-Publication Data

Ferris, Monica.
    Cutwork / Monica Ferris.
        p. cm.
    Originally Published: Waterville, ME : Wheeler Publishing, 2004.
      ISBN 1-58724-665-1 (lg. print : sc : alk. paper)
    A Needlecraft Mystery.
      Subjects: 1. Women detectives — Minnesota — Fiction.
2. Artisans — Crimes against — Fiction.   3. Needlework — Fiction.   4. Large type books.   5. Minnesota — Fiction.
6. Mystery fiction. I. Title.
PS3566.U47C87 2004
    813′.6—dc22   2004041568

CUTWORK

As the Founder/CEO of NAVH, the only national health agency solely devoted to those who, although not totally blind, have an eye disease which could lead to serious visual impairment, I am pleased to recognize Thorndike Press* as one of the leading publishers in the large print field.

Founded in 1954 in San Francisco to prepare large print textbooks for partially seeing children, NAVH became the pioneer and standard setting agency in the preparation of large type.

Today, those publishers who meet our standards carry the prestigious "Seal of Approval" indicating high quality large print. We are delighted that Thorndike Press is one of the publishers whose titles meet these standards. We are also pleased to recognize the significant contribution Thorndike Press is making in this important and growing field.

Lorraine H. Marchi, L.H.D.
Founder/CEO
NAVH

* Thorndike Press encompasses the following imprints: Thorndike, Wheeler, Walker and Large Pr int Press.

Acknowledgments

I am exceedingly grateful to a lot of people who helped with the many details of this novel. Julie Norton designs and teaches Hardanger (and cutwork). Ivan Whillock taught me a lot about the art of carving wood. Tom Yarborough let me try his electric welding torch. A dear relation who wishes to remain anonymous explained to me how the world of modern art works. Deb Hart allowed me to "help" with Excelsior's annual Art on the Lake fair so its details as presented here are mostly accurate. My writers' group, Crème de la Crime, made me work really hard, for which I thank them. And Ellen Kuhfeld, as ever, did her wonderful "invisible editing," thereby improving my reputation as a detail-oriented mystery novelist.

Prologue

It was a few minutes after ten on a warm June Sunday. Art on the Lake, Excelsior's annual art fair, had started yesterday, so those who simply had to come had already been; and the threatening weather today had made others decide to wait and see if it cleared. Still, it was a very popular fair in an attractive location; so when the rain started, there were several hundred shoppers wandering the outdoor aisles. Then thunder boomed and the aisles cleared as customers hustled into the nearest booths for shelter.

Betsy Devonshire was a member of the volunteer committee who ran the fair. A small-business owner, she'd really been pressed to find time for the planning meetings, and because her needlework shop was open on Saturdays, she had only Sunday to offer her services. Deb Hart, chairman of the fair, had been ruthless with her schedule. Betsy had been in the service building on The Common since daylight, which came very early in June. Artists could not open to the public until ten — but there was cleanup, rearranging, and restocking to do, the enter-

9

tainers wanting to know where they could set up, and the food vendors needing to get cooking. Betsy had fielded a steady stream of artists and workers, coming for the free donuts and coffee she had laid out for them on the counter and to ask questions: Was it against local ordinances to —, could they run a line from —, was there a mechanic in town who could fix —, would she mind if the balloon artist stored his spare balloon inflater in here?

"Here" was the information booth in a corner of a brick building on the southwest corner of the big field in which the fair was held.

Betsy was surprised at the number of times she had to refill the urns and make more coffee.

But with the approach of ten o'clock and customers, the stream slowed to a trickle. Betsy unplugged and washed the coffee urns, put the six remaining donuts into a paper bag, then stocked a big refrigerator with soft drinks and the counter with T-shirts, both for sale to the public.

The intense downpour cooled the air but raised the humidity, and only dampened slightly the scent of broiled pork, popcorn, whipped fruit, hot dogs, blooming onions, and other delectables being sold from stands around the corner from her, out of sight but not nose.

Right in front of Betsy, glittering under a wash of rain, was a big red fire truck, the kind with a cubicle back end. It was at the fair as a boast and exhibit; the art fair was sponsored in part by the Excelsior Chamber of Commerce, and the fire truck was new. Despite the rain, a few adults stopped to show the truck to their children, and a fireman in a yellow raincoat and helmet answered questions.

Suddenly the fireman jerked around and hurried to the front of the truck. He climbed up and in and its engine roared to life. Adults and children scattered. A man appeared from the other side of the truck, hauling a toddler by his arm, splashing through a puddle hidden in the grass. No hard feelings; he laughed as he ran for the porch of Betsy's building and the toddler, now over his shoulder like a sack of grain, was doing a happy imitation of the siren.

Instead of coming back past the building to the street, the fire truck did a Y turn and went forward, down between booths, past the little band shell, toward the lake. Shelter seekers in the shell waved as it went by, but Betsy frowned. The only place the fire truck could go from there was along the lakefront. Surely none of the artists' booths could be on fire, not in this rain? So it must be a medical emergency. Here at the fair, or perhaps, thought Betsy, it's headed for the docks

11

where big excursion boats and smaller private craft tied up. People sometimes fell on wet decks, or had heart attacks lifting sails.

Betsy heard another siren approaching distantly. It got louder, then cut off. The sound seemed to come from the opposite end of the field, in the direction of the docks.

Here and there, artists or their assistants were braving the storm to check guy lines. One stood on tiptoe, then hurried back inside to push up on his sagging roof and dump water off it. Another was replacing short tent pegs with long ones, kneeling in a big puddle to feel for the ground, his wristwatch pushed up past his elbow. The faint "tink, tink, tink" of his hammer could be heard over the rain.

The booth at Betsy's end of the row was a singleton, set apart from the others. The sides were rolled up all around and the artist was sitting in the very middle, on a wooden folding chair. She had a big artist's sketch tablet braced on her lap, and was drawing swiftly. Caricatures hung all over the inside of her booth, but she didn't have a customer at present. She seemed to be looking off toward the band shell, toward which another young man was wading. Betsy smiled; the little dog with him was swimming. Lightning cracked and thunder boomed, and the young man grabbed his dog by its collar and waded more swiftly for the band shell.

It rained hard for fifteen minutes, less hard for another ten, then the storm began to rumble north across the lake, headed for Wayzata, Saint Louis Park, and Minneapolis. A watery sun appeared, and everything sparkled as if freshly painted. The little crowd on the porch stepped out, looking upward, blinking in the sunlight, smiling at one another.

Betsy decided she needed a Diet Coke and was bent into the refrigerator for one when someone said in an excited voice, "Betsy, have you heard?"

Betsy looked around the refrigerator door to see Irene Potter looking wilder-eyed than usual, an accomplishment so unlikely that Betsy came to her at once. "Heard what, Irene? Is something wrong?" she asked.

"It's Mr. McFey." She added proudly, "I found him. I screamed so loud my throat still hurts. Did you hear me? I was really loud."

"No. Why did you scream — Irene, what's happened?" Betsy tried to think if she knew who Mr. McFey was. And suddenly remembered the fire truck going off in the wrong direction.

"I told you, it's Mr. McFey. He's dead."

"Did he have a heart attack?"

Irene shook her head vigorously. "It was *murder,*" she said solemnly. She leaned closer, eyes gleaming. "I walked over to look at that carving he did of the lion, so powerful, and

13

he wasn't in there, which was wrong because the fair was opening, but then I saw blood, and then I saw him." Her hands went over her nose and mouth, and froze like that a few seconds, until she made a snoring sound as she tried to take a breath through her fingers. She took her hands away, uncovering a mouth pursed into an O as round and nearly as small as her eyes, and took a deep breath. As she let it out, she whispered, "I have never seen anything like that. Ever, ever, ever. Poor man," she added, an afterthought.

"Perhaps it was an accident of some kind," said Betsy, not sure if she believed this strangely told story.

"Oh, no, no, no, no. Someone cut his throat." She made the old-fashioned gesture for that, drawing a skinny forefinger across her own throat. "No one knows who did it. The police are there, but of course I thought of you. You will look into this, won't you? It can't go unpunished. Oh, he was *such* a good artist! His work, *so* magnificent, *such* a loss!" She rolled her eyes heavenward.

Irene saw the world in a very peculiar way, Betsy knew. Still, it couldn't be possible Irene was making a joke in *such* poor taste. And the sirens had been real. And her mention of a carved lion . . .

Back in March, when the slides and photographs of artwork arrived from artists seeking a place in the fair, Betsy had been allowed to sit in on the jurying process one evening. Some of the art she thought was pretty good didn't move the jury. Other stuff that made the members gasp and exclaim in pleasure meant nothing to her. Then, *click,* and up on the screen came a magnificent wood carving, seen a little to the left from head-on. A murmur of pleasure swept the room.

A big-maned lion was in a fully extended run, one big paw reaching out for the back leg of a fleeing antelope. The artist had cleverly used a natural dark place in the wood to place and accent the lion's flowing mane. But it was the terror in the antelope's eyes, and the businesslike intensity captured in the lion's, that had been remarkable.

"Well, are you coming or not?" asked Irene impatiently, pulling Betsy out of her reverie.

"I thought you said the police were already there," said Betsy.

"Oh, yes, and they've been talking to me and taking pictures and all. I sneaked away to get you."

"They won't want me over there," said Betsy, "and besides, I have to stay here, I have things to do here."

Irene stared at her. "I can't believe you don't care if a murderer gets away."

"I doubt very much if a murderer could kill someone in a place as crowded as this and get away with it," said Betsy truthfully. "There are probably all kinds of witnesses. Including

15

you, right? Shouldn't you get back over there? They're probably looking for you."

Irene looked over her shoulder. "Yes, I imagine they are. Very well, I'll go back. But you call me when you're ready to take over the investigation."

Betsy watched her go, a skinny woman in a long, shapeless brown dress and old-fashioned sneakers. It was true. Betsy had been involved in several murder investigations, but strictly as an amateur. How could Irene think the police would be eager to have her barge in? Besides, this probably wasn't a murder at all. Irene was growing more eccentric every month, it seemed, now that her needlework inventions were being taken seriously by the art community. No, Betsy would stay right here and wait for someone more reliable to come and tell her what was going on. Murder, indeed!

Chapter 1

For a while, Detective Sergeant Mike Malloy thought this was going to be another one of those screwy cases, the kind his amateur nemesis would get involved in. (Mike couldn't have defined "nemesis," not exactly like in the dictionary, but he was certain it described a certain woman who was messing up his career by interfering where she wasn't needed.)

It started Sunday morning, during a thunderstorm. The town of Excelsior had only two investigators in its little police department, so in addition to normal working hours, Malloy and his partner had twenty-four on–twenty-four off standby duty. Today Malloy was on, and so had to restrict his fishing to Lake Minnetonka. Which was fine, Minnetonka was the finest bass lake in the state, one of the finest in the country, probably. Plus, the weatherman Malloy had come most nearly to trust said it would clear before eleven.

Excelsior was also a very quiet town, so when his beeper went off while he was still in the garage loading up his boat, he was surprised.

Walking to the kitchen to phone, he decided it was probably another in the short series of burglaries plaguing the town. Someone was climbing into unlocked cars parked over at Maynard's for Sunday brunch and, if there was a garage door opener on the visor, checking the glove box for insurance cards that gave the home address. Then when the folks came home from brunch, they'd find someone had gone in through the garage and stolen all the easy-to-fence stuff.

So instead of going fishing, Mike would have to spend most of the day taking statements and filing reports. Damn.

He dialed the number and got an answer on the first ring.

"Sergeant Cross," said Jill Cross.

"Malloy here, whatcha got?"

"A homicide down at the art fair on The Common."

This was so far from what he was expecting that all he could say was *"Huh?"* He hated when he did that; it made him sound dumb.

Jill repeated herself in that cool voice of hers — she had never said "Huh?" in her life, probably — adding, "The reporting person is Irene Potter —"

"Oh, Christ!" he interrupted. Because Irene Potter was Excelsior's craziest lady. And the only time Irene had been in his office on official business, she had brought along Betsy Devonshire, AKA Mike Malloy's nemesis.

18

(That had been when Mike began to learn he had a nemesis.)

But just as if he hadn't interrupted, Jill continued, "And the person in charge of the fair is Deb Hart. Ms. Hart is here at the scene, which has been secured. I'll ensure that Irene is here for you, too. The forensics team is on its way. Be warned, the scene is kinda, um, messy."

Oh, Jeez. That last, coming from the unflappable Jill Cross, didn't help. "I'll be right over."

Mike called the woman next door to tell her he had a call and could she keep an eye on JR and Mary Beth until he or his wife got back? The woman sighed but then said sure, send them over.

Mike got into his wife's voice mail at the nursing home and left a message, then drove his blue Chevy four by four over to the park. It was only six minutes away, but the rain had about quit by the time he got there. He pulled into the single vacant parking space on Lake Street that overlooked the park. A wilted cardboard sign marked it as reserved for emergency vehicles. Since he was wearing faded jeans and a chambray shirt with fraying patches on the elbows, he turned his ID folder inside out and hung it on the shirt's pocket so the gold badge showed. Just like the cops on TV. He remembered to take his lucky fishing hat off and leave it in the truck.

The storm's purple clouds were only a short distance out on the lake, lightning still visible in them, and there were still audible rumbles of thunder.

He stood a minute at the top of a plain wooden staircase leading down to the park, to look the scene over. Lake Street, which he'd just come up, ran along the lake until The Common began. Then the park stayed down near lake level while Lake Street climbed a steep hill. People alighting from their cars halfway along had to come down a bluff via the staircase. The street then went downhill until at the far end it was level with the park again.

This section of park, a grassy field at the bottom of the stairs, was covered with hundreds of square white tents in neat double rows, with a single row along the lakefront. The tents were like stores, open at the front and full of art stuff for sale. The art fair was an annual event; Mike's wife had gone last year and come home with a sheet-iron sunflower that weighed twenty pounds and rusted so bad it killed her favorite rose-bush.

Mike had no doubt where the problem was: An ambulance, two squad cars with their lights flickering, and Excelsior's new fire truck were at the far end of a vertical row. Mike could see the deep grooves cut by the tires of the vehicles in the soggy grass, and decided to leave his pickup where it was. He ducked back in it briefly to get a notebook and pen from the glove box.

The sun broke through as he went down the wet staircase, a slim man in his late thirties with a freckled face and a thin but sensitive mouth.

The tents were emptying of people who had sought shelter from the rain. The artists were talking fast to the last of them, holding up items and gesturing. The tent he was passing was full of felt hats with floppy brims and fabric flowers. The artist wore one himself; he looked ridiculous. In the next tent there were glass cases on white pedestals under bright lights. In the cases were clumsy-looking rings and pins, some with colored stones. The prices on little cards in the boxes indicated the metal was real gold, the stones real gems. That didn't keep them from being, in Malloy's never-humble opinion, ugly. The next tent held kites. Not regular kites; there was one shaped like the Wright Brothers airplane that even had a silhouette of a man lying on it. Another was a three-dimensional pirate ship whose sails provided the lift like a box kite, probably. A really big one shaped like a dragon was being sailed skillfully higher and higher in the clearing sky. JR would love it if his dad brought one of these home. But not right now.

Mike turned his attention away from the

kites to focus on the tent at the end of the row.

Three men whose shoulder patches said they were from Shorewood were keeping a crowd back, a crowd that had been small when Mike first spotted it, but was growing fast now the rain had stopped. Mike edged his way through and started to say something to one of the uniformed officers, but heard another already on his radio asking for yet more help. Thank God for the agreement that all the little departments in the towns around Minnetonka would come to one another's aid.

Mike went to the tent for a look. There were three men in civilian clothes standing with their backs to the tent, forming a screen of sorts. They were carrying the cases of equipment necessary for collecting evidence. Mike recognized one as an investigator from the state crime team, so probably the others were, too. Inside, a man with a video camera was recording the interior. The video operator moved aside and Malloy leaned way forward and got his first glimpse of the victim, sprawled on the floor in a big red —

Malloy immediately turned away, wiping his face with one hand. Jesus! Jill's description of "um, messy" was, um, right. He squeezed his eyes shut, blew gently, and saw Sergeant Jill Cross looking at him. She was all crisp and calm, like this was something you ran across every day. She nodded at him and came over.

"What happened here?" he asked.

"A knifing. This is the victim's booth." Sergeant Cross was a tall woman, a natural ash blond, not at all skinny but somehow not fat, either. She had a face that went with her voice, cool and showing nothing of her thoughts. She wasn't an investigator but a supervisor, and so was in uniform. Mike had gone from not liking her when she signed on as a patrol officer — he disliked female cops in general — to an uneasy admiration. She rarely put a foot wrong and had all but aced the sergeant's exam a few months ago. On the other hand, she and his nemesis were good friends, and his nemesis was an interfering civilian, old enough to know better.

"Any idea who the victim is?" Mike asked.

"Robert McFey. He was a wood carver, and it seems his throat was cut with one of his own knives." Jill glanced sideways at the tent, which had shelves in it with carvings of animals on them, and a couple more on a long table set like a counter across the open front.

"Any idea who might've done this?" he asked.

"Not yet. The weapon appears to be the small knife beside the body. There's an overturned cash box in there that seems to be empty."

"And Irene Potter saw it happen?"

"No, she found the body. She's here selling her needle art, she's got a booth just up the way. She came over for a look at his work and went off like the noon siren."

"How long ago?"

"Just before ten, the fair was about to start." Mike checked his watch. Ten-fifty. "You want to talk to her?" Cross asked. "She walked off a while ago, but she's back."

Mike sighed. "Okay, I'll start with her."

"You want me to stay?"

"No, no, just bring her over and then go back to crowd control or whatever you were doing."

"Yessir," she said coolly. Had he put that clumsily? Mike had never felt comfortable around Cross. He didn't want a sexual harassment suit, which in his opinion every female cop in the country was spring-loaded to bring. He looked at her, ready to give a friendly smile, but she was already walking away.

Irene Potter was the same skinny little woman with shiny dark eyes and very curly dark hair he remembered. She wore a light brown dress and pink Keds. Her earrings were shaped like tiny scissors; they glittered in the fresh sunlight. Like her eyes.

"Hello, Sergeant Malloy," she said cheerily. "Isn't this just dreadful?"

Mike pulled his notebook from a back pocket and slipped the ballpoint pen clipped to its creased cover off. He opened the note-book to a blank page, noted the time, date, and Irene's name. He said, "How did you come to find the body?"

"I believe I was summoned by a Greater Power," she chirped, and he repressed a sigh. She continued, "I was arranging my pieces in my booth when all of a sudden I had this . . . *urge,* a powerful urge, to go look at Mr. McFey's work, even though it was raining hard. I took my umbrella and . . ." She gestured awe by raising both hands. "So beautiful! Such energy! I wanted to ask him how long he'd been doing his art. At first, I thought he had stepped out. But he hadn't. Because then I . . . I *saw him.* I think I screamed, but I don't know for sure, except my throat is sore, and it wasn't sore before. So I really think I must have screamed." She put one slim hand to her throat and smiled like a schoolchild with the right answer.

Mike didn't write any of this down. "Did you notice anyone hanging around his tent before you got this urge?"

"No, I was busy with my own arranging. It's so important to get everything just right, so the eye travels naturally from piece to piece until it reaches the one that pleases the eye, that one *must buy.*" Her eyes had gone dreamy and her hands moved upward again, this time arranging invisible works on an in-visible wall.

"Yeah, okay, you weren't looking," said Mike. "I understand. But you got your stuff arranged and came over to look at this man's wood carvings and you saw him. What time was this?"

"It was just a few minutes before the fair opened, though there were customers already starting to come through. It was raining simply buckets, but I had my umbrella, so I wasn't afraid to go out of my booth. The fair opened at ten." Mike kept looking at her, and she blinked and said gently, as to an obtuse person, "It was about five minutes before ten that I went to talk to him."

He nodded and wrote that down. "Did you go in to see if he was still alive?"

She looked horrified. "No, of course not! He looked dead — he *was* dead. There was so much blood, he must have been dead. But I must've screamed because two people came running. I think one of them went in. I felt — ill, so I went back to my booth and sat down." She nodded at his notebook to encourage him to write. He made a brief note to find those two people who came when Irene must have screamed. Satisfied, she went on, "And someone must have called 911, because pretty soon there was a police car, and an ambulance, and the fire truck came, too; it had been on the grounds, it's the new pumper. Or maybe the fire truck came first, I don't remember. And I wasn't looking, I'd

26

gone back to my booth to sit down, and my heart was going at a terrific pace, quite frightening. A squad car came, then Jill, and last those people who are taking pictures. And now you. I wonder why Betsy Devonshire is not here. I mean, she's here, she was working in the information booth earlier this morning. But she's not *here*."

Mike said firmly, "Ms. Devonshire has no business at the scene of a crime."

Irene stared at him. "But she can help you, I'm sure she can. She's so very clever about murder. You know that, Sergeant Malloy."

Mike found a patient smile somewhere. "How about you let the professionals have a go at it first, okay? Then if we need to talk to her, we will. Now, did you see anyone running away from this tent?"

"No. All I saw was the body. And the blood. There seems to be a great deal of blood, doesn't there?" She wrinkled her nose.

"Yes," said Mike, trying not to grimace back. "That's all I have to ask you right now, but would you mind waiting here for a while, in case I have more questions later?"

"I can't, I have to go back to my booth. People are moving around again, with more arriving now the rain's stopped. Shopping. Shop*lifting*. I'm across the row, up three booths, easy to find. Number forty-nine." She nodded her head toward a tent up the way and started off.

"Wait! Do you know, uh . . ." He checked his notebook. "Deb Hart?"

A voice behind him said, "I'm Deb Hart."

Mike turned around to see a sturdy woman with her hair pulled back tightly from her face, which was innocent of makeup and carefully blank of expression. She was wearing a loose-fitting blue denim dress under a clear plastic raincoat whose snap fastenings were all undone. "Are you in charge of this shindig?" Mike asked.

"Yes. Unfortunately." Her blue eyes were intelligent and steady. "Mr. McFey was a very talented artist, and it is a terrible thing that he should be murdered here."

"Did you know him personally?"

"No. Well, I talked with him yesterday after he was set up, but only briefly. He hadn't been to many of these fairs, and this was his first time here. He won an award from us for his work, but I wasn't his judge." She looked around toward the tent, and Mike saw her dark blond hair was in a very long braid down her back.

"But you're sure the body in there is his. McFey's."

Her head came back. "Yes."

"Do you know where he's from?"

"He's from around here, Golden Valley or Hopkins, I can't remember. Or Minnetonka?" She frowned, a little disturbed that she couldn't remember.

"Do you know how to spell 'McFey'?"

"Yes," she said and did so.

"Is there next of kin to be notified?"

"Yes, a wife. He gave a separate phone number and address for her, out in Maple Grove, so maybe they're divorced; but he listed her as the person to be notified in case of accident. I haven't made the call yet."

"That's all right, we'll take care of it."

"Thank you." Ms. Hart was relieved about that.

"Have you had a problem with stealing here?"

"Once in a while. Someone will take a piece, something small enough to fit in a purse or pocket, or up a sleeve, and walk away."

"I was thinking of the money. Stealing from the cash boxes."

"Oh. Well, no, not for several years. The fair is pretty well attended so it's hard to do something like that and not be seen. Artists tend to put the cash box somewhere hard to reach, so other customers notice when someone tries to get at it. Is that what happened here? A robbery?"

"We don't know yet. I understand there's an emptied cash box in the tent."

"Booth."

"What?"

"Booth. These aren't tents, they're booths."

"That's right, that's what Sergeant Cross called it, too." He nodded and repeated,

29

"Booth, then. There's an empty cash box in there."

"Oh. No one told me that. Interesting." Ms. Hart looked thoughtful. "And stupid, really."

"Why's that?"

"Because nobody brings cash boxes in with yesterday's receipts still in them, of course. And the fair was just getting under way today when this happened. There would have only been starting-up money in Mr. McFey's box, just what he needed to make change."

"How much would that be?"

"Not more than forty or fifty dollars, I'd say. How incredibly, incredibly stupid if a very fine artist is dead because somebody needed to steal fifty dollars."

Mike wrote some of that down while she waited, but at last she said, "I — I'd like to go back to my other duties now, if that's all right." She wasn't looking at him anymore, but he could see that was because she was trying not to show how sad and angry she was.

"Yes, all right. How can I get back in touch with you, if I have more questions?"

"Look for my staff, people carrying walkie-talkies, I've got one, too." She touched a big pocket on the skirt of her dress that was bulging heavily. "And I'm carrying a cell phone as well." She gave him the number, then turned and walked away, her sandals squishing a bit in the sodden turf.

Mike reviewed his notes. Okay, the dead man was Robert McFey, one of the artists selling his stuff here at the fair. His throat had been cut, probably by one of his own carving knives. His money box had been emptied, which probably meant this was about robbery. On the other hand, this guy wasn't selling gold jewelry like the guy up the way, and had maybe fifty dollars, max, in cash, so why pick on him?

Maybe because not many people were around when the robber was looking for a mark. Or maybe because the robber was an amateur. Mike didn't like amateur murderers for the same reason he didn't like amateur sleuths: They don't play by the rules. Like here. Only an amateur would go after a man in a place crowded with people, and so unprepared he had to borrow the murder weapon from his victim.

Of course, it was possible the victim was out of his tent — booth — for a while and came back in time to surprise someone getting into his cash box.

Poor schnook, with the accent on poor. After all, selling wood statues out of a tent, that wasn't any way to get rich. Harmless guy, probably, without an enemy in the world, who didn't deserve to die like this.

Which might mean this would be difficult to solve. Such a dumb amateur as this murderer could be hard to find, because he was so far off the pattern most perps followed.

Truth be told, Mike preferred his victims also to be criminals. Dope dealers, for example. Pimps. Burglars. Loan sharks. The kind of pro with obvious enemies — and friends and associates who didn't know what loyalty meant — all of them willing to drop a dime on the perp.

(Funny how slang sometimes got stuck in a time warp, he considered. Snitches still dropped a dime on people, even though pay phone prices had long since gone trotting past fifty cents in the Twin Cities.)

Of course, amateurs were sometimes careless about leaving clues behind and, once confronted, tended to blurt out incriminating details. So maybe this would be one of those times.

It would have to be crazy Irene who found the body. Her bright but careless embroidery — to Mike, any decorative stitchery was by definition embroidery — had been pronounced Important Art, which only confirmed Mike's opinion that the smoke in her chimney didn't go all the way up. Most artists were at least a little crazy, weren't they? She hadn't helped her case by asserting that he ought to send for Miss Nemesis.

Deb Hart, Mike knew, owned an art supply store that catered to artists, but she wasn't one herself. Also, she had run the art fair since it began twenty years ago, and both the store and the show did well, so it all went to show, right? *Not* an artist, *not* crazy.

She had said this McFey fellow was from one of the Minneapolis suburbs. He had written that down, gratefully certain there weren't many Robert McFeys in the phone book. Now, if he'd been Robert Larson, that would have made his life miserable. The Twin Cities was lousy with Larsons.

About then, Sergeant Cross came back and said the police photographers had finished making their record of the scene on film and tape. Mike thanked her and walked slowly along the table, looking into the white tent. Booth.

It was just like all the others at the fair, square, the size of a kid's bedroom, straight-sided, and so tall you could stand up in it, with metal bracing under its peaked ceiling that made it look like it went up easy, like opening an umbrella. A heck of a deal, he thought enviously, having camped for years in a low, slope-sided, rip-stop nylon tent that was hard to put up and easy to blow down. He looked back up the aisle. Not one tent — booth — had blown down in the storm just over. Heck of a deal.

On the table were wood statues, one of a lion about to take down an antelope that was very nice, very nice. And beside it was another one, of those little birds that chased and were chased by the waves on the seashore. Mike had seen those birds in movies and on television and once in person when he went to Atlantic City for a lawmen's convention. The seashore was represented by a smooth, wavy piece of wood with the birds stuck on it by their wire legs. It had five birds, one with its beak driven like a nail halfway into the wooden seashore. Nice, but not as nice as the lion.

Beyond the lion, at the end of the table, was a little clear-plastic holder with a couple dozen business cards reading ROBERT MCFEY, ARTIST IN WOOD, with a post office box and an email address. Mike wrote that information down in his notebook.

Surrounding the holder were a dozen small carved pieces, some knocked over, that were different from the serious pieces. They were like from a cartoon. A wolf, a crow, a possum, and other little animals, all standing up and dressed in human clothes with human expressions on their faces. Comical, clever. Mike would have liked to pick one up for a closer look, but he had better get on with the more important piece of information waiting farther back in the tent. Booth.

That's what the murder victim was now. A source of information. Mike braced himself with that thought and went for a look.

The dead man was thin, medium-height, with graying brown hair pulled into a pony tail and a graying light brown beard trimmed rather long. He was lying in an uncomfort-able-looking position, halfway to face up, one foot across the other ankle. He had on a big, loose navy blue T-shirt with LET THE CHIPS FALL WHERE THEY MAY printed in white letters on it, faded blue jeans, and an old pair of penny loafers that might have cost a lot when new. And his watch was a Rolex, though not the famous Oyster. Possibly significant that it hadn't been stolen. But too bad it was not helpfully broken by his fall to record the time of death. Mike checked it against his own Timex: eleven twenty-three, right.

The man had very obviously died from a big cut that slanted crookedly across his throat. From it, his life's blood had spilled onto a kind of floor on which he lay. He, or someone, had laid down the big square of plywood — no, two pieces of plywood, side by side, to make the floor, and there were a great many gory footprints made by the first responders anxious to save him. The floor didn't cover all the inside of the tent; there was a border of grass around it that was widest at the back. A tipped-over director's chair was surrounded by tiny pieces of wood — the chips mentioned on his T-shirt — and a partly finished cartoon animal was under the table. It looked like a shaggy dog, the kind whose ears tipped over at the ends, the kind who herded sheep, what breed was that? He couldn't think, though he recalled that they made bad pets because they always had to have something to do. Oddly, the fur on the back of the dog looked like it had been braided. He frowned at that and then suddenly thought, *That's supposed to be Deb Hart.* And he smiled, because it gave him an insight into her personality, or what the artist had thought of her personality. Then he looked at the lifeless hands of the clever man who had carved it and felt a stir of anger. The little carving knife he'd apparently been using had been taken and used on him, then left beside him on the plywood. It had a curved handle and a darkly clotted, not-long blade. But long enough.

Though Ms. Hart's identification didn't really count, legally, since she wasn't a relative, Mike was satisfied that this was almost certainly Robert McFey, whose name appeared on the business cards, the man who had carved the statues on the table and on the shelves back here. That one on the bottom shelf, of the fox with its front feet on a log, that was another nice one. The look on its face was alarmed, as if it thought it heard dogs barking in the distance.

Mike bent forward. In front of the fox statue, on the plywood floor, was the cash box. It was of gray-enameled steel with a little key-operated lock on it. He'd seen them at outdoor sales before, where a cash register wasn't necessary but you needed something to keep money in. The lid was open but the box was upside down. Mike took his pen out of his pocket and very carefully turned it over.

It was empty, of course. But the box had made a very nice protective cover for another footprint. Mike looked around but didn't see that pattern anywhere else on the floor. There were some smears on the grass, but they were unreadable.

Mike stood and said to the uniform standing outside the tent, "Ask if anyone remembers moving or tipping over the cash box. And get the guys with the camera back in here."

His thin mouth was pulled into a tight, satisfied smile. If the box hadn't been tipped over by the crew, a major clue was right here.

He looked at the print. He knew that kind of pattern. It came from one of those very expensive sports shoes young males liked — and it wasn't a brand new pair. Shoes that had been worn awhile developed wear marks on their soles, marks as distinctive as a fingerprint. Mike had dealt with many young criminals and was pleased at how many of them didn't realize this. They'd climb through a window from a grimy alley or freshly spaded flower bed and leave a sharp footprint on a windowsill or the floor.

No, this wasn't screwy after all. Only sad.

Chapter 2

Of all the unpleasant duties of police work, one of the worst is going to tell a family that one of its members has been killed. *That,* thought Jill, *is probably why Mike shoved the job off onto me.* She nearly shoved it off again, onto a patrol officer, then reconsidered.

She had joined the police with the notion of becoming a detective. In Excelsior that couldn't happen until one of the two investigators left. Jim was seven years from retirement, and Mike was looking for a job opening as sheriff in some quiet upstate county, one with a lake full of bass. He'd been looking for that position for a very long time, and there was no hint that it was going to happen anytime soon.

Meanwhile, Mike was hot on the trail of a suspect — but hot suspects sometimes cooled off. Jill decided that having an experienced peace officer — herself — taking the initial measure of the victim's family couldn't hurt. And it would give her a chance to do a little investigating without Mike feeling she was walking on his turf.

Excelsior was a small town, with a tiny police force. During the daylight and evening hours, there were only two squad cars on patrol — late at night, only one. But law enforcement rules dictate that making an official call took two officers. Since Jill could not take half the street force out of jurisdiction, she called the current graveyard-shift patrol officer from his bed to drive her in the spare squad car to Maple Plain. He was a lanky man named Nelson, and she filled him in on the drive out.

The McFey house in Maple Plain was one of those elaborately windowed clapboard mansions the upper middle class was building. An itinerant wood carver never bought a place like this. Nelson agreed. "Maybe his wife has money," he suggested.

The house was pastel green with white trim and a for-sale sign on the broad, professionally landscaped front lawn. The door was opened by a thin teenaged girl in outsize overalls. She had a nose ring, spiky hair, and blue fingernails. Her pro-forma sulky look turned authentically wary when she saw their uniforms.

"Is Mrs. McFey at home?" asked Jill.

"Sure. I mean, I guess so. Is something wrong?"

"Yes, I'm afraid so. Is Mrs. McFey your mother?"

"Yes." The girl's eyes widened. "Is this about Coy?"

"Who's Coy?" asked Jill.

The girl looked relieved. "Come in, I'll get Mommy." She led them into a beautiful parlor done in shades of brick, colonial blue, and cream. "Wait here." She walked away and Jill noticed she was barefoot under the enormous legs of her denim overalls.

They took their hats off and looked around, at the blue leather couch and complex window dressings, the cream silk flowers in a big Chinese vase. "Nice," Nelson murmured.

Jill took her notebook out, wrote something in it.

Three minutes later a trim woman in a white silk shirt and dark blue trousers came in alone. Her hair was streaky blond, freshly combed, her lips lightly touched with color. She wore a clunky gold necklace and earrings. "Is there something I can help you with?" she asked, only a little anxious, her light blue eyes wide with concern.

"Are you Pamela McFey?" asked Jill.

"Yes, what is it?"

"Won't you sit down, please, Mrs. McFey?"

The look of concern deepened to fear. "What's wrong, what's happened?" she asked.

But Jill insisted gently, "Please, sit down, I'm afraid I have some bad news for you."

Mrs. McFey obeyed, perching on the very front edge of the couch, her eyes flicking from Jill to Nelson and back again. "Is it Coy?"

"No, ma'am, it's Robert, your husband."

She looked so relieved, Jill hated to say it. "I'm afraid he's dead."

She blinked rapidly, but the relief was still there. "Oh, my, that's sad. I suppose Dr. Moore was right the first time." She looked up at Jill, and was surprised at Jill's look of surprise. "I mean, he's had this liver disease for a long time, he's already lived two years longer than Dr. Moore thought he would."

"Oh," said Jill. "Well, I'm afraid he didn't die of liver disease, ma'am."

"No?" She floundered for words, gesturing helplessly. "Well, then, what? Car accident? No? Not . . . suicide, surely?"

"No, ma'am. He was at the Excelsior art fair, and I'm afraid he was found in his booth a few hours ago. I'm sorry to tell you this: He was murdered."

Mrs. McFey gaped at Jill, then at Nelson. "No," she said. "Robbie? Oh, no, that's ridiculous!" A new thought came and was swiftly suppressed. "That's ridiculous," she repeated, and looked down at her fingers, which had clasped themselves without her volition. She pulled them apart, rested them on her knees. "I don't understand," she said, asking for more information.

"He was stabbed," said Jill. "Another artist found him and raised the alarm, but . . ."

41

She gestured helplessness. "Nothing could be done for him."

"Oh!" She made a face, a twist of disgust, horror, and dismay. "Why would — who did this terrible — who would do such a terrible thing?"

"We don't know, not yet. It may have been a robbery. We're investigating, of course, and a detective will be by later to talk to you. Do you know of any enemies your husband might have had?"

"Enemies? No, of course not! I mean, who would hate Rob enough to — stab him?" She seemed surprised even to ask such a question, to connect his name with such a deed. "But you said it was a robbery, right? I mean, he had money with him, he had this metal box, to make change out of." She gestured the shape of the box with both hands, accurately.

"Yes, ma'am, the box was found, and it had been emptied."

"Yes, I see. Was, was there a struggle?" Her eyes widened as her imagination glimpsed an unpleasant scene.

Jill recalled the small amount of disorder in the booth. "I don't think so. He was probably taken by surprise, perhaps walking in on someone emptying the cash box. His death was quick."

Pam grasped that crumb of comfort. "Yes. Thank you."

"What did your husband do?" Jill asked. She raised her ballpoint pen, prepared to write.

"Well, you saw them, didn't you? Those animals he carves? He does big and small pieces — he did big and small pieces —" She stopped to swallow, overtaken by the need for past tense, and touched two trembling fingers to her lips.

Jill looked around the expensively furnished room in this big, costly house. "He didn't have another job?"

She nodded. "Yes. Well, he used to. He owned Information Please, an advertising agency. But he sold it a few years ago."

Jill wrote that down. "Who is . . ." Jill went back a page. "Coy?"

"Coy?" Her head swiveled toward the door to the entrance hall, as if the pause had been to query someone's sudden appearance in the doorway. Finding it empty, she looked back at Jill, saw the notebook, and said, "Oh, Coy is our son. Coyne is his name, actually." She spelled it. "He's named after his grandfather. He's not here right now."

"You have just two children?" asked Jill.

"Yes, Coyne and Skye. You met Skye, she's fifteen. Coy just turned twenty. They're good children, we're proud of them."

"Yes, ma'am." Funny what people found relevant at times like this. "Do you know where Coy is?"

"Out looking for a job. He's enrolled at Northwestern University. He got a scholarship, but it's a small one, and he has to make up the rest himself now, since I can't afford his tuition." She saw incomprehension on Jill's face and said, "Since the divorce. Rob quit working in advertising, you see, when he found out he was dying. But then he" — she lifted her hands and shoulders in a bewildered shrug — "didn't. Die, I mean. The company was doing well, he sold it for cash and stock but the buyer went belly up six months later." She shrugged again. "Rob always wanted to be an artist, he'd carved those things for years as a hobby. He was good at it, some of his work surprised me because it was so good, and when the doctor said six months, he got out of advertising as fast as he could and started growing his hair and he bought some expensive wood and started going to art fairs and galleries.

"When all the money was gone, and he hadn't died, I said, 'What about the house, Coy's college expenses, Skye's tuition at Blake School?' He said, 'I guess I should've told you I'm not going to die of hepatitis after all. So you won't be getting my insurance as soon as you thought, huh, Pam.' As if it were a joke. And he said I'd better find a job, hadn't I. Well, goodness, what kind of a job could I get? I haven't worked outside our home for twenty years! So now we're

44

losing the house, and Coy has to work his way through college and Skye's going to have to quit Blake and start all over making new friends with new teachers at a public school this fall . . ." There was the slightest emphasis on public, as if she were forced to say a rude word.

She shrugged again and frowned. Then, as if replaying all she'd said, she looked up at Jill and said in mild amazement, "I'm sorry, this isn't why you're here, is it? To hear all our petty little problems." But now she saw the pen moving, looked away again, and continued, "But really, I don't know what I'm going to do. And now, Rob's dead, and it's really all on my shoulders. And he's not dead the way he was supposed to go, but murdered, actually murdered. I don't know what to say — but I just can't seem to stop talking."

She made a fist and put it in front of her mouth, pressing hard, clearing her throat to give a reason for the gesture. Her other hand clenched hard onto her knee. "This is embarrassing, it's as if I don't know how to shut up!" She took the fist down, opening her hand to stare at it, as if she'd never seen a hand before. She pressed her lips very firmly together and swallowed, trying to gather herself.

Jill said, "It's all right, Mrs. McFey. You've had a very bad shock. Perhaps a drink, or a cup of tea, or coffee — ?"

"Yes. Yes, that's a good idea. I'll ask Skye . . ." Her eyes widened. "Does she know?"

"No, ma'am."

"Oh, dear, this is going to be hard, she loved her father very much." She raised her voice. "Skye? Skye darling!"

The shush of denim on a wooden floor was heard and the teen came into the room. She stopped short at the sight of her mother's pale, set face. "Mommy, what's wrong?"

"Come here, darling." She held out her hand and Skye came to take it. "Listen very carefully to me. Your father is dead. He's been murdered."

Skye gave a little shriek and pulled her hand free. "No, no, no!" she cried. She turned to Jill with a look so angry Nelson stepped up beside Jill. "That isn't true! That can't be true!"

Jill said, "I'm so sorry, Skye, but it is true."

Skye's eyes searched Jill's face. "How? Where did it happen?"

"At the art fair in Excelsior."

"Excelsior? Oh, yes, he said he was going to be there. He always tells me where he's going to be. Sometimes I come and sit with him . . ." She turned on her mother. "I told you I wanted to go, but you wouldn't drive me!" There were tears in her eyes, and in her voice.

46

"I told you, darling, the real estate agent is coming today and I have to be here for him . . ." She thrust her fingers into her hair. "I suppose I should call and cancel. Or should I? This is important, I think he has someone seriously interested. But of course our plans may change now, with this happening. Or will they? I can't think, my brain is simply whirling! I don't know what to do, this is impossible, I can't take it in!"

"It's *not* important, *nothing's* important! Oh, what does anything matter! Daddy's dead, my daddy's dead! If I'd been there, this wouldn't have happened!"

"What could you have done?" The two stared at one another for a horrified second, and Mrs. McFey said, "For heaven's sake, darling, if you'd been there, I might have lost you, too! Oh, my God, *I might have lost you, too!*" She reached to touch her daughter, but the child flinched away. Mrs. McFey looked at Jill. "You suggested a drink, I believe." She looked back at Skye, who had covered her eyes with both hands. "Darling, could you go get your mother a little brandy?"

Skye dropped her hands and said dully, "I could have stopped it, I know I could have stopped it. I should have been there."

"No," said Jill firmly. "Don't take any blame for this. This is not your fault. It's a very sad thing, losing your father, but I doubt very much if you could have done any-

47

thing to help him. And your mother's right, you could have been hurt yourself."

Mrs. McFey began suddenly to weep, folding herself in half so her forehead rested on her knees, hands falling to her ankles. Skye sat down beside her, touching her lightly on her back. "It's all right, Mommy, I'm here." She looked up pleadingly at Jill.

Jill was not very good in situations like this. Her own reaction to pain or sorrow was to become silent. When others abandoned themselves to grief, her first reaction was to step back.

Nelson was different. He moved to kneel beside Pam McFey, placing his hand on her shoulder. "This is scary and awful, and I know you're hurting," he said. "But it's very important that you try to get it together and listen to us, just for a short while. Then you can take the time you need to be alone, and to cry. But you see, we can't leave until some questions we have are answered."

Mrs. McFey didn't straighten, but the weeping began to slow. "Yes, yes," she muttered. "I understand." Nelson stood, nodded at Jill, and went back to his place.

"Now, first of all," said Jill, "are you and Mr. McFey divorced?"

Mrs. McFey straightened with a huge effort. "I've filed the papers, but the decree hasn't gone through yet," she said tiredly.

"When did you last speak with your husband?"

She sat up, thinking. "I don't know — wait, he called me last week, something about a court date, a conflict. He was going to another fair, somewhere in Wisconsin."

"I talked to him yesterday," said Skye in a low voice.

"What did he say to you?" asked Jill.

"He — he wanted to know if I could come sit with him in his booth on Sunday, today. I said I'd ask, but Mommy said she couldn't leave the house, she had to be here all day." Tears were streaming down her face, but she was speaking coherently.

"So you've both been here?"

The child wiped her eyes with both hands. "Well, no. I called my friend Jessica and her mother came and got me and picked up Chris and we swam in their pool all morning."

"What time was that?"

Skye shrugged, but when Jill only waited, she narrowed her mascaraed eyes and thought. "It was early." She smiled, just a little. "It's such a drag but I like getting up early and so does Jessica. But we had to get Chris out of bed and then wait for him to eat and get dressed, so I guess around nine, maybe before. I just got back home when you came. We had lunch over there."

Jill made a note and asked, "Who else

49

needs to be notified of this? Is there some way you can get hold of Coyne?"

Skye stared at Jill. Jill suddenly could see freckles delicately strewn across her nose and cheeks. "I don't know where he is," the girl said. "He went out before I did this morning. I don't think he said when he'd he back."

Pam McFey blinked slowly at Jill. She looked dreadful. "There isn't any way to get in touch with him right now," she said. She thrust her fingers into her hair and clenched them. "I really could use a drink, I'm afraid."

Skye said in a strange voice, "I'll get you a tot of brandy." She rose clumsily and started to turn away, but her ankles twisted together and she fell boneless onto the heavy carpet on the floor.

"No, no!" exclaimed Mrs. McFey, moving in a single, athletic motion to her daughter's side. "Skye? Skye! What's wrong? Are you all right?"

Jill stooped beside the unconscious girl, seeking and finding a shallow, rapid pulse in her throat, noting the unlabored breathing. "She's fainted, that's all." When Mrs. McFey started to lift her, Jill said, "No, don't move her. Hand me a pillow from the couch, please."

Mrs. McFey obediently reached for a crewel-worked pillow from a corner of the couch and handed it to Jill, who put it under Skye's feet. She began to pat and rub Skye's hand. "Wake up, honey," she said gently. "Everything's all right, you're all right."

"Come back to us, baby," said her mother, stooping beside her daughter on the other side. "Mommy's here, everything will be fine."

"Hum?" murmured Skye and her eyes fluttered open. "Mommy!"

"I'm here."

"What happened to me?"

"You fainted, that's all. You're going to be all right. Isn't she?" Mrs. McFey asked Jill.

"Of course, she's just fine. No, no, don't get up yet," she added to Skye.

"But . . . Oh! Oh, Daddy's dead! My daddy's dead!" Tears welled up and slid down her temples to vanish into the thick, dark hair.

Jill said, "I'm so sorry, Skye. But the police are investigating, and don't worry, we'll catch whoever did it."

Skye stumbled on a sob and exchanged a swift glance with her mother. "Mommy, where's Coy?" she asked.

Pam said quickly, "Yes, he needs to be told right away." Her eyes darted to Jill. "I think we should tell him, rather than the police. It's going to be such a . . . shock."

"Yes, a terrible shock," said Skye.

Pam said to Jill, "Thank you for coming in person to tell us, Officer."

"Sergeant," corrected Jill, too new to the

51

stripes on her sleeve to allow that to pass. "And you're welcome. Your son needs to be told soon, before this gets onto the news. Does he carry a cell phone?"

"He has one, but it's shut off. He was told it's very bad manners to have a job interview interrupted by a call."

Jill said, "He's got job interviews on a Sunday?"

"Why yes. Well, one, anyway. It's at Prestige Auto, and they work on Sundays just like any other day of the week. He's going to be a junior this fall, and he doesn't want to switch schools, so he has to find something, and not just as a bag boy, even at Byerly's." Byerly's was an upscale grocery chain.

"What time was his interview?" asked Jill.

"I don't know. And it may not be the only one. He did say he'd probably be gone all day. Do you really need to be here when he comes home?"

"No, I have other things that need doing. But here . . ." Jill reached into her pocket for a slim pack of crisp, new business cards. "This has my name and a phone number where I can be reached. I'm sure someone from the department will want to talk with him. And if Coy has any questions, after you talk with him, he can contact me, or the investigator who is in charge of the case. His name is Mike Malloy, Detective Sergeant Mike Malloy. He'll be the one to get in touch with you." She scribbled Mike's name on the card. "The phone number is the same."

Mrs. McFey nodded, and took the card. "Thank you."

Skye was sitting up now, her color mostly returned. "Is Daddy — I mean, what will happen now?"

"There will be an autopsy. Then the body will be released to you. But you'll be hearing from Detective Sergeant Malloy before that happens. He can answer any questions you may have at that time."

"Is an autopsy . . . icky?" asked Skye, who, like her mother, had a mind that went in an odd direction when under stress.

"No," lied Jill. "It's something like an operation. You won't notice anything at the funeral."

"Funeral," repeated Skye, and suddenly she was crying, huge gulping sobs. Her mother gathered her up onto the couch, murmuring gentle words, stroking her hair.

Jill and Officer Nelson left them weeping together.

In the car on their way back to Excelsior, Nelson noted quietly, "Interesting how they're both scared Coy did it, isn't it?"

Chapter 3

It was two o'clock; the Monday Bunch was in session. Mostly women, they gathered in Betsy Devonshire's store, Crewel World, to work on needlepoint, counted cross-stitch, and knitting projects while chatting. There were nine members present, an unusually large number, brought out by the news of Sunday's murder at the art fair.

"You were there, weren't you, Betsy?" asked Martha, a plump, cheerful-faced woman in her seventies. She was doing a counted cross-stitch pattern of fledgling blue-birds sitting on a wire fence. Flick, flick went her needle, and a bluebird's beady black eye appeared.

For a change, Betsy was sitting at the table herself, working on a needlepoint pattern of wild mustangs charging in a cloud of dust, the dust so thick the horses were mere sil-houettes in the midst of it. She was working it in wool with the wasteful but sturdy basketweave stitch because she wanted to use it as a chair seat. She said, "Yes, but I had no idea what had happened until it was all over."

"You mean, Mike didn't even come over and talk to you?" asked Alice, a big woman with a man's broad shoulders and a chin not to trifle with. She sounded indignant on Betsy's behalf.

"Why should he? I couldn't have told him anything useful."

Bershada, a slim black woman with magnifying glasses well down her nose, said, "That's not what I hear. What I hear is, you can take one look at a crime scene and know who did it."

"Where did you hear that?" asked Betsy, amazed.

"Shelly told me. She admires your detective work very much." Shelly Donohue taught in a local elementary school, and worked part time in Betsy's shop.

"Anyway, it's not true," said Godwin, Betsy's chief clerk and her one employee present. He was a trim young man with fair hair and guileless blue eyes, knitting another in his endless series of white cotton socks, his fingers making swift, economical movements. "It's not the *scene,* it's the *people.* She has to talk to people, listen to their stories, sort out the lies. *Then* she knows."

Betsy nodded. "Sometimes it works like that. But there's no reason for me to get involved in this one. The police have already arrested the person who did it."

This created a very satisfying sensation

around the table. Virtually everyone in Excelsior loved gossip, none more than the Monday Bunch.

"Who did they arrest?" demanded Alice in her deep voice.

"I don't want to tell you his name, but it's a teenager from right here in town."

"I bet it's Chris Martinsen," said Idonis, naming a notorious window breaker.

"I agree," said Alice.

"No, more likely Billy Swenson," said Emily. "He's been hanging out with that tough bunch from Wayzata."

"How did Mike solve it so quickly?" asked Godwin — slyly, because the group understood that Mike Malloy wasn't the brightest crayon in the box.

"Mike's very sharp when it's a criminal type of crime," said Betsy, echoing her source. "And that's what this was. His theory of the crime is that Mr. McFey set up his booth for the day, then left for a few minutes. Along came this young man, who saw the cash box unguarded and decided to help himself. But Mr. McFey came back and caught him in the act, possibly tried to detain him. The young man panicked, grabbed one of Mr. McFey's whittling knives, and swung it. He probably didn't mean to kill Mr. McFey, but . . ." She shrugged. "It was one of those stupid, stupid crimes. All he had to do was turn and run, but . . ."

"So how did Mike figure out who did it?" asked Godwin. "Did the kid leave his fingerprints all over the cash box?"

"He left a footprint in Mr. McFey's blood," said Betsy.

"Ewwwww!" said several women immediately.

"Go on, go on!" said Alice impatiently, flashing a quelling look around the table.

"Well, the young man apparently saw the blood on his shoes and threw them in one of the Dumpsters behind the food vendors. Several people saw him running up the street in his stocking feet. Two of them recognized him."

"Stupid is right," remarked Godwin. "All he had to do was take his socks off, too. Then he'd just be barefoot, and hardly anyone would have noticed him."

"But you don't know who he is?" Emily asked Betsy.

"She didn't tell me his name." Which was true, but Betsy had guessed, and had been told she was right.

"Who didn't tell you?" asked Martha.

"Jill, of course," said Godwin, when Betsy hesitated.

"I didn't say a name!" said Betsy too quickly. She realized her mistake and her heart sank.

"We won't tell, will we, girls?" said Godwin, trying to come to Betsy's rescue.

"No, no, of course not," several murmured quickly. The rest nodded, their eyes flashing from face to face. They were already calculating how soon they could leave without everyone guessing how urgently they wanted to tell someone else, in strictest confidence, what they'd learned in Betsy's shop.

Excelsior was noted for its gossipy ways, and the first person to supply a shiny new grape for the vine was honored and envied. It would be on the evening news that Mike had arrested the murderer, but not that Sergeant Jill Cross, a police official of great probity, who never, ever gossiped, especially about police business, had told Betsy something she shouldn't. *That* was gossip worthy of the name!

And it was symptomatic of how quickly it was spread that by midafternoon several customers alluded to it, hoping for more details. Which Betsy very determinedly didn't give them.

Around three, the shop door went *Bing!* and Betsy looked around to see Irene Potter standing just inside the door. Her dark eyes were shining, her curls positively vibrating with excitement.

Now that Irene was actually earning good money as an artist, she had quit her old job running the shipping department of a small local manufacturer. And she no longer had to save loose change until she could come in and buy a quarter yard of twenty-six-count linen and a skein of Anchor 1006. Now she could — and did — special-order unusual fabrics and rare silks, writing checks with a wonderful insouciance. So Betsy was pleased on several levels to see her, from the simple pleasure of watching her bloom to the joy of depositing a large check that never bounced.

"What can I do for you today, Irene?" Betsy asked.

Irene bustled up to the big desk that was the shop's checkout counter. "I've come to be interviewed," Irene announced.

"What, is a reporter meeting you here?" That was great news; he might mention the shop and Betsy loved getting free publicity.

"No, no, I'm here for *you* to interview me."

"What about?"

Irene stamped an impatient foot. "About the Rob McFey murder, of course! I was the one who found the body, you must have some questions for me!"

"Irene, the police have already arrested the murderer."

"Oh, that boy didn't murder Mr. McFey."

Betsy felt her ears growing big points that swiveled toward Irene. "What? How do you know that? What did you see at The Common?"

Irene writhed in pleasure at Betsy's keen interest. "Let's go sit down in back, it's more private."

"All right. Godwin?" Betsy called. The young man came out from the back, where he'd been sorting a new order of Anchor floss into the cabinet of little plastic drawers. "Take over out front, I want to talk with Irene."

Goddy's eyes sparkled, but he only said, "Of course."

Betsy and Irene took seats on little padded chairs around a very small round table. "Now, what is it you want to tell me?" said Betsy.

"I saw that boy who was arrested going by my booth toward Mr. McFey's, but that isn't the order things happened in. There were other people at the booth first."

"And you think one of them murdered Mr. McFey?"

"I don't know that for sure. But there was an argument earlier, and there wasn't any sound like that when the boy was there."

"That doesn't mean — well, wait a minute, maybe it does." Betsy thought a moment. "Would you like a cup of coffee, or tea?"

"Tea, please. Do you have some of that delicious raspberry?"

"Yes, I think I do." Betsy went into the small back room and filled two of her prettiest porcelain cups with hot water from an electric kettle, put a teabag each on the matching saucers, and refilled the kettle from a jug. She considered Irene's words while she did that. Irene was a very imaginative person, and growing more so all the time. But she was also a keen observer of the passing scene, and while inclined to draw strange conclusions about the motives of the people she observed, she did not ordinarily lie about what she actually saw. Betsy added a soupçon of imitation sugar to her own cup, and went back to the little table.

"Who was the boy you saw?" Betsy asked.

"Mickey Sinclair. I knew he was up to no good, skulking around like he was. Looking for something to steal, I'm sure. There should be more police on duty at the fair — some of the jewelry items are easy to stick into a pocket, and are quite valuable."

"Did you see him take anything?"

"No, of course not. I made sure he saw me looking at him, so he didn't dare take anything. He saw me and all of a sudden he was just a boy on his merry way to someplace, not a thief looking for something to steal. He was very obvious about it."

Betsy had a sudden recollection of a young man strolling the grounds, hands in pockets, whistling tunelessly, very ostentatiously playing the innocent. Was that Mickey Sinclair?

"What does he look like?"

"Well, he's not very tall, and he's thin, with curly brown hair that's too long for a boy and a ring in his nose." Her own small nose wrinkled in distaste. "He was wearing jeans with holes in them and a black T-shirt with a skull on it, disgraceful."

That matched Betsy's recollection.

"Did you see Mickey at Mr. McFey's booth?"

"No, but he went past my booth headed in that direction."

"And then you heard a quarrel?"

"No, the quarrel was earlier. Two men shouting. It wasn't very loud or very long."

"Could you hear what they were fighting about?"

"No. I think I heard one man say, 'You can't have it,' or maybe it was, 'You can't take it.'"

"'It,' not 'that'?"

Irene reflected while sipping her tea. "Yes," she nodded. "I'm almost positive he said, 'You can't have it.'"

"And there wasn't any sound like even one shout when Mickey Sinclair went past Mr. McFey's booth?"

"No. That's why I was so surprised when I went down there to look at his lion carving and found him." Her hand with the cup came down involuntarily, the fingers twitching. "There was a great deal of blood, it was very disturbing. Even Mike Malloy, though he's a policeman, was upset by it. When I tried to tell him to talk to you, he was rude to me." She turned those shining eyes on Betsy. "But there's no reason *I* can't talk to you, and now I'm sure you'll be able to discover who really murdered poor Mr. McFey."

Betsy was in her shop after closing that night. A large box had been delivered right at five by UPS, and she decided to unpack it before going upstairs. Her super-size cat, Sophie, didn't approve of the delay. The animal was in the back room beside the door to the back hallway, whining at intervals for someone to take her up to the apartment and feed her. Betsy ignored the whine.

She had tried to forbid food in her shop, both because it soiled fibers and because Sophie too often succeeded in garnering a share. In the last few months, by strenuous enforcement of the no-food rule, Betsy had reduced losses thirty percent and helped Sophie reduce her weight to nineteen pounds; the cat's role had been to complain that she was fading away to a wisp. But the shop's customers complained and so many persisted in bringing food along, especially when shopping during their lunch break, that Betsy had loosened the reins. And apparently believing Sophie's complaints, they resumed slipping the occasional tidbit to the cat. Just this afternoon, Betsy had seen Sophie eat a corner of a Hershey bar, a quarter of a sugar cookie, and a fragment of lettuce leaf coated with ranch dressing. God knew what else she'd eaten without Betsy noticing; certainly over the past few weeks she had regained two of the lost pounds.

So while Betsy still fed Sophie her official dinner scoop of dry cat food, she felt no urgency in getting upstairs to do so.

In the box Betsy was unpacking were a variety of baskets. When her sister Margot Berglund had owned Crewel World, she had used baskets to display items such as skeins of yarn and small needlework accessories. The baskets had grown shabby, and some had become a source of snags for anything placed in them. Baskets were expensive, so Betsy tried to ignore the problem. But then a customer had indignantly displayed the splinter in her finger. The customer, a Band-Aid on her finger and a free skein of overdyed silk in her bag, had departed only somewhat mollified — and Shelly Donohue had come in with a basket on her arm.

Shelly was a good friend as well as a sometime part-timer in Betsy's shop. She had a curvaceous figure, beautiful hazel eyes, and a great deal of light brown hair worn in a fat bun at the nape of her neck. A divorcee, she hadn't married again, and Betsy sometimes wondered why.

The basket was neatly woven, about fifteen inches deep and with an unusually high handle. "I don't think I've ever seen one like that," Betsy had said. "Where'd you get it?"

"In a place called Dell Rapids, South Dakota," replied Shelly. "I collect baskets, and I used to just display them, but lately I've been using some of them. This is just right for a quick trip to the grocery store. I no longer have to choose between choking a fish or killing a tree."

Betsy chuckled dutifully at the worn jest, and asked, "What were you doing in Dell Rapids, South Dakota? Is it near Mount Rushmore?"

"No, it's a little north of Sioux Falls, where I went to visit some friends. There's no needlework shop in Sioux Falls, but there's a nice one in Dell Rapids. And the owner carries baskets made by a local woman, Marcy Anderson. I bought this one and a double-rim."

Shelly gave Betsy the name of the owner of the needlework shop, and the owner in turn kindly gave Betsy Marcy Anderson's address so Betsy could deal with the basket weaver directly.

And so the box Betsy was unpacking held a big round wool-drying basket on short legs, two double-rimmed baskets, an egg basket whose bottom was shaped like a human bottom, and a mitten basket.

She enjoyed making displays and soon was deep in design mode, humming to herself, loading the baskets with goodies, and trying out places to put them, when someone tapped on the door to her shop. The sound was as if the person was using a key or coin, and Betsy knew before she looked around who it was. She saw a pair of long, dark-trousered legs and a light blue shirt standing at the door. The head was hidden behind her needlepointed closed sign, but Betsy grimaced. It was Jill, all right.

She went slowly to the door and lifted the sign to see if she could tell how angry Jill was. There was no expression at all on the woman's face, but Jill had a way with her face — the less it showed, the more she was thinking. Betsy braced herself and unlocked the door.

"Hello, Jill," she said. "Come on in."

Jill came in, removing her police cap as she did so.

"I thought when you got to be sergeant, you didn't have to work nights anymore."

"I'm just coming off duty, not going on," said Jill.

"Then you'll have time for a cup of coffee, or tea?"

"No. I just wanted to say . . . how disappointed I am in you."

Betsy nearly put on a surprised face, but caught herself in time. "I'm disappointed in me, too. I'm sorry I broke a confidence, Jill. It won't happen again."

"I'm glad to hear that. Good night." Jill put on her cap and turned for the door.

"Jill?"

She turned. "Yes?"

"Are we still friends?"

Jill's expression had not changed throughout this conversation, nor did it now. "Of course." She left the shop.

Betsy turned back to her task, but her heart was no longer in it.

At home, Jill sat down to her dinner of beef stew over a big biscuit. Jill never dieted; she wasn't particularly slim, but hadn't gained or lost an ounce since she was twenty. Tonight, however, she skipped the additional treat of frozen yogurt with strawberries she had planned on.

Though her surname was Cross, Jill was seven-eighths Norwegian, and had been raised in the cool-tempered traditions of that culture. Except to cheer at Twins and Viking games, she had never heard her parents raise their voices. When disagreements arose, the household settled into a frosty silence until someone was willing to apologize; and even then, there was a distinct chill until hurt feelings healed.

Jill used to envy people who shouted at one another over trivialities, then quickly got over it and embraced as warmly as they'd quarreled. She was pleased when she started dating an Irishman raised in that kind of family. But she quickly came to dread the no-warning flare-ups and found she had to fake the hasty, easy, sentimental making up that followed. She let the Irishman go and started dating Lars Larson, whose dogged, low-key emotions matched her own.

Lars had been asking Jill to marry him for well over a year, but Jill knew he didn't just want a wife: Lars wanted children, lots of them. He once confessed that he hoped Jill would get pregnant on their honeymoon.

This would have been fine with Jill, except that she was a patrol cop. It was very difficult to chase fleeing suspects or handcuff angry, struggling drunks while pregnant. So Jill had wanted to wait until she got a desk job.

Well, now she had the desk job, or anyway mostly a desk job, or at least she was no longer engaged in foot pursuits. To get the job, she'd passed the sergeant's exam.

Then came the catch. Excelsior had a no-fraternization rule. If Jill and Lars had been married, or even engaged, there would have been no problem. But they weren't. So unless one of them quit the police force — which wasn't going to happen — they couldn't date anymore. Well, if Lars passed his own sergeant's exam, then they could date, but that wasn't going to happen, either, because Lars refused to take it on the grounds that he loved the variety and action of patrol.

Interestingly, it never occurred to either of them to break the rule and see each other secretly. This was first because they were Scandinavians, who were second only to Germans in their passion for obeying the rules; but also because Excelsior had a citizen spy network second to none, and they never would have gotten away with it.

Which brought Jill to her second serious disappointment: Betsy Devonshire.

Jill had been introduced to Betsy by Betsy's sister Margot. Margot had been Jill's friend for seven years, her best friend for nearly four. Then Margot had been murdered, and Jill drew closer to Betsy for Margot's sake. The tie had strengthened when Betsy uncovered Margot's murderer. It was perhaps because the tie had never been questioned or even tested that Betsy's betrayal of Jill's trust had been so shattering.

That's how Jill saw it, as a betrayal. Even though she was a civilian, Betsy had successfully involved herself in criminal investigations and so, in Jill's mind, had a special status. So naturally Jill had told Betsy that a juvenile had been arrested for the murder of Robert McFey.

And Betsy, like any common gossip, had told the Monday Bunch meeting in her shop. Which would have been all right, but she had let slip that Jill was the source of her information. Within hours it was all over town.

The fault was partly Jill's, too; she should never have told Betsy about the arrest. In fact, she hadn't specifically told Betsy not to repeat it. So all right, the fault was mostly her own. The thought was enough to make her dinner a cold, unpleasant lump in her stomach.

Chief Nygaard had not been pleased. Jill had been reprimanded a time or two when she first joined the force, but for nothing more serious than mistakes any rookie might make — and far fewer of them than normal. Never before had an error of hers been called to the attention of the chief.

Even now, remembering his words (which were few) and his tone (which was cold), Jill felt a painful blush rise from her throat and spread upward to her ash-blond hairline.

It said much about Jill's integrity that she hadn't decided never to see or speak to Betsy again, but rather had gone to see her and in a calm voice expressed her disappointment.

But it would be a while before she could feel the same warm attachment.

And dismayingly, she couldn't go for comfort to Lars.

Chapter 4

Betsy tried to continue arranging the baskets, but at last shrugged and shoved some yarn in the remaining three of them, scattered them all around the shop, then went upstairs to feed her cat and herself. Like Jill, she didn't much appreciate her meal, and had no appetite for dessert.

After dinner, to remind herself she'd turned from proprietor of her shop to a student in it, she changed into jeans and a pink cotton shirt before she went back down to wait by the door for people to come to an evening class.

Charlotte Norton arrived first, as befitted the teacher. Char, a trim woman in her early forties with dark brown hair and hazel eyes, had been a customer of Crewel World long before Betsy had inherited it. Betsy had discovered that Char knitted and was fond of small, quick counted patterns, which she did as gifts for friends. But Char also bought a lot of white, green, and natural linen and a large number of balls of number five and number seven DMC Perle cotton in white and ecru — but nowhere near enough patterns to account for this amount of material. It wasn't until she asked if Betsy had a certain brand of scissors — Davos — which she didn't, that Betsy decided to ask just what it was Char was stitching.

"Hardanger," Char replied. Betsy had heard of Hardanger, but had never seen any. She asked Char to bring in a sample of her work. A week later she did, a spectacular table runner of her own design. Well over a yard in length, it was stitched on platinum-colored Cashel linen with threads matching in color — "Hardanger is usually stitched color on color," said Char, meaning white on white, buff on buff, or some color on a matching color.

The piece was composed of three geometric motifs made up of tiny squares filled with very fine, lace-like designs. These were interrupted by star-like satin-stitch motifs, and the whole surrounded by a border pattern made of more of the little squares in geometric patterns that identify Hardanger.

"I know it looks complicated," said Char, "but it isn't. It's made up of squares surrounded by five simple stitches on a side. The centers can be left alone, or snipped out entirely, or you can snip the weave threads and leave the warp threads so they look like little stripes, or you can wrap the threads into shapes called 'bars.' "

Yes, well, Betsy thought, bending to discover that what appeared to be tiny beads attached to some of the bars were, in fact, a loop of thread. She touched one gently. "Those are called picots," said Char, which she pronounced *pea-koze.*

Delicate rows of triple cable stitch flowed along the outer edge, just inside the buttonhole binding. Every stitch was as flawless as its sister, yet there was an indefinable feel and look to the pattern that said a human hand had done this, not a machine.

Running her fingers over the luxuriously textured squares, Betsy, feeling more than a little overwhelmed, said, "How long does it take to learn to do all this?"

Char shook her head. "Not long. If you can count to five, you can make a Hardanger kloster block. After you learn that, the rest is just patience."

And Betsy, who at this stage of learning needlework should have known better, believed her. "Would you be willing to teach me? No, let's do this right: Would you be willing to teach a class here at Crewel World?"

Char's hazel eyes darkened with pleasure. "All right."

So here she was, carrying a basket filled with beginner kits: fabric squares, fibers, needles, and a sheet of instructional text. "Is everyone coming?" she asked as Betsy let her into the shop.

"I suppose so. At least, no one's called to cancel." Four people in addition to Betsy had signed up. Betsy needed five in order to break even — she didn't count herself — so this was a bit disappointing.

Char went to the library table in the middle of the room. She put her materials on it, and stood with her back to Betsy for a moment. "Betsy, can I ask you something?" she said without turning around.

"Sure," said Betsy, but before Char could continue, there was a knock at the door.

It was the first of the other students; the rest followed in quick succession. They were Shelly Donohue, retired librarian Bershada Reynolds, and regular customers Ivy Jackson and Doris Valentine. After they were seated, Char asked each one to introduce herself to the others and tell what kinds of needlework she already knew how to do. Bershada was explaining that she'd done counted cross-stitch for "twenty years, at least," when there was a knock on the door.

Betsy went to open it, and found Godwin standing there looking near tears. "What's wrong, Goddy?" she asked in a low voice.

"I had another fight with John and it was my turn to go for a cooling-off walk, but I don't feel like walking. I remembered we have a class in Hardanger starting tonight and thought maybe I could try it."

"You're really upset. Do you think you'd

get anything out of it? No, no, wait a minute! This may be just the thing! It's one of those kinds of needlework that takes a little concentration and a lot of patience. Very soothing to the distressed mind. Come in."

"I'll write you a check tomorrow."

"Oh, don't worry about that." She gave him a quick hug. "I'm glad you came by."

"Thank you, my dear," he murmured, and squaring his shoulders and assuming a cheerful face, he went to the table and sat down. "Hi, Char," he said with a smile, "hi, Bershada; hi, Shelly; hello, Mrs. Jackson; hello, Ms. Valentine."

Char giggled. "I guess this is one person who doesn't need to introduce himself." Then she continued, "In theory, Hardanger isn't difficult." She handed the small squares around the table. "Hardanger cloth is a variety of Aida, which is a two-thread weave, so be careful not to split the weave or it will throw your count off." Ivy, the senior woman present, moved down a chair so she could use the Dazor light attached to the table. She snapped it on and held the cloth square under it, looking at it through the big magnifying glass in its center.

"You make a kloster block by placing five stitches side by side, working over four threads," Char said. "Everyone cut a length off the Number Five Perle floss." She handed balls of floss and blunt needles around the table. "You're less likely to split the fabric if the needle is blunt," she explained. She noted with satisfaction that no one reached for a needle threader from the jar of them Betsy kept on the table; that meant there were no beginning stitchers present.

"Now, stitch a row of five vertical stitches near the center top of your fabric." She picked up her own fabric square, pinched it to mark the center, and began to stitch. Heads came together as bottoms rose off the chairs and everyone looked at Char's stitching. Satisfied, they all sat down and began to stitch. When everyone had done five stitches, Char said, "Now, bring your needle back through the bottom of the last stitch, and let that be the start of five horizontal stitches. You want them at an angle of ninety degrees to the vertical stitches." She began stitching on her own cloth, but this time the others watched only the very start before sitting back down and doing their own.

Char had them do five vertical stitches across the bottom of the forming square, and five horizontal stitches leading back up the other side. "There, that forms the square that is the basic shape of Hardanger." She told them to run the end of the thread under the original kloster and cut it off short, "So when you're finished, it will be hard to tell the top from the underside of the project. In fact, I recommend that once you start your real project, you run a short piece of thread in near the border, bring it back up, and tie the two ends, so when you come back to it after a break, you'll know which side is the top."

She brought out the small heart-shaped project they'd be working on, and everyone started in. "It's much more important that the stitches be placed correctly than that you finish this in one sitting," said Char.

Everyone settled in to stitch; Char went around the table answering questions and pointing out errors. Betsy found it easy to do and went around quickly. But as she was forming the last kloster block, she found she only needed four stitches instead of five. It didn't seem important, so she ran the end of her thread under the first kloster and sat back with a smile. She was the second one finished, behind Shelly.

But then Char told them the next step: Snip the fabric at the bound edge of one kloster block and the corresponding block on the other side of the pattern from it. The idea was to pull the threads out. And in Betsy's case, that was not possible, because the two blocks were one thread off.

So Betsy had to start pulling out her stitching until she came to the mistake that caused the error. She began stitching from there — and it still didn't match. She had counted carefully this time; there was no mistake.

Char came by and at a glance saw that Betsy had made two errors originally and had corrected only the second one. She had to go even farther back to the first mistake.

Rattled now, Betsy found that no matter how carefully she counted, she kept making mistakes. The others were happily snipping threads while she was still working on the doggone outline of the heart.

"Oops," said Godwin. "Rats."

"Also," Char pointed out, taking Godwin's project from him and holding it out as an example, "you have to be careful to cut the proper side of the kloster block, which Godwin has done. Good for you. But not to cut beyond it, which he also has done. That's why I recommend a really good pair of little scissors."

Char had brought along several pairs to lend, but Shelly, holding out her piece admiringly, said she thought she'd buy a pair. Bershada, also smiling, said, "Me, too." Betsy pulled two pairs from a spinner rack of accessories. Shelly set to clipping with hers. Shelly paused long enough to look at the price and sigh, but she didn't give them back.

By the end of the class, everyone but Betsy and Godwin had finished pulling threads, and he was in the process of making his first snips. Shelly, who was halfway through a second heart, wanted to know how to make the little lace-like pattern in some of the squares on Char's big piece, but Char said that was for a later class. Betsy was thinking of getting another piece of fabric and starting over. She'd pulled her thread out so often the weave of her fabric was becoming distorted.

At eight-thirty, the class broke up. As the others filed out, Char lingered. Betsy, tired after a long day and frustrated by her first attempt at Hardanger, hoped Char wouldn't remember she had not asked the question she started to earlier.

But she did. "Betsy, I really need to talk to you."

"What about?" asked Betsy as politely as she could.

"Did you see the Channel Four news tonight?"

"No, I didn't have time. I am hoping to stay awake long enough to watch at ten — but I'm awfully tired." Hint, hint.

But Char was determined. "Did you see where they arrested a juvenile for the murder of that artist at the art fair?"

"Was it on the news? Someone told me about it."

"Yes, I heard that Jill told you." Char either didn't see or ignored Betsy's wince. "Betsy, the boy they arrested is my nephew.

My sister and brother-in-law are frantic, as you can imagine." Char took a strengthening breath and said, "They want to know if you can help."

Betsy didn't want to say yes to anything that would add to her burdens right now. "I don't know how I could help. I don't know any of the people involved in this. And Sergeant Malloy is sure he's got the right person."

"Yes, I know he's sure. That's what's got Faith and Greg so frantic. You see, Mickey's been in trouble ever since he was eleven. He's been arrested half a dozen times for stealing bicycles and shoplifting, for getting in fights, and for smoking marijuana at school. But he's never done anything like this; this is *murder.* He's sixteen and the police told Greg that when it's a homicide by a sixteen-year-old, the county attorney automatically petitions that he be tried as an adult."

Betsy said, "That's too bad. I'm so sorry."

"Yes, and you know Malloy, he's as sure as he can be he's got the person who did it, so he's not even looking at any other possibility. Mickey swears he didn't do it, but he's scared and angry and so he's acting out, which isn't helping a bit. Please, Betsy, won't you just talk to him?"

"To who? Mickey's father? I'm not sure that's a good idea; he may think I'm willing to help, but I don't know if that's true."

Char said, "No, they want you to talk to Mickey."

"Why? Do they think I can make him behave?" Betsy really was tired.

"No, no, no. Listen to me, please. They don't think he's guilty —"

"I'm sure they don't. Parents always want to believe their children are good and obedient creatures."

"Betsy, they know better. I've told you that Mickey is a very troubled young man. But what if he didn't do this?"

Betsy couldn't think of an answer. Her reputation *was* for clearing the innocent of criminal charges. "Is he out on bail?"

"No, they're not going to let him out. For one thing, he's run away from home twice in the past six months, so he's what they call a flight risk. But even if he weren't, he's charged with murder while committing a robbery, which makes it automatically first degree, so if they set bail, it's going to be an enormous sum, which his parents won't be able to raise. Betsy, if he gets convicted, they'll send him to prison for life. Mickey's parents really, really need help. Could you just please talk to him?"

"How? I mean, is he allowed visitors?"

"His attorney says he'll take you with him if you will go. Please, Betsy. Maybe if he talks to someone who isn't his family and not a police investigator or a lawyer, someone who's coming in as a friend, he'll say something helpful, instead of mouthing off and denying he was anywhere near The Common that morning."

"Was he in the park?"

"He says he wasn't. But they found a pair of shoes his size in a Dumpster behind the food vendors, and Faith says a pair just like them is missing from his closet."

Betsy sighed. "This doesn't look good, you know."

"I know."

"If I get involved in something like this, I may have to drop out of your class," she warned, a last-ditch plea.

"Fine," said Char, and she hugged Betsy hard.

So Betsy didn't get to go shopping on Thursday, her day off. Which was annoying, since she needed new underwear and there was a sale at Penney's.

It was a beautiful Minnesota summer morning, the temperature just approaching eighty and not much humidity. She drove with her windows down to the eastern edge of downtown Minneapolis, where the new Juvenile Detention Center on Fifth and Park was. She parked in a lot between the Center and the Metrodome; the Twins were out of town, so the lot was half empty.

The Center was a modern building of

large, dark bricks. The main entrance was in the middle of the building, its tuck-in entrance marked with fat concrete pillars.

A short young man, his light brown hair cropped close, stood just outside the dark glass door. He wore a nice lightweight suit, very modern eyeglasses, and an expensive new briefcase. There was an aggressive set to his mouth. He gestured impatiently as Betsy walked up and opened the door more to encourage her to keep moving than to be polite. "Glad you could make it," he said as he nimbly stepped ahead of her to open a second door into a small, diagonal lobby and again to show her to the window with a tray under it and a man in Dockers and a blue polo shirt behind it.

"I'm attorney Gerald Wannamaker," he said to the man.

Betsy thought for a moment to give a false name just to wipe that too-confident look off Wannamaker's face, but only said, "I'm Betsy Devonshire."

The man behind the glass queried his computer and found they were authorized for a visit. He issued them each a plastic pass on a lanyard and told them to wear it "visibly at all times," and they obediently hung them around their necks. While they waited for yet another door to be unlocked, Betsy said, "Thank you for arranging for me to come with you to see Mickey."

"No problem," he said, managing to indicate in those two words that it had been a problem, which he had solved with his usual skill.

A man in khaki trousers and a green polo shirt came to unlock the door. He led them down a broad corridor to a metal door set with a thick glass window that had chicken wire in it. He unlocked the door to let them into a tiny room with concrete block walls painted cream and a dark cafeteria-style table. Two dark chairs were on either side of the table. The napless gray carpet of the corridor continued in here.

Wannamaker sat down facing the door, gesturing briefly at the chair beside him, and put his briefcase on the table. He opened it and lifted out several legal-size documents, stapled to blue backs, and photocopies of official-looking reports.

Betsy, old enough to be affronted by this continued lack of manners, sat down in the chair indicated.

"Do you know Mickey's parents?" she asked.

"You mean personally? No."

"What do you think about this case?"

"Open and shut."

"You mean you can get him off?"

He stared at her, momentarily nonplused. "You're kidding, aren't you?"

Before Betsy could reply, the door's lock

rattled and it opened to admit yet another man in polo shirt and khaki trousers — this shirt was red — leading by the elbow a short young man with narrow shoulders, a trace of mustache, and a surly scowl.

"Mickey Sinclair," announced the polo shirt. "Knock when you're finished," he added and left, locking the door behind him.

Mickey had dark brown hair shaved to a shadow on the sides and grown into unruly curls on the top. His pale blue eyes were half veiled behind the lids. His hands were very large but delicately formed, neither knobby nor work-thickened. He wore gray scrubs that hung off his shoulders and were too short in the legs.

Wannamaker indicated one of the chairs on the other side of the table and Mickey took it a little too casually. He folded his big hands loosely and studied the thumbs.

"Mickey, I'm Betsy Devonshire," said Betsy, since Wannamaker apparently was not going to do the honors. "Your parents asked me to come and talk to you. Did they tell you about me?"

"Yeah," said Mickey with a rude glance up and down her.

"We need all the help we can get, from whatever source," said Wannamaker, agreeing with Mickey, by his tone, that she wasn't much. "You are in very serious trouble."

"They can't convict me," sneered Mickey. "I didn't do it!"

"They found your shoes in the park —" began Wannamaker.

"They aren't my shoes," said Mickey.

"They found money hidden in your bedroom, an amount that matches what was taken from the cash box at the scene of the murder."

"No, it don't, not exactly. Anyhow, money's money. It's my money, and I didn't steal it."

"You have a job?"

"No, I saved it up out of my allowance, plus some aluminum cans I collected. I didn't steal it. Plus I didn't kill anybody. They can't put me in prison for something I didn't do."

"Do you ever watch the news on television?"

He gestured dismissively. "News is boring."

"Then you may have missed those stories about people sentenced to death row, people who were later found innocent."

Mickey stared at him, and some kind of idea came to him. "Yeah, wait a minute, I did hear about that. It was a DNA test that proved they were innocent. That's a kind of blood test, right? They took some of my blood already, could they give it that kind of test?"

"It wouldn't help you," said Wannamaker.

"Why not?"

86

"DNA will tell them whether you left some skin under the fingernails of Mr. McFey."

"Which I didn't," Mickey interjected.

Wannamaker kept going. "It will tell them if you raped Mr. McFey. It will tell them if you are the father of Mr. McFey's baby."

"Dammit, quit making fun of me! Tell them I want a DNA test."

"They're already doing one. Now, listen a minute. Whose skin or hair will they find on Mr. McFey's body? Yours or someone else's?"

"Not mine! I never touched him! And he never touched me! So you see? That could prove it, couldn't it?"

Mickey seemed in earnest, but Wanna-maker sighed and consulted one of the reports. "Now, they found a pair of shoes in a trash container behind the food vendors."

Mickey threw his head up in an angry gesture. "So what? Everyone wears shoes, don't they?"

"Yes, but these shoes seem to match a pair you own, and your own shoes have gone mysteriously missing."

"Someone took them," mumbled Mickey. He was staring hard at his thumbs.

"Why would someone steal a ratty old pair of shoes?"

" 'Cause they were really good Nikes? Anyway, maybe they didn't steal them, maybe I loaned them to someone."

Wannamaker didn't even bother to ask for the name of a possible borrower. "Do you ever wear those shoes without socks?"

Mickey thought a few moments, trying to think what Wannamaker was getting at so he could choose the least damaging reply. "Hardly ever," he guessed.

"So there may be little traces of skin inside them. They are looking for little traces of skin in the shoes they took out of the Dumpster. Skin has DNA, and they are testing scrapings from the inside of those shoes, to see if your DNA is in them. They are also doing a DNA test on the blood that was on the outside of those shoes. They already know the blood type is Mr. McFey's, not yours. If they find your DNA inside the shoes and Mr. McFey's DNA on the outside, that will put those shoes on your feet at the scene of the crime."

Mickey threw his arms up and Betsy leaned backwards and sideways, sure he was going to reach for Wannamaker. But he was only giving himself room to fill his lungs and yell, "I thought you were on *my* side!"

Wannamaker, unafraid, barked, "Shut up!" Mickey dropped his arms. "I am on your side," continued Wannamaker. "I'm only stating the facts. Let me ask you this: When the DNA test results come back, will they help you or the prosecution?"

"I wasn't there," Mickey grumbled doggedly. "I wasn't in the park, I was supposed to but I changed my mind, and I didn't go." He said it as if saying it often enough would make it so.

"You're a fool to stick with that story."

Mickey sat back with an unhappy sigh. "What else can I do?"

"We should talk about your options. There are at least two eyewitnesses who saw you running up Lake Street wearing socks but no shoes."

"They're lying, they hate me, everyone hates me. They saw someone else, someone who looks like me." This was said with no conviction at all. He rubbed one eye sleepily. "All right, you're supposed to be my lawyer. What do you think I should do?"

"I think you should consider a plea bargain."

Faint hope dawned. "Yeah, I did that once before. I didn't have to say I did it, even. Can we do that again? Last time I got probation. Can we get that same kind of bargain?"

"Not a chance. But maybe we can do the kind that has you home in eight or ten years."

Mickey came out of his chair as if lifted by a rope. *"Ten years?!"* He pirouetted on one foot, arms spread. "What kind of a lawyer *are* you? Ten freakin' *years!* I don't *think* so! I didn't *kill* him! *Ten years,* when I didn't freakin' kill him!"

"Sit down," Wannamaker said quietly.

But Mickey's face suddenly twisted with hatred. "You're just like everyone else, you aren't here to help me! I tell you I wasn't there, I didn't kill him, but you don't believe me. You don't want to help me, you *want* me to go to prison!"

"I said, sit down." Wannamaker spoke no louder than before, but something in his voice was not going to permit argument.

The boy sat. "I'm done talking to you, you're no help to me. Why don't you just freakin' leave? And don't come back."

"Fine, I'll do that. And I'll tell your parents you don't want me to represent you anymore." Betsy thought this an obvious ploy, but Wannamaker underlined it by beginning to sort the papers he'd laid out on the table into two stacks.

Mickey sneered, "Go ahead, quit. You're no good anyhow."

Wannamaker picked up a stack of papers and bumped them lightly on the table to align them. Without looking at her, he asked Betsy, "Do you want to ask this loser anything?" He didn't think so, his behavior suggested, he opened his briefcase and put the stack into it.

So Betsy, tired of being treated as a nuisance at best, said, "If you don't mind." She turned to Mickey. "Despite all the evidence against you, despite the bloody shoes, despite the money they found, despite the eyewitnesses, what if I told you I believe you did not murder Robert McFey?"

He stared at her, unable to speak, then his face suddenly rumpled in all directions, his eyebrows going up and drawing in, his eyelids turning down at the corners, his mouth twisting oddly, as he struggled not to burst into tears.

"Yeah, right," growled Wannamaker, and as suddenly as it rumpled, Mickey's face pulled smooth, then twisted with anger. He proceeded to show that while the young are fluent in all manner of scatology and pornography, they often lack imagination.

Well before he was finished, Wannamaker went to the door and rapped sharply on it. The man with the key appeared so promptly that Betsy suspected a hidden microphone or camera.

"That's enough, Mr. Sinclair," the guard said, and Mickey subsided at once, not even offering a parting shot at Wannamaker as he passed him on his way out.

"Sorry about that," sighed Wannamaker.

"Are you going to withdraw as his attorney?" asked Betsy.

"No, that was an empty threat. He's not the one who hired me," said the lawyer, amused. He consulted his watch and used what he saw as an excuse to hustle out ahead of her.

On her drive home, Betsy growled to herself about the rude attorney, and then about the dreadful young man whom she was supposed to help. But as she cooled a bit, she recalled the brief but utter transformation of Mickey's attitude when she offered to believe his denials. She'd blindsided him with that offer, so his reaction was very likely honest. Could it possibly be that he was, in fact, innocent?

She decided to talk to his parents.

Chapter 5

The Sinclairs lived in a modest brick house on a small lot fronted by a hedge that needed trimming. A corner of the lot was cut off by one of Excelsior's ubiquitous diagonal alleys that once had served as fire lanes. This one was unpaved, and had a slight curve punctuated by mature trees. Early pink peonies and the many colors of bearded iris thrust between the slats of backyard fences. The yards without fences marked their borders with lilac bushes or bridal wreath, the latter so heavy with white blooms the branches dipped to the ground as if caught in a fragrant blizzard. The lilacs were in their brief purple glory, the scent of them and bridal wreath and — What was it? Yes, mock orange — heavy in the air.

Betsy's shop carried a counted cross-stitch pattern of a romanticized country lane that was not as pretty as this, nor could it capture the heady fragrance. No wonder people paid ridiculous prices for houses in Excelsior!

She suddenly remembered why she was there, and her pleasant reverie faded. She collected her wits and went up the sidewalk to ring the doorbell.

The door was opened promptly by a short, thin woman with dark brown hair tucked behind her ears. There were brown shadows under her brown eyes, but her sleeveless white blouse and pale plaid shorts were crisp. "Yes?" she said.

"Faith Sinclair? I'm Betsy Devonshire."

"Oh, of course. Won't you come in?"

"Thank you." Betsy smiled to herself. Faith had never met Betsy, and was probably expecting a tall, thin sleuth with piercing gray eyes and a lot of presence. But Betsy was not tall, or slender, and the only thing gray about her would have been her hair if she didn't make regular trips to a hairdresser.

The woman led Betsy into a small, warm living room — no air-conditioning. The place looked and smelled immaculate, but the furniture and carpet were badly worn. On the couch were a girl and a young woman, and standing in front of an easy chair was a good-looking man in a nice suit and thick hair, all one shade of brown.

"Ms. Devonshire, these are my daughters, Kristal and Kathy, and that is my ex-husband, Greg." There was the slightest emphasis on *that*.

"How do you do?" said Betsy.

The girls mumbled something, then became interested in how their arms crossed their chests. There was an unhappy tension in the air that somehow did not seem linked to her visit.

"How do you do?" said Greg, stepping forward and extending his hand. His grip was firm, his expression that of someone hoping his show of pleasantness would disguise the tension. She noticed a few gray hairs in Greg's eyebrows and, when he stepped back, a shiny new wedding band on his left hand — a reason to dye one's hair, certainly. But the girls narrowed their eyes at him, not liking his false show, or perhaps the man himself, their father with a shiny new wife.

"Won't you sit down?" said Faith. "May I bring you something? A Coke? Bottled water?"

"Water would be nice," said Betsy. Greg stepped away from the easy chair and gestured that she should take it. He looked at the couch, but the hostile eyes of his daughters warned him off, so he went to a wooden chair with a flat pillow tied to its seat and sat down.

"I understand you've done several successful investigations," he said.

"Yes." Betsy disliked bragging and didn't elaborate.

"I hope you're able to help us."

"Me, too."

"Did you talk to Mickey in the jail?" asked the younger girl, Kathy. She was an attractive creature, with curly brown hair like her brother's, and his blue eyes, but her forehead was wrinkled with distress. She wore cutoff jeans, thick-soled sandals on bare feet, and a tube top that made a display of her budding breasts. She looked about fourteen and so was probably around twelve.

"Yes, just briefly. He's . . . angry."

"Of course he is," said Faith, coming into the room with a glass and a green bottle on a tray. She put the tray down on a little side table beside Betsy's chair. "It's perfectly understandable."

"Yeah, that's how he always reacts when he gets caught," said the older girl, Kristal. She had her mother's dark hair and eyes, and was pretty in a little pink knit dress with spaghetti straps, but her voice and expression were hard. She was that young-adult age, which can be anything from seventeen to twenty-four; whatever, she was Mickey's big sister.

Betsy, surprised, stopped pouring to say, "I thought you were sure he was innocent!"

"He is innocent!" said Faith, frowning at her daughters. "Innocent of murder, certainly. But I have no doubt he was at The Common."

Kristal made a disparaging face and nudged her sister, who nudged back, imitating the face.

"He denies that," said Betsy.

"Faith has no faith in our son," said Greg.

"I have more than you!" said Faith, so sharply Betsy was sure this was the source of the tension, and that it was a continuation of a quarrel that had begun at least as long ago as Mickey's arrest, and possibly before Greg became Faith's ex-husband. She looked at Betsy. "But I'm sure he was there and doing something . . . inappropriate. He told me the night before that he was going to The Common to meet some of his friends. I didn't want him to go, but he went."

"Do you know the names of those friends?" asked Betsy.

"The police have talked to them already," said Faith, "and the boys said they didn't see him there. But by then they knew Mickey had been arrested, and I'm sure they were lying for him, the way boys do."

But Betsy, feeling she'd at last asked a question that might lead somewhere useful, rummaged in her purse for a pen and a little notebook. "Tell me their names anyway," she said, opening the notebook and clicking out the point of the pen.

"Well, there's Noose, I don't know his real first name; his last name is Levsky. And there's the Martinson boy, I think his first name is Chris, though he likes people to call him Thief. And Billy Swenson, though I'm not sure he was there, the other boys said they didn't see him, either; and I've told Mickey he's not to hang out with him anymore."

"A fine set of friends," noted Greg, "Noose, Thief, and Bad Billy Swenson."

"I've been doing the best I can!" said Faith, taking the remark as criticism of herself. "May I remind you that you haven't exactly been holding up your end?"

"How could I? You almost never let me have him! Always some excuse — he's sick, he's going someplace with his friends. It's wrong, you're wrong. He's a boy, and a boy needs his father."

"A boy needs a stable, two-parent home, which Mickey doesn't have anymore, and a father with some integrity, which he *never* had!"

"Excuse me," said Betsy, trying to head off the storm that was about to break over their heads. "I'm here to discuss Mickey and what you want me to do for him."

"Yes, of course, I'm sorry," said Faith, contrite.

"Whatever," muttered Greg.

"Can I say something?" interjected Kristal. When everyone looked at her, she brushed shyly at the brief skirt of her pink dress, but then raised her chin to say, "I don't think Ms. Devonshire should get involved. We've tried long enough to do something for Mickey; nobody can help him now."

"Don't say things like that," said Faith.

"Face it, Mother," argued Kristal, "he's gone from stealing to murder. It's the logical next step for someone who's been in trouble ever since his voice broke and he started turning into a 'man.' " There was a bitter twist on the last word.

"That's enough!" said Faith, too sharply. She paused long enough to replace her frown with a false smile at Betsy that asked her to ignore Kristal's words. But there was real concern in her voice when she asked, "Are they treating him all right? He catches anything that's going around, and being in close quarters with all those other boys, some of them . . ." But now she was in danger of becoming politically incorrect, so she let the sentence trail off unfinished.

"That's because he smokes pot," announced Kathy. "Pot makes you sick and stupid."

"Just being Mickey makes you sick and stupid," said Kristal.

"Hush up, both of you," said Greg.

"You aren't the boss of us anymore!" said Kristal, her contempt now reaching to her father.

"Not one more word," warned Faith, and the girls recrossed their arms and slouched deeper into the couch.

"Tell me about Mickey," said Betsy.

"Well, he just turned sixteen three weeks ago," said Faith. "He'll be a sophomore in high school this fall —"

"Yah, he flunked fifth grade," sneered

Kathy, with the superior air of someone who would be in sixth grade come fall.

"Kathy, if you can't be quiet, or at least helpful, you may go to your room!" said Faith.

"Okay, I will!" Kathy rose to her feet, her face twisted with anger. "Mickey is a bad person, I hope he stays in jail forever!"

Kristal stood in solidarity, but she tried a reasonable tone when she said, "We can't afford to throw more money away on him, Mother. Kathy and I always go without so you can buy Mickey out of trouble, and we're sick and tired of it. Besides, not even the miracle worker here can help Mickey this time."

Betsy said, surprised, "I'm not a miracle worker — and I don't charge anything for my investigations."

Kristal was surprised in turn. "Then why are you doing this?"

"Because I have a talent for discovering whether someone innocent has been accused of a crime."

She and her sister offered identical snorts of incredulity. "Mickey's never been innocent in his life!" said Kristal.

"Yeah!" agreed Kathy.

"I think perhaps he may be in this case."

"I give up, you're all crazy," said Kristal, and she left the room, Kathy marching in total agreement behind her.

"Okay, now the disrupting influences have left the room," remarked Greg, as if beginning a sentence. But he didn't finish it, only cast a wary eye on his ex-wife.

"Do you really believe Mickey is innocent?" Faith asked Betsy, desperate to hear "Yes" in reply.

"I think perhaps he is. You said you were sure he was at The Common, but he says he wasn't."

"He's . . . a bit of a liar," said Faith.

"He's a big fat liar," amended Greg.

"Why is that?" asked Betsy.

"Because he wants to be a man, and doesn't know how," said Greg. "Faith has no idea how to help a boy become a man."

"Not being one yourself, neither do you!" said Faith.

Surprisingly, Greg didn't reply, and she continued to Betsy, "Mickey's just like his father, always trying to prove himself. I tried to tell him that real men have flaws and weaknesses just like women do, but he wouldn't believe me. He brags about how strong he is, and lies about how well he's doing, always denying that he's scared or tired or unable to handle a situation. Greg told him he was the man of the house —"

"Once. One time," interrupted Greg.

"So he started trying to boss us around. I told the girls they don't have to take orders from him, so he fights with them all the time. *And* me. And after a fight he storms out of the house, and next thing we know, he's done something *really* inappropriate."

"Is that what happened last Sunday?" asked Betsy.

Faith sighed. "Yes. It wasn't a worse fight than usual, but it ended with the usual slamming door."

Greg said, "I think Faith has some kind of notion about 'testosterone poisoning,' which started as a feminist joke but has become gospel. She used to get angry with Mickey when he was little because he was loud instead of quiet, messy instead of neat, and ran instead of walked. He was just a normal boy, but she couldn't see that, all she could see was that he wasn't like Kristal when she was his age. It got worse, a lot worse, after the divorce. He had just turned twelve and didn't know how to handle his anger and resentment — and I wasn't there to show her that acting out is part of the struggle toward manhood, and show him how to handle the feelings he was having. He's my son, and I was proud to have a son, but we both failed him."

"It got worse *because* of the divorce," amended Faith.

"You were the one who wanted a divorce," Greg reminded her.

"You were the one who started staying out at night!" she flared.

"You're the one who kept running me out of the house!"

"We're talking about Mickey," said Betsy, trying the heading-off technique again.

"This *is* about Mickey!" snapped Faith. "It's about boyhood and manhood and, all right, the whole testosterone thing!" She flung herself down on the couch, propped her head on one hand, and took several deep breaths. "I'm sorry, Greg's right, it wasn't just him, we both handled it badly." She raised her head. "But I can tell you from my heart, I absolutely know that Mickey didn't murder that artist!"

Driving home an hour later, Betsy shrugged several times and moved her head around, trying to make her shoulder muscles loosen up. What a family! No wonder Mickey Sinclair was in trouble, coming from a home like that.

She grabbed that thought and decapitated it. Plenty of children had come out of worse homes and done well.

Once, long ago, Betsy had had a friend who was a dog breeder. This friend explained that breeders were — or should be — as interested in behavior as in looks, and could select for both. She told Betsy that the Doberman was bred to guard territory — unlike the German shepherd, which was bred to interact with people — and that its indifference to people made it a dangerous animal, much more savage in its attacks on an intruder, or what it considered an intruder. People who loved the aerodynamic lines of the Doberman nevertheless wouldn't buy one because of its reputation for ferocity. So breeders responded with selective breeding that produced a warm and friendly personality with the same sleek silhouette.

In Betsy's mother's day, human babies were thought to be very different from animals. They even had a term for it — *tabula rasa,* the blank slate — meaning a baby was a creature on which any personality might be written. It was during those dark times that a child who turned out autistic, homosexual, criminal, cowardly, a pedophile, or even just lazy was thought to be the product of bad mothering. Betsy's mother hadn't believed it. Her best friend, she said, had a lazy son who even in utero was so lumpish she had twice gone to the doctor, certain the child had died in her womb. Betsy's mother had pointed to Betsy and her sister as examples of two very different girls who had been raised in very similar surroundings by the same two parents.

But people were very adaptable, Betsy thought. Just look at the variation in culture around the world. Personality, she was sure, might be colored or channeled by environment; but the environment had a person's innate character to deal with, which produced different results with different characters. A television program had pointed out recently that almost all serial killers were sociopaths, which is a personality defect that makes its victims unable to empathize. On the other hand, a person born with that defect normally didn't turn into a serial killer unless he also survived a sickeningly cruel upbringing. Was sociopathy itself a genetic defect, inheritable? Because sociopaths made terrible parents.

Mickey's parents weren't sociopaths. He had a mother who disliked, maybe feared, men and taught her two daughters to be the same way. He had a father who couldn't manage to be there for his son. But Mickey had a personality that couldn't compensate for that, and so he was the kind of child who began behaving inappropriately at age twelve.

Betsy's mouth twisted. What a word, "inappropriate"! Like a lot of euphemisms, it was imprecise; but this one was wildly so. Especially considering the long list of Mickey's sins, as detailed by his parents. Yelling at his sisters was inappropriate. Smoking in the school lavatory was inappropriate. Getting tattooed was inappropriate. Shoplifting, stealing bicycles, punching a classmate's front teeth out, running away from home — once as far as Kansas City — all inappropriate. That description made them seem all equally bad behaviors.

But had Mickey escalated his bad behavior all the way to the top, to murder? Mickey was an angry boy, a troubled and troublesome boy. An unlikable boy. And the evidence seemed convincing — even his mother was sure he'd been in the park. But stir in the facts that the parents were also unlikable, his sisters aggravating snots — Betsy didn't need this. Maybe she should just back off, say she didn't have time for this investigation. She felt a rush of relief at the thought. She wasn't a professional, assigned to cases. She could pick and choose.

But there had been that little glimpse, hadn't there? That brief look at a terrified child grabbing at hope when someone had offered to believe he was innocent.

But that mere glimpse wasn't evidence, or not evidence enough. Mickey had every reason to be afraid, and to hope desperately for someone to believe he wasn't guilty. Betsy needed more than that.

Well, Mickey had pointed out that the money found in his room wasn't the same amount as the money stolen from the victim. His explanation of where it had come from was lame, but that might be because it was the product of marijuana sales. A kid who needed money for pot might well get it by becoming a dealer.

On the other hand, if Rob McFey's fingerprints had been found on the money . . .

She wished she could ask Jill what Malloy had found out in his investigation. But Jill was done talking about police business to Betsy, that was for sure.

Well, then, what else? There were those bad-influence friends of Mickey's. Faith had said the police had talked to Noose, Thief, and Bad Billy Swenson, all of whom said they hadn't seen Mickey in the park. Faith was sure they were lying to protect Mickey. And maybe they were. But could one or more of them be lying to protect themselves?

So okay, there were a few angles she could investigate — provided she decided to investigate. Which she wasn't sure she was going to do.

Betsy was coming up Lake Street toward her shop. Parked in front of the door was a large, square-cut green car of ancient vintage. It had a single brass lantern for a taillight, and the wheels had wooden spokes painted a bright yellow. A wisp of steam was coming from near the rear underside. Betsy began to smile.

The car was a 1911 Stanley Steamer belonging to Lars Larson, whom Betsy had sponsored last year in an antique car run. She had been the only person of his acquaintance to find the car fascinating, and still enjoyed going for a ride in it. The car's boiler had been damaged last year, and Betsy had thought Lars might sell it. But he hadn't, and people were getting used to seeing the pioneer machine in the area.

She pulled into the driveway that led to the back of her building and parked, still smiling. A short, swift, silent run up a highway in the old car would be just the thing she needed to blow the cobwebs of indecision out of her brain.

She went in through the back door, into the back of her shop. Lars, a very big man with blond hair and enormous hands, was standing in front of the old desk that served as the shop's checkout counter. Behind it was Shelly Donohue, her part-time employee at Crewel World. She was smiling up at Lars and tucking a stray tendril of hair into the big knot at the nape of her neck — Lars belonged to Jill Cross, Shelly knew that, but he had a virile Viking charm that made a woman remember whether she'd put on perfume while dressing that morning.

"Hi, Lars!" called Betsy, starting forward.

But when he turned toward her, he wasn't smiling. His face went red and clenched into a furious display of anger. "Where the hell have you been?" he demanded. "And what the hell were you thinking about?"

Chapter 6

Lars was a large, aggressive police officer, quick to rise to the defense of the weak or threatened — which Betsy felt both of at the moment. Confused, she took a step back. Then clarity struck. "Did Mike Malloy send you over to talk to me?"

Apparently not; her question bewildered him so much that his anger faded from red to pink while he tried to figure out why she had asked that. Then he understood. "You've been investigating one of his cases again," he said accusingly. "I bet it's that murder at the art fair."

"I've been asked by Mickey Sinclair's family to look into it, yes," she said, nodding. "But that isn't why you're here, is it?"

"No." The anger came back, but not in a scary form. "No, it's not! Jill's having enough trouble with me without you aggravating her, too!"

"What have you done?"

He was aggravated by her always wandering from his point of ignition. "Nothing, dammit! *You're* the one who made her mad. You're the one who needs to make up with her!"

"Then tell me how!" Betsy retorted. "She's mad at me, I'm not mad at her!" She continued, less sharply, "I don't blame her for getting angry with me, but I apologized and promised not to do it again. I don't know what else to do until she cools off and lets me talk to her." Betsy waved that turn of phrase away. "I mean, warms up. She was about seventy degrees below zero the last time I saw her. Could you talk to her on my behalf, Lars? Explain that I'm really, really sorry?"

"Nope." Lars shook his head. "We can't talk anymore."

"Why, is she mad at you, too? This is terrible, her being mad at both of us!"

Now he was woebegone as well as annoyed. "She's not mad at me. She made sergeant, and there's a no-fraternization rule. I can't date her anymore."

"Oh, no!"

"But that's stupid!" said Shelly, coming out from behind the desk. "Surely they can't mean to break you two up! You've been dating for years, since long before she was promoted!"

Lars tugged at an earlobe. "Yeah, I know. Everyone knows. But it's a rule. If we were engaged or married, it would be all right."

"Well, can't they promote you, too?" asked Betsy. "You've been a police officer as long as Jill."

"I'd have to pass the test, and there won't

be another one for a long while. Years, maybe. Openings don't come along too often in a small department. Anyhow, I don't want to be promoted! I like what I'm doing on patrol. It's rotten that we can't see each other . . ." He was suddenly recalled to his original purpose. "And it's worse when her best friend gets her in trouble on the job!"

"On the job?" echoed Betsy.

His anger rose from its ashes. "You sure did! The chief called her on the carpet for talking to civilians about police business. He was really PO'd, and it'll probably go in her personnel file. It's the first time that's ever happened to her, her first black mark on the job, and she's really sad about it."

Betsy was reduced to a shocked and shamed silence.

Shelly said, "If you can't talk to her, how do you know this?"

"I had to talk to her on official business, and she was looking like she was coming down with flu or something, so I asked her if she was feeling all right, and she told me about it. I thought she was gonna break down and cry. She's got two kinds of trouble on her plate and I've never seen her like this before."

Betsy had seen Jill sad but never tearful. "That's terrible! What can I do? She's my best friend!" She thought of Jill, cool, unruffled Jill, distressed to the point of tears —

and it was all Betsy's fault! Betsy felt her own eyes filling. She turned away to grope blindly for one of the little chairs around the small table in the back half of her shop. She fell into it and put her elbows on the table, resting her face in her hands, trying to control her breathing, which threatened to turn into sobs.

"Aw, now, don't you start in," said Lars, coming to pat her on the back. His big hand was hard as a board, and he brought with him a whiff of kerosene and oil — his antique car took constant maintenance. The pain of his sympathetic thumping shocked away the incipient sobs.

"Th-that's all right," she said. "But there must be s-something that will help."

Lars stopped thumping. "I dunno what it could be," he said. "I can't help her and I can't arrest you." But the thought of an arrest made him grip her shoulder.

"Arrest!?" Shelly said indignantly. "What would you charge her with, Lars, failure to yield?"

After a startled moment, Betsy laughed, and Lars, surprised, let go. Betsy said, "That's funny, Shelly: failure to yield!" She looked up at Lars's pink, sad face and sobered again. "I'm sorry, I apologize. My emotions are all over the place. I'm just coming from a terrible interview with the Sinclairs, and when I saw your car, I thought

I was going to have fun going for a ride, but when I came in, you were so angry it scared me, and all because Jill's in a pickle at work . . . I'm just feeling a bit of whiplash, that's all." She stood up, wiping her cheeks. "Lars, do you think writing Jill a letter would help?"

"I'm a lousy letter writer — oh, you mean if you wrote to her? I dunno, maybe." He sighed and rubbed the back of his neck. "Hell, when we used to fight, nothing worked to change her mood. All I could do was wait her out. After a week or two, she'd decide she liked me more than she was mad at me, and she'd call and we'd get back to normal. I suppose that's what you've got to do, too."

Betsy grimaced. Two weeks seemed like a very long time to just wait. "Well, if you say so. I guess I'll have to be patient with her." Seeking to become businesslike, she said to Shelly, "Has the mail come yet?"

"Not yet. But that shipment of Crystal Rays you ordered is here. And Mrs. Wilcox phoned to ask if her special order of merino wool has come in yet. I couldn't find it, so I said no."

"Oh, golly, I meant to call the supplier about that, we've been waiting for that order for nearly a month. I'd better phone them. No, wait a second, this is Saturday, they aren't open on weekends. Write a note, Shelly, use my red pen and all capital letters,

113

reminding me to call them first thing Monday."

Lars said, "I'd better get out to the Stanley before someone tries to steal her."

"Wait a minute, Lars." Betsy didn't want to be patient. "Isn't there something we can do? I know, I'll send her a gift, nothing big, some little thing from the shop. Maybe a couple cards of Crystal Rays?" Jill liked exotic fibers, and that shipment of Crystal Rays tubular ribbon included the new solid colors.

"For cripe's sake, don't do that!" Lars said. "After the way the chief laid into her, she'd turn you in for attempted bribery."

Betsy shoved her fingers into her hair. "But there has to be something I can do to help her warm up to me again! I can't just sit quietly for weeks!"

"Well, hey, isn't there a Sophia Designs trunk show coming in soon?" asked Shelly from behind the desk, red-ink pen raised to her cheek. Trunk shows were sent in sturdy cases from shop to shop across the country. They featured new designs, new patterns, new fabrics and fibers — and special prices.

"Yes, I've already done a mailing about it."

"Did you mention that this one features C. Bethel's work?"

"Yes, of course. Oh! Shelly, you are a genius!" C. Bethel's needlepoint canvases often featured exotic women in Art Deco–style clothing: strangely shaped hats or turbans, brightly patterned dresses with peacock-feather trim, complex jewelry. The hand-painted canvases were costly, but beautiful and popular. Jill loved them. "That would be just the thing to lure her back into the shop."

"But wait, I'm not finished. Why don't you have a special early opening for it, inviting only your best customers? Jill certainly qualifies, doesn't she?"

"Well, of course! And I'll set aside a Lady in Blue for her. Last time I had one, someone else got it ahead of her. Now when she comes in, I'll . . ." Lars caught her eye and she quickly amended that thought. "I'll be just ordinary to her, no special attention at all."

Lars nodded approval of her swift grasp of the rules. "If she acts like nothing was ever wrong, you should be just as usual back."

When the door went *Bing!* they all turned to look at a man standing just inside the shop. He was a stranger, about forty-five, handsome in a broad-faced, burly way, his eyes marked with laugh lines and his mouth inside a goatee already in a smile as he looked around with pleased interest. He was tall and dressed like an old-fashioned hippie in broad-strapped sandals, too-short trousers, and a collarless shirt big enough to drape gently over his paunch. His hair was brown lightly mixed with gray; thick, curly, and long, caught in a trio of scrunchies down his back. His eyebrows were dark and bushy, a contrast to the well-kept goatee. He had a fat bandage on one hand, just the last joints of two fingers showing.

"May I help you?" Shelly asked before Betsy could.

He turned a powerfully charming grin on her and said in a pleasant growl, "Are you Betsy Devonshire?"

Shelly turned to gesture at Betsy. "No, this is she."

Betsy said, "May I help you?"

"I'm Ian Masterson," he said with a slight bow, his tone indicating she should perhaps recognize the name. When she didn't, he said, "I'm an artist and an old friend of Rob McFey's. I was helping him get a gallery show in Santa Fe when . . . all this happened." His smile dissolved into an unhappy look. "I hear you know something about the case, so I decided I should talk to you."

Lars said, "I gotta go. You want a rain check on that ride?"

"Yes, please. Thanks, Lars."

Ian held out the bandaged hand sideways to stop him. "Hey, you the owner of that Stanley sitting out front?"

"Yeah, why?"

"I always wanted to see one of them up and running. You from around here?"

"Yeah."

"Would it be possible to talk to you about

your car? I can't believe you actually drive one of those things on the public streets. Aren't they dangerous? Is it hard to keep it running? What kind of fuel do you use?"

"Naw, it's safe, and it's not hard. I use Coleman gas and kerosene, though I'm thinking of changing the pilot light fuel to hexane, because it runs cleaner than Coleman. Your pilot light clogs easy, and that can lead to real trouble."

"Can you use regular water for the boiler, or do you need distilled?"

"Hell, I can suck it up out of a ditch if I need to. Here . . ." Lars was reaching into a front pocket. "Here's my card. I really gotta go, but give me a call sometime and I'll tell you anything you want to know." Lars handed over the card and went out.

Ian looked the card over, and one eyebrow lifted. "He's a *cop?*"

"Yes." Betsy nodded. "Of course, the department uses internal combustion automobiles."

Ian looked blankly at her, then suddenly broke into such complimentary laughter that Betsy felt herself blushing. His laugh was infectious, and Shelly began to laugh too. He stuffed the card into a trouser pocket. "I'm sure the local criminal element is unhappy to hear that!" he said, still laughing. Then he sobered and asked Betsy, "Tell me, can I help you in any way with your investigation?"

"Who told you I was investigating?"

He looked embarrassed. "Uh-oh. Am I wrong? The woman I talked to, she, uh — she does some interesting fiber art, but she's a little . . ." He broke off again with a swift glance around the shop, worried that now he'd put his foot in yet another wrong direction.

But Shelly said, "Irene Potter! Honestly, that woman is a worse gossip than I am!"

Ian turned to look with interest at Shelly. "That's her name. You know her?"

"Everyone knows Irene," said Shelly. "She's a fantastic needleworker, and starting to get famous. I heard she's not going to take a booth at the art fair anymore, because she's getting above them." Shelly blushed. "There, see what I mean? Gossip."

Ian grinned. "But she as much as told me the same thing." He turned back to Betsy. "It was your Ms. Potter, all right. But is that some kind of fantasy she was spinning, about you looking into Robbie's murder? I mean, she said you solve murders all the time . . ." He let that trail off, looking Betsy up and down.

There was that lack of intimidation again. It wasn't that Betsy was a frump, nor did she have a vacuous face. But she was short and plump, with a pleasant, middle-fifties face. No thin, hawk-like profile here — nor a darkly powerful costume. She was wearing a pale green pantsuit with a cross-stitch pattern of flowers on the collar and pocket.

Shelly said, "Irene exaggerates, but in this case, she's absolutely right. Betsy's amazing. She's solved several murder cases, some of them right here in town."

Betsy hastened to say, "I don't know yet if I'm going to get involved in the Rob McFey case. I've talked with the boy the police have arrested, and his parents, but I'm not certain whether or not there's anything I want to do, or even can do."

"I see," said Ian, but not as if he really did. "This is kind of awkward. Ms. Potter seemed very sure you'd want to interview me."

"Well, since you're here, you might give me a new perspective by telling me about Mr. McFey."

"I'd be glad to. Robbie was a good friend."

"Did you see him at his booth at the fair?"

Ian nodded. "On Saturday. I came by to see how he was doing. He seemed happy, said he'd been selling pretty well. He liked the setup in Excelsior, said the park was a pleasant venue, so it attracted lots of people."

"How long had you known him?"

Ian calculated, his eyes cast upward. "Six, going on seven years."

"Did you meet because of your mutual interest in art?"

Ian grinned. "No, we met because I didn't

know the difference between advertising and publicity. He used to own Information Please, and I'd been told by my agent that I needed a publicist, so I made an appointment for lunch with Robbie. It must've been halfway through the duck at Five-Ten Groveland when he explained that a publicist was not someone who worked at an ad agency. But by then he was intrigued by someone actually making enough money from his art to hire a publicist, and we've been friends ever since. I mean, until . . ." He shrugged and looked away, his face sad.

"You said you were helping him get into a Santa Fe gallery?"

"Yes. It's Marvin Gardens, the same one that represents me. They've done very well by me, making sure I get seen by the right reviewers, timing my shows for maximum effect, and most important, paying me promptly." He expanded a little, literally, rising onto his toes, filling his chest, lifting his bearded chin. "Thanks to them, I've developed a national reputation." He let some of the air out. "I was hoping they could do the same for Robbie."

"Do you know his family? Was he married?"

"He was in the process of getting divorced when this happened. It was his wife who filed. She wasn't in favor of his new lifestyle *at all.*"

"I don't understand."

"Then let me back up and explain. Like I say, Rob used to be in advertising. About ten years ago he and another fellow started their own company, Information Please. They were doing pretty well, making real money, everybody was happy." Ian went over to the library table in the middle of the room. He used his good hand to turn the three-tiered holder of scissors, a measuring tape, scrap fabrics, a needle holder bristling with needles, and other gadgets associated with stitchery. He made it go around one full turn, then turned around himself and said, "Then Robbie was given a sentence of death."

Chapter 7

There was a shocked silence. Robbie asked, "Have you ever heard of hepatitis C?"

"I have," Shelly said, pleased to have something to contribute. He turned to her, his eyes warm and interested, which caused a confusion of emotions in her breast. She touched her hair in its knot and continued, "Last year a child in my classroom had it, got it from his mother before he was born — at least, I think it was hepatitis C. It could have been A or B. I do recall he was a very sick little boy."

Betsy said, "I think they're up to letter what, G? H? Why do you ask? Do you have hepatitis?"

Ian shook his head. "No, no. But Robbie McFey did. He was told he was dying of it."

"He did? There was no mention of it in any of the news reports."

"The doctors were wrong. He wasn't dying."

"I don't understand."

"I'm sorry, I guess I'm not explaining very well." Ian leaned back against the table and stroked his goatee while he considered how to tell his story.

Shelly slipped over a few feet so she could look at him in profile. He was attractive in a homely way. His nose was strong and only a little too big. His chin, under the goatee, was square — and double, which might explain the hairy cover he'd grown over it. His hair seemed to be thinning at the crown; when he tilted his head, the tied-back part was lifted and showed how carefully he'd combed it to disguise the thinning area. She smiled at herself when she realized she found this sign of vanity touching.

Shelly didn't believe in love at first sight — not true love. On the other hand, she'd experienced that powerful, unexpected, inexplicable attraction to a member of the opposite sex twice before — she'd married the first one — and so she recognized it when it happened again now. Ian Masterson, a big, masterful-looking man, was not at all her type. Nevertheless, he radiated some variety of sex appeal, charm, charisma, or whatever-it-was that brightened her eye and rattled her heart.

Ian continued, "A few years ago, Robbie got sick — muscle aches, vomiting, temperature. He thought it was flu, and went to bed; but when it didn't get better, his wife sent him to his urgent care clinic — and they put him in the hospital. A blood test had come up positive for hepatitis C."

Shelly said, "So they're the ones who made the mistake."

Ian shook his head. "No. They did a liver biopsy, and found some very early signs of cirrhosis. They asked him if he drank, which he did, but he lied about how much, so they concluded the cirrhosis was from the hepatitis."

"Anyway, drinking doesn't give you hepatitis," said Betsy.

Ian smiled at her. "No, it doesn't. But they asked him about his sex life and drug use, because unprotected sex and dirty needles are the two most common ways of getting the disease. He said he hadn't messed around on his wife, and the only people who stuck syringes into him were doctors and nurses."

Shelly asked, cocking her head pertly, "So did he have it or didn't he?"

Ian said, "The virus was there. The blood tests showed that."

Betsy asked, "Did they learn where he got it?"

"It turned out he'd had a blood transfusion back in the late eighties after he ran into someone's elbow during a touch football game and ruptured his spleen. Back then they didn't test donated blood for it."

"I never heard of a disease that has an incubation period that long," said Shelly. "Well, except maybe AIDS."

"Hepatitis is another one, it seems."

Betsy said, "And so they told him he was dying. Are you saying this was a motive for murder?"

"No, I'm just telling you how he came to be at the art fair, instead of writing ad copy."

"I still don't understand."

"What happened was, they told him he had a year to live, maybe two if he took care of himself. They got the symptoms under control, gave him some medicine that made him damn sick, and released him."

"How long ago was this?" asked Betsy.

"Three years."

"Well, hey, didn't he ask about a new liver?" asked Shelly.

"Hepatitis C lives in your whole system, so all that would happen was that the new liver would be infected, too — and much faster, because of the immune-suppressing drugs he'd have to take."

"You seem to know a lot about all this," remarked Betsy, and Shelly managed to drag her attention away from Ian to Betsy. Normally, Betsy had the quiet, helpful demeanor proper to a small business owner, but now there was an edge to her pleasant alto voice, and a keen look in her light blue eyes. Shelly was thrilled to get this glimpse of the sleuth she knew resided in her friend and employer. And Ian was supplying the clue! She returned her attention to Ian.

Who, oblivious, was nodding. "We had some deep conversations, Robbie and I. But he didn't die. It turns out that whatever made him sick wasn't hepatitis C. They think maybe it was what he thought he had in the first place: flu."

"They had faulty equipment for testing," guessed Shelly, wanting him to look at her.

"No, he really had the disease, he was just one of those people who carry it around without getting sick from it."

"But you said there was liver damage," said Betsy.

"Yes," nodded Ian. "I told you, he lied about his drinking. I mean, I'm a party animal from way back, but he put whiskey into his morning coffee, and thought a four-martini lunch was for folks on the wagon. He stopped when he got the diagnosis, of course. Spent three weeks at a clinic drying out, but never went to an AA meeting. Said he didn't need them to motivate him to stay dry, he had a powerful motive already." His tone became more emphatic. "But he did quit his job. He told his wife that if he was dying, he was going to spend what time he had left doing what he always wanted to."

"Carve wood," said Shelly.

"And sell his work." He asked Betsy, "Did you see any of it?"

"I saw slides. That lion was wonderful." Her voice was sincere.

Ian's head came up. "It's a masterpiece!" he declared, than looked sadly at the floor. "And the hand that wrought it is stilled forever." He cheered up a bit — he's like an actor, Shelly noted, or at least someone with a sense of drama. "Of course, now it, and all his other remaining work, should increase in value. There isn't going to be any more of it."

Shelly said, "I guess I should have bought that raccoon when I had the chance, huh?"

Ian turned to her. "What raccoon?" he asked, and again she felt the power of his interest.

"The one with the crayfish in its front paws, he was kind of standing on his hind legs — but oh, it doesn't matter; I couldn't afford it then, so I certainly couldn't now."

"Crayfish?" he asked, apparently drawing a blank.

She came out from behind the desk, gesturing the size of the piece with both hands, holding them about nine inches apart. "I liked it, I liked it even more than the lion. The way it looked as if it were turning toward something that suddenly caught its attention, about to drop the crayfish because it was so distracted. You almost turned around to see what it was looking at."

He smiled at her. "How very perceptive of you!" he said warmly. "Yes, his talent for capturing emotion in animals was remarkable, but he had the even more remarkable ability to make the work live in a world bigger than itself. Do you draw or paint?"

Shelly looked down so she wouldn't see the

disappointment in his face when she said, "No, I just do cross-stitch."

Ian looked around the shop, at the models on the walls. "Don't say 'just.' Some of this stuff is wonderful. It's made from patterns, right?"

"Yes, that's right," said Shelly.

"Well, did you draw any of them?"

"No."

Betsy said, "But sometimes you take parts of several patterns and combine them to make a piece that's all your own."

"Well, yes, I do."

"That's very artistic, and completely in the spirit of this age, to combine parts of the work of others to make something entirely your own." Ian was again warmly approving, and Shelly smiled her gratitude at Betsy.

Betsy asked, "Were there two raccoons among his pieces?"

Shelly said, "I only saw the one."

Ian said, "I didn't even know about the one." He asked Betsy, "Is there anything else you want to know?"

"What do you know about Mr. McFey's family?"

"Not a whole lot. I think I might have met them twice. Except his daughter Skye, I saw her perhaps a dozen times — he'd bring her along once in a while to dinner, and he liked having her in his workshop. She was quiet and serious, and showed early promise as an

128

artist herself. Did some interesting things in pencil. She was a lot like him, actually, even when she was just a little kid. Intense, funny, hardworking. She's in high school now. There's a boy about four years older than she is, his name is Coyne. One of those kids with a scientific mind. A real sobersides, but with a temper if he feels pushed. This is all from Robbie, of course, but he said Coyne was angry because Robbie refused to go back into advertising, back to making good money. I offered to pay the boy's college tuition, but Robbie turned me down."

"I should think it was his wife who would be angry."

Ian nodded. "Very likely. But I don't know for sure, I think I met her exactly once."

"But you saw Robbie often."

He held out and wobbled his bandaged hand. "Off and on. We'd meet almost every day for five days or a week, then not see each other for months. One of us would get into artist mode and disappear."

"You mean, go out of town?" asked Shelly. "Like to art shows?"

"No, more like going to the back of a big, dark cave to have a deep conversation with your muse. When you come out, you stand blinking at the sunlight, or surprised at the snow, and wondering what's been going on. I think I was probably among the last Americans to hear about the twin towers in New

York coming down, because I was working on a piece during that time. The muse had me by the throat, and when that happens, it's like the only real thing in the world is the piece I'm working on."

Shelly nodded. "Like stitching binges. Lots of our customers go on them, I've done it myself — neglecting the house, turning the dogs out in the backyard instead of taking them for long walks, just so I can finish a piece."

Again that warm approval. "You do understand."

Betsy asked, "Was Rob McFey serving his muse lately?"

"Definitely yes, until just a few months ago. When he came up for air, he called me to come see what he'd just finished. It was that lion. I saw it and I went right home and phoned Marvin Gardens in Santa Fe to say they really had to take a look at Robbie. They said on my recommendation they would, and he should send them some items. He was in the process of selecting some pieces when . . . this happened."

"That's too sad," said Shelly. "Maybe you, or maybe his family should send the pieces anyway?"

Ian shook his head. "I don't think there are a lot of unsold pieces, and just that one really brilliant one isn't enough to anchor a real show. But his work should have been in a gallery, not an art fair, if only because the prices would be better. Problem is, there won't be any more. My gallery is the kind that likes to take a new artist and publicize him, bring him in for events and get him interviews in magazines, build him up, so his pieces really escalate in price. Robbie would have been really good at that, he was photogenic and could talk a great game. But Marvin Gardens won't consider him now, because he isn't available for interviews." He stood abruptly and went to look out the front window, peering around the canvases and patterns at the sunlit sidewalk. A jogger came by, unmindful of anything but the pain in his legs. Ian's hand went to his face for a few minutes, then he sniffed lengthily and his elbow worked as he rubbed his nose.

Shelly glanced at Betsy, whose face was sympathetic, and they waited in silence until he turned back. "It's sad when anyone dies, of course, even some poor old sap who never had kids or made anything else worth keeping. But when it's someone like Robbie, who would sit and study a piece of wood until it spoke to him of anger or fright or deep mourning, well, it's just too bad. Robbie thought he was dying, which in a way was good because, like the saying goes, a sentence of death concentrates the mind wonderfully — and he really worked hard. And then he found he wasn't dying, which was wonderful, because he then had more time to reach the height of his talent; but he's gone now, and that's the *damnedest* shame!" He drew a deep breath and let it out in a heavy sigh. "Sorry, I pontificate. It's one of the things that happen to people who start to get a name, they think the world is actually interested in anything they have to say."

Shelly said, "What kind of art did you say you do?"

She realized instantly the insult of this question, but after a single flashing glance, he began to laugh. Shelly decided she didn't mind asking foolish questions if they brought this infectious response. He said, "Welded art. I started out in sheet metal, then got into big-beam work, not at Don Gummer's level, but corporations and some local governments bought my work. Then about five years ago I had this rush of inspiration and went haring off after it, so now I'm into smaller pieces again. And they're doing pretty well, with private collectors and a couple of museums buying all I can produce."

Betsy said, "I've seen some of those steel girder things on the grounds of Minnesota Mills and Sweetwater. Are they yours?" She pushed two fingers from one hand against three from the other, forming a quintruped shape.

He nodded proudly. "Some of them." He

made a restless gesture. "But I didn't come in to talk about myself. I've taken up enough of your time, I ought to be going."

Shelly didn't want him to go. She asked, "How did you get started in metal? Were you a construction worker?"

He shook his head with a wry smile, and held up the bandaged hand. "As you can see, I'm not skilled enough to earn a welders' union card. It started back when a friend who had a small arc welder in his home workshop let me have a go." Ian's eyes grew dreamy. "Even that first time, when I drew a bead along two small pieces of steel, I looked at the wavy, interlocking lines — I wasn't very good at it and had to do two passes to make a solid weld — they were beautiful. Silvery, delicate, and yet powerful. That little welder had melted the ends of the steel, knitted them together like scar tissue, and the join was as strong as if the two parts had been cast as a single piece. Strength and beauty. That's my art. I was hooked and I've been hooked ever since."

"I saw some metal art at the fair last weekend," said Shelly. "Fish and birds done in stainless steel. Was that some of your early work?"

"No, no," said Ian with a gesture of dismissal. "I don't do art fairs. Not that there's anything wrong with them," he added hastily. "Some of them, anyway. Some are more craft

133

fairs than genuine art fairs. The Excelsior one is juried, which makes a difference, but even they have" — he gestured again — "bird houses and kites."

"Do you have any idea," asked Betsy, "who might have wanted Rob McFey dead?"

His head came back around. "Uh . . . no, of course not."

"Not his son? Or his wife?" she pressed.

He looked a bit disconcerted and backed off a little. "Well, they were resentful, or so Robbie said, but that's understandable. I mean, it's one thing when a person is dying and wants to fulfill a lifelong dream before he goes, and another when he just doesn't want to get back in harness after galloping free for a while." He cocked his head as if mentally replaying those words, and gave a little nod of appreciation at his turn of phrase. Again Shelly was touched at this boyish show of self-regard.

"So his whole family was unhappy," prompted Betsy.

"Well, no, not Skye. She thought the sun rose and set on her father. But Coyne, yes. I think he'll have to drop out of Northwestern now, he can't afford the tuition. Robbie said Coyne was angry about it, but . . ." He shrugged, possibly an echo of the shrug Robbie had given. "Robbie was in love with art, and allowing that love to guide him. And it wasn't as if they were going to have to live in their car. His wife has an MBA, even if she hasn't used it in a while."

"And there's nothing wrong with the University of Minnesota," said Shelly, Class of '85.

He bowed in her direction, his face amused. "Not at all, not at all. I went there myself, a century or two ago."

Shelly touched her upper lip with the edge of a forefinger to hide her smile. He really was a most attractive man.

A few minutes after Ian Masterson left, Shelly went into the back to get more of the drawstring plastic bags the shop put merchandise into for customers. She found Betsy back there, stopped halfway through the making of a cup of tea, her spoon stirring and stirring while she looked off into the distance, perplexed about something.

"What's the matter?" asked Shelly.

"Hmmm? Oh, I was just thinking about Mr. Masterson."

"Isn't he hot?"

Betsy turned her perplexed gaze on Shelly. "Ian Masterson is *hot?*"

"Don't you think so? Well, no, I guess not, you being so wrapped up in Morrie." Betsy's on-again/off-again romance with her retired police investigator was currently back on, now he was up here from his winter home in Florida.

Betsy nodded. "Yes, I suppose so."

"I think he's like a big ol' teddy bear, with that growly voice and hairy face."

Betsy laughed softly. "You sound really smitten!"

Shelly smiled and touched the back of her hair. "I could be. Not that I have a prayer, really. He's all wrapped up in his artist thing. I wish I were an artist, then I might have a chance to get to know him."

"Maybe it's just as well," said Betsy, her faraway look coming back.

"Why? What's the matter with him?"

"Probably nothing. But I wonder why he came to see me."

Shelly felt herself growing defensive. "Irene told him to, silly! And *he* told you, he wants to help any way he can with your investigation into Rob McFey's death."

"Yes, he told us a great deal about Robbie, didn't he? And how his wife and son were angry with him. Yet he was surprised when I asked him who he thought might have done it."

"I didn't notice that he was," Shelly lied, but added strongly, "I suppose he might not have expected you to ask him to name names."

Betsy nodded. "Yes, I suppose that's possible," but not as if she believed it.

"After all, he's not a sleuth, like you are."

Betsy nodded. "True."

"Well, what possible reason could Ian Masterson have for murdering Robbie McFey? They were friends! Ian was doing Robbie a favor, getting him a chance to show his carvings in Ian's gallery!"

"Yes, that's right, isn't it?"

"Yes, it is right! And if you keep stirring like that, you'll wear a hole in the bottom of that cup."

"What? Oh!" Betsy lifted the spoon up to let it drip into the cup. "Wouldn't want to do that," she said. But when Shelly left with an armful of bags, Betsy was stirring again.

Chapter 8

Jill used a coffee break to go see Mike Malloy. "Do you know Betsy Devonshire has been asked to look into the McFey murder?"

"Who by?" demanded Mike.

"Mickey Sinclair's parents. Well, the mother's sister, Char Norton, is the one who asked her."

"Oh, well!" Mike scoffed, waving it off. "Parents always think their darling little boy couldn't possibly have done the deed we caught him red-handed at. So let 'er take a look, what difference will it make?"

Her sergeant's stripes gave Jill the nerve to persist. "Mike, is it possible that he came upon the crime scene after the murder and took the money from the cash box?"

Mike hesitated. She could tell he wanted badly to say no. But leaping to a conclusion too early led to ignoring any evidence to the contrary, a surefire way to have a case blow up in your face. Even Mike knew that. But he didn't like it. "All right then, who killed McFey?" he argued. "And if not for the money in the cash box, then why?"

"Well, when I went to break the news to

McFey's wife, the setup made me think she might be mad at her husband for giving up his ad agency to be a starving artist. Their big house is for sale, their son now has to work his way through college, and their daughter is going to have to quit Blake and go to public high school, poor thing. Plus, I don't think she has an alibi that would hold water for a minute. She was hinky as a fox in a chicken coop — but not for herself, for her son, Coyne. What's more, her daughter was just as anxious to help cover for Coyne. The boy is home for the summer and was, they said, out job hunting at the time Robert McFey bought it. They were very explicit that I didn't have to come back to talk to the boy, they wanted to tell him themselves about his dad."

"When did you go talk to them?"

"On Sunday."

"He was job hunting on a Sunday?"

"At a car dealership, they said. Which may be true, some of them are open on weekends. His mother said he needed a well-paying job because tuition at Northwestern is so high."

"So all right, they're hurting for money. How would McFey's death benefit them?" He held up his hand again. "Wait, wait, don't tell me: insurance." He leaned back in his chair. "Do you know if there's a big policy?"

Jill shook her head. "It's your case. All I did was what you asked me to, go tell the

139

family about McFey's death. But the house they live in speaks of a high income bracket, which almost always means a big life insurance policy."

"Well, hold on a minute. Didn't he get a golden parachute or something when he left his agency?"

Jill brought her notebook out. "He didn't leave, he sold it. He was the owner. It went to a bigger agency for cash and stock. But the bigger agency went bankrupt, so his stock is worthless. And since the house is for sale, I would guess the money part either has run out, or will soon."

"How long ago was the ad agency sold?"

Jill again consulted her notes. "Something over two years." She looked at Mike. "The story is, he caught a terminal case of hepatitis and wanted a shot at being a professional artist before he died. But he was living longer than anyone thought he would, including his doctors. If there's a big policy, maybe someone got impatient."

Mike nodded and leaned on his forearms to think. He started to say something, and stopped himself. Jill grimaced; Mike was notorious for being surprised when a female showed herself competent. Still, he was not a stupid man, and suspicious behavior needs to be looked at no matter who reports it. He pressed his palms onto his desk, stood, and offered a sincere and more proper compliment. "Want to come along while I go talk to them?"

Jill smiled and said she did.

Mike phoned and found Pam McFey at home. He drove, of course; he said it made him nervous to ride shotgun. On the way he asked, "Has your friend Betsy found out anything good about this case?"

Jill replied evenly, "I don't know."

"She hasn't told you?"

"I haven't asked."

"Well, why the hell not?" This came close to an admission that Betsy Devonshire was good at sleuthing, and he added hastily, "She's quick enough to tell everyone else what she knows."

"I know."

Mike glanced at her. "Oh, that's right, you're mad at her for blabbing what you shouldn't've told her in the first place. How mad? Are you at least on speaking terms?"

"No."

"You aren't going to let that be a permanent situation, are you?"

"I don't know."

"What's the matter, she won't say she's sorry?"

For once, Jill couldn't resist biting back. "Mike, if you're so anxious to know her thoughts on this case, why don't you go talk to her yourself?"

Mike, surprised, let loose a defensive snort.

141

But he didn't press further, and the rest of the ride was made in silence.

When they pulled up the long, gentle slope of driveway, Mike said, "Nice house," with only a trace of envy.

He'd talked to Pam McFey when he'd called, but the door was answered by a very handsome young man in preppie clothes: chinos, penny loafers, light blue long-sleeved shirt. His hair was bleached blond, but was dark close to the roots. "Hello, I'm Coyne McFey," he said. "My mother is expecting you." His expression was a polite blank, and he showed them into the beautiful living room, where Pam waited with an equally bland, polite face.

The girl, Skye, was not in evidence.

"How do you do, Sergeant Malloy?" said Pam McFey from her seat in a high-backed wing chair, offering a slim, cool hand. She wore a simple navy dress and an elaborate necklace of silver and turquoise. "And Sergeant Cross." She gave a little nod of recognition. "Won't you sit down? May I offer you coffee?" There was a magnificent antique silver coffee service on a tray on the coffee table, with four paper-thin porcelain cups and saucers.

"No, thanks," said Malloy, so it sat there unused the whole interview. But the display, and the throne-like chair Pam sat on, did what they were designed to do: Malloy was, if not deferential, polite. Or perhaps it was not the powerful show of wealth; perhaps he, like Jill, sensed the advice of a good attorney at work. And good attorneys, even more than money, can make a cop wary.

"I'm glad to have this opportunity to clear up any questions you might have," said Pam. "I want very badly to see the person who murdered my husband caught and punished."

"I appreciate that," said Mike, reaching into an inside pocket for a notebook and pen. "Do either of you have any idea who might have wanted your husband dead?"

Pam's eyes widened at this directness. "No, of course not. Rob was a good man, well liked by his many friends."

Coyne nodded and seconded his mother. "Everyone liked Dad."

The two were tense, Jill noticed. Which was understandable; people of this class were rarely of professional interest to a homicide investigator. The boy was more tightly wound than his mother. He looked at Pam only in the briefest of glances, keeping his eyes on Malloy, trying to read Malloy's receptiveness to their answers.

No, Coy said, he was not home when the bad news came. He had gone to talk to the sales manager at Prestige Auto in Saint Louis Park. He was there a little ahead of the appointed time, ten-thirty, but they'd let him wait awhile. He also thought the interview had gone well, but — grin — they hadn't offered him a job on the spot. He'd gone across the freeway afterward to see if they needed someone at Saturn of Golden Valley. Saturn needed a mechanic, but Coy didn't know anything about repairing cars. Nearby Lupient Cadillac needed someone to wash and vacuum their used cars at base wages, a job he frankly couldn't afford to take. He'd eaten at the Taco Bell up the frontage road — no, he hadn't applied for a job there, though they were advertising for counter help — then gone to see some friends, to watch a rental movie with them. Home? Well, probably a little after six, to hear that his mother had been frantic to reach him with the terrible news. "I was just shocked, blown away, to hear it," he said, and bowed his head.

Malloy, Jill noted, let him have a very brief moment to display his mourning, then asked, "How long did you have to wait at Prestige for that interview?"

"Well, they told me to be there at ten-thirty and talk to a Mr. Allan Silk. I came in, oh, about twenty after, but I didn't know where Mr. Silk's office was, so I kind of wandered around for, I don't know, fifteen minutes, then someone came over and showed me to his office. But Mr. Silk was on the phone, I don't know with who, but I sat in the customer waiting room for a long time. By the time I was called in for the interview, it was eleven or a little after."

Coy produced Sales Manager Allan Silk's business card, and another from the Saturn dealership, from his shirt pocket and held them up. Malloy could call them to confirm he was there, if he liked. But Malloy only nodded and didn't take them. Coy didn't know what to do with them, and finally dropped them onto the coffee table, beside the silver tray.

Malloy said, "And how about you, Mrs. McFey? Where were you Sunday morning?"

Pam McFey put on a surprised face. "Me?" She affected a careless little laugh. Coy bumped her arm by reaching to rearrange the business cards. She flinched at his touch, then laughed more naturally. "I'm a little nervous," she admitted. "I don't have a, what do you call it, an alibi? I was here at home with Skye part of the morning, dusting and putting things out of sight. Our house is for sale and our realtor said she might bring someone by."

"Did she?"

"Yes, but not until after two."

"Was your daughter here all morning?"

"Well, no. She wanted me to take her to Excelsior so she could sit in the booth with her father, but as I said, I couldn't leave the house. So instead she called one of her friends and they went over to a neighbor's to swim in their pool."

"What time was that?"

Pam appeared to think a moment and said, "About nine, I think. Maybe a little later."

"May I talk with her?"

Pam shrugged. "I'm afraid she's not here right now. She's over at the Warners' pool again. I didn't think you'd need to talk to her, since Sergeant Cross already has."

"How old is she?" asked Malloy.

"Fifteen."

"Did you get an offer for your house?"

That question seemed to surprise her, and Jill saw Malloy make a brief note. "No. Well, yes, but it was a ridiculous offer. It was as if . . ." She cut the rest of that sentence off by pressing her lips closed.

Malloy said, "As if they knew how badly you need the money?"

"We don't —" began Pam.

"Don't lie, Mother!" said Coyne sharply. "Especially after you told the truth to Sergeant Cross here." He said to Malloy, "We do need the money. Father quit earning a decent living at a very bad time. The house isn't paid for, the car isn't paid for, I have college tuition, and Skye has Blake School for two more years. Mother isn't in a position to take up the slack, and it'll be two more years before I can. It's not exactly a secret around the neighborhood, but it was stinking of our real estate agent to tell a prospective buyer that we were anxious to sell."

"Were?" Mike said just as Jill also noted the past tense.

"Well, now there's life insurance, isn't there?" Coyne produced that fact with a slightly defiant air, as if he knew the significance of it.

Pam said quietly, "That's enough, Coy." She took a breath, gathering her courage, as if at last facing the object of her fears. "Coy is right, however. Now that Rob is . . . dead, there is the matter of life insurance. We will probably still sell the house, but are no longer anxious about it." Her chin came up. "Yes, I know that means you could consider us suspects, but you see, we both have alibis. Neither of us could possibly have mu-murdered my husband." She stumbled over the word and pressed the fingertips of one hand to her mouth. But after blinking rapidly a few times, she regained control. The hand came down. "Is there anything else you want to know?"

"Do you know how much life insurance your husband carried?" asked Mike.

"Of course. There are two policies that total something over a million and a half dollars. His company paid the premiums until Rob sold it, but because he thought he had only a short time to live, he kept up the premiums."

There wasn't much else to inquire into. Mike got permission to talk with Skye if it proved necessary — in her mother's presence, of course. "Thank you, I'll be in touch if anything develops or if I need to talk with you again."

Mike picked up the cards Coyne had dropped, and they left.

"So," said Mike on the highway back to Excelsior, "Mrs. McFey and her son Coyne are not exactly iron clad in their, um, what do you call 'em, alibis."

"I don't think Coyne could have done it at ten and been in Saint Louis Park by ten-twenty."

"You've never been in a new-car show-room, have you?"

Jill glanced at him. "No." Her current car was an elderly Buick, inherited from her grandmother, and her previous cars had all been bought used.

"No one ever walks around a new car showroom for more than two minutes before a salesman has him by the elbow. Coyne may have had to cool his heels in the customer service waiting room after he was taken in hand, but he didn't arrive early. I suspect he arrived a little after his appointed time. I'm going to call Mr. Silk to see if he remembers what time he began that interview, and if anyone else remembers what time young Master McFey actually arrived."

"What about Mrs. McFey?"

"Well, her alibi isn't worth spit either, but

realtors aren't reliably tardy. I got the realtor's name off the for-sale sign. I'll check to see if she did call Mrs. McFey to say she was bringing a prospective buyer over, and if she gave a time."

Godwin came back from lunch with a cardboard bowl of chicken noodle soup, and half a turkey sandwich on whole wheat bought at the request of his boss. The sandwich had lost its low-calorie status by being spread with cranberry jelly and cream cheese, an Antiquity Rose Tea Room special.

He put the bag of food on the big desk and, after looking around to make sure the two customers in the place were out of earshot, leaned forward to ask in an undertone, "Have you made up your mind about helping Mickey Sinclair?"

"His mother called last night and I said I'd look into it." She opened the bag, inhaled gently, and smiled. "Yum, thanks."

"If I know you," said Godwin slyly, "you've already been looking into it, and found out something that got you interested."

"Let me take care of Mrs. Hamilton, then we'll talk."

Mrs. Hamilton wanted a fat quarter of an evenweave plaid in shades of orange, three skeins of black floss, and a card of gold metallic.

The other customer was deeply involved in

comparing three knitting pattern booklets at the library table, a heap of knitting yarn in several pastel colors at one elbow.

Godwin came to watch Betsy looking over bills. "All right, what have you found out?"

"I talked to Mickey Sinclair, who seems to be making good time down the road to a life of crime. And his family seems specially designed to encourage that journey. But right at the end of my visit to the juvenile detention center I offered to believe Mickey's claim that he did not murder Robert McFey, and he looked at me with such gratitude and hope that I felt as if I'd tossed a corner of this sandwich to a stray dog."

Godwin's face lit up with amusement. "You should write that down, that's pretty good."

"I'll put it in my journal this evening," promised Betsy gravely.

"Okay, what else?"

"Not much. A friend of 'Robbie's' — he called Mr. McFey 'Robbie' — stopped in yesterday. This friend is an artist, too; he does those big welded beam things and is apparently becoming an important person in the art world."

Godwin nodded and said, "John represents a sculptor who works in metal. He earns big bucks at it but he's kind of a spendthrift."

"Is his name Ian Masterson?"

Godwin shrugged. "I don't know. John loves to share juicy tidbits about his clients but won't name names."

"Well, Ian said Irene Potter told him that I was investigating and he came by to see if there was anything he could do to help me. He did say one interesting thing: Robbie McFey was supposed to be dying of a liver disease, but was disappointing his wife and son by not getting on with it."

"I don't understand," said Godwin.

"He said that Robbie used to own an ad agency that earned big bucks, but when he found out he was dying, he sold it to follow his dream of being a woodcarver. But it turned out the disease wasn't going to kill him. And that now he wasn't earning anything like the money that he used to make in advertising. Ian said he offered to pay Coyne's college tuition, but Robbie turned him down."

Godwin's eyes widened. "So he bought a viatical, didn't he? Oh, my God, oh, my God, he did!" He twirled around twice and stood with his arms out and a big grin on his face. The woman selecting a knitting pattern looked over to smile at him, then went back to her booklet.

"What?" asked Betsy. "Ian didn't say anything about a viatical."

"He didn't?" It was as if someone let the air out of his balloon.

"What's a viatical?"

"Excuse me." It was the customer, ready

151

now to buy two skeins of very pale yellow yarn, three of very pale green, and a pattern for a baby blanket. Godwin, though anxious to see the knitter on her way so he could answer that question, nevertheless took a moment to share a joke: "Do you know why they won't allow you on an airplane with this?" he asked. When the customer said she didn't, Godwin said, "Because you're going to knit an afghan!"

The customer laughed all the way out the door.

The instant the door closed, Godwin said, "I bet Ian is John's client."

"You think so? But I didn't see any signs of big bucks; I mean, he wasn't wearing fancy clothes or lots of gold jewelry."

"Yes, but how many rich artists try to help their poor artist friends?"

Betsy raised her eyebrows and one corner of her mouth in a kind of shrug. "Rob McFey wasn't — well, all right maybe he was. But Ian said Rob turned him down."

"He didn't take Ian's offer to pay for college tuition. But how about a viatical?"

"Wait, wait, I think I remember reading about them." Betsy thought a bit. "It was a way to invest money, right? Something to do with gay men and AIDS and — and insurance policies? With a high return . . ." She frowned, trying to recall the details.

Godwin nodded. "You start with the news

that you have a terminal disease and a hefty life insurance policy. You need money, but suppose there's not much cash value in the policy. So you find an investor who will take over the premiums. He gives you a lump sum and you change the policy to make him the beneficiary. Gay men with AIDS sold them because they needed the money to pay for medical care. Years ago, they died pretty quick, and the investors made a decent profit. Everyone was happy, in a gruesome sort of way. The gay men got decent medical care in their final days, and the investors made a fast buck or two. It wasn't like the gay men had wives and babies who needed the money." His face grew sad briefly.

"What I remember is a magazine article that said it wasn't a good investment anymore," said Betsy. "They were finding medicines that really worked and the AIDS sufferers were living years longer than . . ." She hesitated.

"The investors were willing to wait," nodded Godwin. "Yes. The deal was, investors had to take over premium payments. You do that long enough, and it's no longer a quick return, plus it can cut deep into the profit margin."

"But what's the connection to this situation? Did Rob McFey have AIDS?"

"Not as far as I know. You don't have to have AIDS to sell a viatical. John told me

153

about this artist client who bought a viatical from another artist who had a terminal disease. He paid sixty-five thousand for a hundred-thousand-dollar policy. And he took over the premium payments. You said Rob McFey was supposed to die of liver disease in a year or two, right?"

"Yes, Ian told us all about it. But he didn't mention anything about a viatical."

"But he wouldn't, my dear. Because then he'd have to admit he had a big, fat motive, wouldn't he? When Rob didn't die, and Ian had to keep making payments, where was the profit going? Down the drain."

"Hmmmm," said Betsy. Because Godwin also said John's artist client was a spendthrift. Maybe it wasn't just a loss of profit; maybe he couldn't afford to wait.

Shelly glanced at her reflection in the mirror, smoothed her hair back, and touched the outsize earrings that twinkled down nearly to her bare shoulders. Her makeup was intense, and her long hair was pulled with seeming carelessness on top of her head whence it coiled and tumbled extravagantly down her back. She was wearing a pale yellow cotton dress that ran a ruffle across the top of her bosom and was tight in the short skirt. Though light-haired, she tanned quickly and easily, so the color glowed against her dark, unfreckled skin. She no longer looked like a clerk in a needlework shop, and even less like an elementary school teacher.

She'd been surprised when he'd called, and flattered. Now she waited a bit breathlessly for the doorbell to ring. At three minutes after seven it did. She opened the door to find him waiting with a small bouquet of flowers, how very charming and old-fashioned.

"Am I late?" he asked.

"No, of course not, Ian. You're right on time."

Chapter 9

Ian found Shelly more attractive than he had expected from their meeting in Crewel World — amusing name for a shop, he thought. He liked them young, whereas she was well into her thirties, perhaps even coming up on forty. He liked them to be lusty, while she taught fourth grade, for heaven's sake. (What did kids learn in fourth grade? Times tables? Geography? He couldn't remember. Was that because he was, oh, how many years past fourth grade? Never mind!) On the other hand, dressed to kill as she was now, he was prepared to change his opinion. She did have a sexy figure, with seductive shoulders and beautiful eyes. He liked her eyes; they were an unusual smoky brown with green highlights.

And there was a grace to her movements he found almost touching. Her upper bosom swelled softly, naturally, not quite too abundantly before it was interrupted by the ruffle. Having taken just about every ride in the female amusement park, he had a good idea what she looked like nude. Her torso, perhaps turned a bit more to the side than it was right now, standing and waiting for their table, would make a nice sculpture. Maybe with an effect at the hip as if the weight were mostly on one leg would be very nice — except it wouldn't capture the grace of her movement. Well, then some kind of kinetic piece . . . He became aware that she was aware of his eyes on her. And not on her face, either. She was smiling as if she knew what he was thinking, which wasn't what he was thinking at all.

That amused him, because his hormones normally were jumping. He took a deep swallow of his wine. "What do you think of modern art?" he asked, since that was what he was thinking about. They were in a nice restaurant near downtown Minneapolis, standing near the bar, waiting for their table.

"I like some things, I don't like others."

He felt his smile become condescending so he squashed it before she could notice that. He shouldn't have spoken; nonartists had such clichéd opinions! "What don't you like?"

"I don't like pretenders."

That surprised him. "Who are the pretenders?"

"You know, the ones who put flashing lights around a ceiling, or pile penny candy on the floor, and call it art."

Oh, that old argument. Well, he'd asked for it. "It could be art," he said with a little shrug. "If the candy were selected for its colors, or its shapes, and if it were piled into a kind of snowdrift of sugar . . ." His eyes kindled. "White saltwater taffy piled against a wall, with blue cough drops making the shadows, that could be interesting." Call it "Saltwater," hmmm . . .

"Perhaps a photograph or painting of it, don't you think?" she asked. "So you could force the viewer to stand at the correct angle and get the perspective right."

"All right," he grudged, not being fond of collaborations, but acknowledging that she might have something there. Actually . . . "Or put it in a big box frame so you could control the lighting, too." This was almost interesting.

"No, if you did that, it would be too much like those corn pictures."

He frowned at her. "Corn pictures?"

"At the State Fair. Well, sometimes it's grain, but most often it's corn. Like a mosaic, with the corn as the pieces of stone. I've seen some that're good, but most of it is awful. But that isn't what I'm talking about. I'm talking about a big pile of penny candy on the floor, not arranged in any special way, and the visitors to the museum are invited to take a piece from the pile, and a janitor comes by every so often with a bucket of candy to replenish the pile. That's not art, that's . . . well, I don't know what it is."

"Performance art, maybe?" suggested Ian, a bit tiredly. Another evening about to be spoiled by an argument over art.

She looked at him, eyebrows lifted. "Well, you're the first person who has suggested something that makes sense! It wasn't advertised as performance art, but if the janitor were actually the artist, then sure, performance art. I like that, perhaps that was what was meant and the report I read had it wrong. So okay, maybe you can explain the cans of poop, too."

"Cans of poop," he repeated in an obedient voice. Piero Mazoni had been a jerk, and the museums who bought his offerings run by idiots.

"Yes, a columnist named Dave Barry wrote about it. He said the artist — I forget his name — the artist's name — anyway, his art was putting his poop into little steel cans. The Tate in London bought a can, and so did MOMA in New York, paying tens of thousands of dollars, but his favorite — the columnist's favorite — was the Pompidou Museum in Paris. He said he wasn't going to cheapen himself by making a joke about the Pompidou."

Ian began to laugh, he couldn't help it.

"But what aggravates me," she said, in a mock-aggravated voice, "is that the cans were 'industrially sealed,' which means they are never to be opened. How do they know it's

159

really poop inside? And if it is, how do they know it's his?"

"Artistic integrity," he replied, and they laughed together, she holding on to his arm. And she didn't spoil the joke by repeating it.

When they were down to chuckles, Shelly said with genuine seriousness, "But you do see what I mean, don't you? That kind of art is by pretenders. Some don't even pretend to be artists. They say things like, 'Everything is art,' or 'It's impossible to express my feelings in art.' Well, if you can't say it with art, perhaps you should go be a carpenter or a bus driver. And if everything is art, then why are museums paying terrific sums for a heap of candy they could buy from a wholesaler for twenty or thirty dollars? It wouldn't be so bad, but most museums are tax supported, and that means all of us are forced into the despicable pretense."

He cocked his head sideways and said, "But aren't teachers paid with taxes?"

She took her hand away, and the twinkle in her eyes turned to a glint. "I'll bet you there's not a school board in the country that would allow its teachers to produce industrially sealed barrels and insist the public take on faith that each contains one properly educated child."

He laughed again, but held up his bandaged hand. "I surrender! You're right, I'm wrong. Truce?"

"Oh, of course. I'm sorry, I do get a bit defensive, don't I?" She studied his face. "Have I offended you? You aren't a supporter of the pretenders, are you?"

He replied strongly, "No, of course not! My art is real and no relation to the piles of cheap candy or tinned excrement or other outrages. On the other hand, I don't do representational art, so that stuff has an unwholesome effect on me and others like me. And it denigrates the difficult work of dedicated curators and critics who *don't* think everything is art."

"What is art?" asked Shelly, a trifle airily, understanding the question was a cliché, and letting him know that she wasn't going to demand a serious answer.

The maître d' approached at that point to take them to their table. Ian followed Shelly across the room with an eye to her backside to see if it was as attractive as her front. It was.

But after they were seated, he went back to her question, and he took it seriously. "Art is a medium of expression, and high art tries to communicate important ideas. Art can talk about life, art can comment on art. Art can also say silly things, playful things . . ." He leaned toward her and widened his eyes. "Sexy things." She laughed encouragingly, but he felt he needed just one more serious statement. "I work hard on my art, and I like to think I have a certain recognizable method and talent."

She said in a throaty voice, "I'd love to see some of your work."

"I'll have you out to my workshop someday, as soon as it's repaired."

"Repaired?" She glanced at his bandaged hand.

"Yes, I was stupid about a hot plate I'd installed, left a pot of coffee on it." He held up the hand. "I like to think I was brave about trying to rescue a model I was building in wood, but anyone who tries to run into a burning building isn't brave, he's stupid. I'm lucky this was the only injury; the back half of the studio roof fell about forty seconds after I realized the danger and dashed out." He opened his menu and made a pretense of looking at it — he knew what he wanted — then glanced around it to see if she was looking properly impressed. She was, but with a twinkle that indicated she knew he was looking for her to disagree, to say he was indeed a brave man. Damn perceptive women! Still . . . He grinned at her and put down the menu. "How come you clerk in that needlework store? Couldn't you find something more challenging?"

"It's challenging enough, to a brain tired of coping with the complex needs of thirty-five nine-year-olds for nine and a half months. Besides, Betsy gives her employees a discount on needlework materials. I have to struggle to keep needlework from turning from a hobby into an obsession. What's good here?"

"Their prime rib. I'm having it."

"Then so will I." She closed her own menu.

"Tell me about her, your employer," he said. "Is she really any good at detecting crime?"

"Oh, yes," said Shelly. "I don't know how she does it, she's never trained to be a police officer. I've watched her solve cases, but I don't really understand how she does it. We can both look at the same facts, but she — well, it's like she looks at the facts from a different angle."

"Different how?"

"A suspicious way, I suppose. She was suspicious of you, you know."

His heart leaped into his throat, sending an alarm of skyrockets into his brain. She was staring at him, so he went with it, feigning extreme amazement, dropping his jaw, pointing to his necktie with his bandaged fingers. "*Moi?* Why?"

She giggled, but nodded. "She wondered why you came in."

"But I told her, I heard she was investigating, and wondered if there was anything I could tell her that would help."

"Have you also talked with the police?"

"No, of course not." He saw that was

wrong and said, "But I expect a visit any day, at which time I'll help them in any way I can, as well. I wouldn't think they'd want people to just walk in and share what they know, unless it had a direct bearing. Or am I wrong?"

"No."

"Does Ms. Devonshire have any other suspects?"

Shelly shrugged. "She suspects everyone at the start of a case. One of her best friends, a police officer named Jill Cross, told me that Betsy's method is to look at everyone as if he or she is guilty, and only cross them off if she can prove they didn't do it. Sort of a 'last man standing' method."

"Has she ever looked at you with suspicion?" he asked.

"No, of course not!" said Shelly, surprised. Then, frowning, she added, "I don't think so, anyway."

"Perhaps you're already crossed off."

"Yes, probably. I mean, I have an alibi, I was working in her shop that day. She was volunteering at the fair, answering questions at the Information Booth."

"Ah," nodded Ian sagely. "On the scene and probably no alibi herself."

Shelly giggled. "I'll tell her that. She has a good sense of humor."

"Irene says she's a divorcee."

"Twice," nodded Shelly.

"She looks a mother type. Does she have children?"

"No."

He smiled. "What about you?"

"No, just students. And three dogs. You?"

"I have two daughters, one married and the other going into her last year of college, thank God for just one more year of child support." He finished the last of his wine. "Does that sound cruel? My ex-wife, the mother of my daughters, has seen to it that they dislike me intensely. After a while, I stopped caring. But the payments go on and on."

"Divorces can be devastating," said Shelly, "especially with children involved."

"Between her store and her investigating, Ms. Devonshire must not have much of a social life," he said.

Those beautiful eyes flashed. "She has a boyfriend who adores her. He wants her to sell the shop and move to Florida with him."

He smiled at this badly hidden show of jealousy. He said, "I take it she's not going to do that."

"I doubt it. She came to needlework late in life, but she's having a ball with it. And owning her own business, actually making a success of it, she says is the American dream. She likes Morrie — in fact, she may be in love with him — but she's not going to give up Crewel World anytime soon. She's enjoying life in Excelsior too much." She smiled slyly over her wineglass. "So you should just relax and enjoy being a suspect."

Betsy was, in fact, not having a ball. She had tried for a while, between customers, to get the hang of Hardanger, but it seemed that the moment she caught the rhythm of it and relaxed her vigilance, she'd make a mistake. And she almost never caught it at once, but went on stitching. Then she'd put the stitching down to serve a customer, and when she came back to it, she'd begin to count to see where she was, and she'd realize the little row of five stitches, the kloster, didn't line up. Sometimes it was because there was a stitch missing in a kloster block, and sometimes it was because she did a stitch two threads away instead of one. Whatever the problem was, the solution was the same: Pull the thread out until she was back to the last correct stitch. She'd done this so many times the thread was getting really fuzzy. She finally ran the fuzzy length under the backside of a kloster and clipped it off short. She cut a new length off the ball and threaded her needle.

It was then that a customer, trying to slip the cat Sophie a corner of a chocolate chip cookie without Betsy seeing her, realized she was spilling the cold cranberry drink in her other hand. The customer shrieked, and Sophie fled, swift and silent as a cloud's shadow, the treat safe between her teeth.

"What, what is it?" asked Betsy, dropping her needle.

"I spilled my drink into that cute little basket," confessed the customer with a humble smile.

Betsy came to look. The basket held four skeins of white alpaca yarn. Correction: pink alpaca yarn.

"Oh, dear, I am so sorry!" said the customer. "But if you hurry, surely you can rinse it out?"

The customer came along and the two crowded into the tiny bathroom off the back room of the shop. Betsy put the skeins into the sink and turned on the cold water faucet. The water in the sink immediately turned pink, too. But cranberry is a tenacious dye; no matter how much water she poured through the yarn, an uneven pink tinge remained.

The customer sighed and apologized again. "Too bad I don't knit," she said, "I could buy that and make myself a pair of mittens and a scarf."

"We have classes," offered Betsy, but the customer didn't take the hint.

Alpaca is a very expensive wool. Betsy wrung it out gently, wrapped it in paper towels, and put it into a plastic bag. She'd take it upstairs and lay it out to dry. Perhaps she could dye it again, properly this time. If not, someone who wasn't fussy about color was going to get a wonderful bargain. So much for Betsy's dreams of profit; between the baskets — which were not selling as well as she'd hoped — and now the damaged wool, there would be no smiles this month.

The customer bought a counted cross-stitch pattern of roses from a sale basket, a single skein of DMC 3722, and departed. Betsy sat back down and tried to figure out which direction the next kloster block went in. Did the first of the five stitches start at the top or bottom of the fifth stitch in the previous row? She sighed, and thought how nice it would be when she could close the shop and go have dinner with Morrie.

The phone rang; she tucked her needle into the fabric and picked up the receiver. It was Brian Forseth, her financial planner. "Don't forget we've got a meeting this evening," he said.

"Is that tonight? Yes, I guess it is. Thanks for the reminder."

Hanging up, Betsy gritted her teeth and called Morrie to tell him she couldn't have dinner with him after all. They commiserated awhile, and finally Betsy was persuaded to say she'd call Morrie after Brian left unless it was after ten.

She hung up and picked up her stitching, but didn't start the struggle with it right away. She was remembering a while back, when she'd first realized she was heir to a fortune. She had quickly realized that it wasn't like fantasies of wealth, in which one gorged a bank account and wrote checks for whatever one wanted. Right from the start there had been tax deferrals and money markets and investment portfolios to worry about.

And over time, it had become even more complicated. She bought the building Crewel World was in and found it needed a new roof. She had moved some money into a batch of high-tech stocks just before the dot-com bubble burst. She couldn't figure out how to keep the IRS from taking most of any profit she made. At last Mr. Penberthy, her attorney, had recommended Brian Forseth as a financial planner. Brian worked at a company she had always connected with insurance but which turned out to be a major financial institution. He proved to be a good-looking fellow with a great smile and an ability to explain things like "reposition of assets" and "cash flow analysis" without making her eyes glaze over.

And under his tutelage she began to understand the ins and outs of hanging on to, and even increasing, her fortune. She had a complex financial situation, he told her, partly inherited and partly the result of her own floundering. For example, there was the strange little company her sister had started in Wisconsin that hunted down bankruptcy estates and bought them at deep discounts to sell at a quick profit. It was doing well, but owning a company in another state complicated tax returns.

She had bought the building that housed Crewel World more because her landlord was a huge, interfering nuisance than because she was interested in real estate. But while it was a good investment — real estate around a prime lake like Minnetonka had been increasing in value since the first white man built a log cabin on its shores — it was also a major drain on her time and her pocketbook. It wasn't just the roof; the mortgage payment was daunting, and there were two other stores and two apartments whose tenants needing constant tending.

Brian Forseth had charged her several thousand dollars for a year of intense education, planning, and constant access to his own and his company's vast store of knowledge and experience.

It was Brian who counseled her to make the building part of Crewel World, Incorporated. For one thing, it made the expense of her general liability insurance policy on the building tax deductible, and it protected her other assets from any claims that might arise from a fire in the deli or the broken leg of a customer in Isbn's Used Books.

Tonight Brian was going to talk to her

about "springing power of attorney," a way to manage her affairs if she should become disabled.

No wonder economics was called "the dismal science," Betsy reflected. So much of it involved thinking of how to divert or manage fiscal disasters!

"You are involving yourself in crime," he said that evening, over a cup of coffee in her apartment. "There have already been attempts on your life. In case one is successful, you have a will — but what if one merely incapacitates you?"

"Well, what if?" she replied — retorted, more like. Thoughts like that were depressing.

"Who could make decisions about your corporation? Who would run the shop until you were able to take over again?"

"Godwin could run the shop, of course," said Betsy promptly. "I'm a silent partner in New York Motto, so that would continue all right." New York Motto was the Wisconsin bankruptcy business. "But I don't know about the other things. I suppose I could name someone to collect the rents and pay the mortgage and upkeep on the building. But how do I do that?" And who would even want the responsibility, she added to herself.

"That brings us to 'springing power of attorney,'" he said, picking up a form. "It's called that because it springs to life only under certain circumstances."

Betsy sighed and prepared to learn something new. She had a needlepoint legend hanging in her kitchen that read: *The only thing more overrated than natural childbirth is owning your own business.* Being rich wasn't all it was cracked up to be, either.

Chapter 10

"*What!?*" shrieked Pam McFey. "I don't believe it! How could he *do* this to us?"

Skye, in the kitchen building a complicated sandwich, dropped the pickle fork she was using to pull a pepperoncini out of its jar, then forced herself to calmly pick it up and continue. She recognized the tone, and had no doubt whom her mother was talking about, though how her father could still be doing things to enrage her mother, she didn't know.

Her mother was now making those little one-word noises people make when they're trying to interrupt. "But . . . well . . . I . . . but . . . yes . . . but . . ."

Perhaps it was the funeral, Skye thought, having pulled the stem from the pepperoncini and now wrapping a slice of prosciutto around it. People sometimes left elaborate, expensive directions. Her grandmother had, she recalled. Her parents, still happy together back then, had complained for weeks afterward, her father about how the service seemed about some saint bearing little resemblance to his mother, her mother about the price of the airline tickets to fly to Baltimore for the service. Skye had been nine when taken to her grandmother's funeral and had thought it astonishing and horrible to put a pretty dress on a corpse and make people come and look at it.

She made a face, not at the slice of stinky cheese she was arranging on the bread, but at the memory.

Her father had hated funerals, just like Skye. She had found this out soon after when she sat with him at work in his studio — one of her very favorite occupations. She would draw and he would carve and they'd talk about everything. Dead bodies were mere husks, he'd said that day, tossed aside like wet and filthy clothes, of no use to anyone, so why all the fuss over them? They should be disposed of in some quiet, sanitary way, and if people wanted to mark the passing of friends or relations, they should gather to celebrate the good memories.

Skye opened the refrigerator and looked among the several containers of mustard for the one with horseradish in it. She knew that the memorial service Mommy was planning for Pop was not going to be a celebration. From what she'd heard of Mommy's plans, it was going to be sad and dreary, with long speeches and awful hymns, and prayers asking a nonexistent God to be merciful to a nonexistent soul. She'd tried to tell her what

Pop said, that the dead were dead, no need to be superstitious about it. Robert Q. McFey was gone forever, why not just accept that? Skye turned and slammed the mustard onto the table. How dare Mommy bring people together to cry? She felt a sob rising in her throat, and banged her fist down hard, using the pain to kill the tears.

But now the thought of food choked her. She threw the pickle fork into the sink and strode off to the living room, where she found her mother still on the phone, but now engaged in pleasant conversation. She must have hung up on the previous caller. As Skye came to a halt, her mother was saying, "But it seems odd that such a thing could have happened without my knowing anything about it!" Her mother saw Skye in the doorway and waggled her eyebrows in a message Skye couldn't interpret, so Skye made an intense face and lifted her hands in a demand to speak.

"Just a minute," Pam said, and put a hand over the receiver. "Yes?" she said to Skye.

"I heard you yelling before. Is something wrong?"

"Mr. Christianson called to tell me that your father sold his life insurance policy to someone else."

Skye felt alarm run through her like an electric current. That insurance policy meant the difference between living well and living very badly. She didn't think much of money herself, of course, but Mommy had no idea how to be poor. "Could he do that?" asked Skye. "I mean, is it legal? Why did he do it?" Life was going to be very complicated if Mommy had to learn to be poor.

"For money, of course, so he could continue playing his ridiculous wood carver's game. I don't know how it could be legal, but apparently it is." Her mother's attention went back to whomever she was talking to on the phone. "My daughter is frightened and wonders what's going to happen to us. Yes, I'll explain, hold on."

Her mother put a hand over the receiver but didn't take the other end away from her ear. She said, "It's all right, darling, we're going to be all right, there are two policies, and your father only sold the smaller one."

"How much is the bigger one?" asked Skye.

"One and a quarter million, he says."

"That's great, Mommy, I'm so happy for you." Skye sighed with relief and went back to the kitchen. So it was going to be all right. Good thing. Mommy had been a mess ever since Pop said he was going to die. At first she'd been upset and frightened because how were they going to live once Pop died? Then she found out there was a big insurance policy, which made things all right — until it became clear the doctors were mistaken and he wasn't going to die. At which point she told Pop he had to give up his art and go back to making some real money. Pop just wanted a little happiness, but all Mommy could talk about was money.

Then Pop . . .

Her hand contracted and too much mustard came squirting out of the plastic bottle onto her sandwich and even onto the counter. She had to get a sponge to wipe off the counter, then a knife out of the drawer to scrape off the bread.

The sight of the knife made her ill again. Someone had taken one of Pop's knives and . . . Skye raised her face to the ceiling, but the tears spilled out anyway and coursed down her face. Mommy said everything was going to be all right now. Oh, how utterly horrible it was that Mommy was glad Pop was dead!

John Nye, Attorney at Law, held out a well-manicured hand to Betsy, who took it briefly. He was tall, spare, and handsome in a square-jawed way, with a long nose and very light blue eyes. Standing behind a beautiful cherrywood desk, he wore a natural linen suit, a tan shirt, and a buff silk tie. Betsy was glad she'd worn her white cotton dress with the puffy sleeves and lace panels, and high-heeled sandals.

"Thank you for seeing me on such short notice," Betsy said, and sat down in one of the two comfortable green leather wing chairs in front of the desk.

"I take a special interest in anyone who is a friend of Godwin's," he said, sitting down himself. "Would you like coffee?" He reached for his phone to place an order. His heavy gold watchband twinkled in the light of his bronze-shaded desk lamp.

"No, thank you, this won't take long."

"That's too bad, I have some time before my next appointment, and if you leave too quickly, I'll be forced to attend to some very tedious paperwork." He gestured at three fat file folders stacked in his In box, then sat back in his big executive chair and tented his long-fingered hands in front of him, resting his elbows on the arms of the chair. He smiled a slightly crooked smile. "Are you here with a complaint about Goddy?"

"Oh, no! On the contrary, he is an excellent employee."

"You don't find him a bit . . . flamboyant?" He gestured upward with one hand, the smile suddenly reaching his eyes.

"No — in fact, his flamboyance, as you call it, is one of his attractions. Gay men are commonly assumed to have an excellent sense of color and design, and by flaunting his sexual orientation, many of my chance customers immediately rely on his advice in selecting patterns and materials. Long-time customers know Goddy has an authentic sense of style — and he's also a very talented needleworker, so his advice in all areas of the craft is reliable."

"Well, I'm glad to hear that. Are you here because of a legal problem?"

"No. Not exactly."

"Well, then, how may I help you?"

"Is it true that you arranged for Mr. Ian Masterson to buy a viatical from Robert McFey?"

The handsome visage turned to stone. "Where did you hear that?" he asked.

"Does it matter? I want to know —"

"Of course it matters!" he cut in sharply. "I take it very seriously when the confidentiality of a client is breached."

"I'm afraid you're the one who breached it," Betsy said. "You told Godwin a story about an artist who bought a viatical from another artist, and later I told him of a visit I had from Ian Masterson, an artist who was friends with Robert McFey, who was apparently dying of hepatitis C. Because Mr. McFey has been murdered, Goddy felt he had to tell me what you told him."

"Ah." He nodded. "And what made Godwin think he could tell you rather than the police this story I told him in confidence?"

"I am investigating the murder of Robert McFey. A young man has been arrested and charged with the crime, but his family has

179

asked me to discover who else might have had a motive. Someone who bought a viatical might find himself anxious about his money when the terminal man proved not so terminal after all."

"Do you often discuss your investigations with people who aren't involved?"

"When I am conducting an investigation, I don't always know who is and who is not involved. I find talking to everyone brings out information — as it did in this case."

"So there are others who know about this?"

"Not so far. I am aware of the sensitive nature of this information, and am not going to casually gossip about it."

The frost in the blue eyes intensified at this slam. "I will remind Goddy of where his loyalty must lie. I suppose this is just the latest example of his tale bearing?"

Betsy clung to her temper with both hands, but the words came out sharply anyhow. "It is the first — but it seems to me, Mr. Nye, that if you don't want private information about your clients shared with anyone, then perhaps you ought to keep it to yourself."

John rose in one motion. His face had turned red, a decided contrast to his light-colored clothing. "You tell Godwin he is fired!"

She stared up at him. "Fired? From Crewel World?"

"That's precisely what I mean! If he can't

hold his tongue about my private business, he isn't to work in a place where he can spread the news" — John gestured widely, a gardener broadcasting seed, a paperboy delivering the *Excelsior Bay News* to a front porch — "to every silly female gossip who happens to stop in!"

Betsy was on her own feet now. "How can you possibly think you have the authority to make me fire anyone?"

"Then I'll make him quit!"

Betsy's chin came up. "Certainly I would quarrel with any attempt you might make to get him to quit."

"You won't win that quarrel."

The two stared at each other across the wide desk. Rather to Betsy's surprise, John's eyes dropped first, and he sat down as they did. "You don't know," he said more quietly. "The alternative is to break off with Godwin, and I don't want to do that. I am . . . very fond of Goddy."

"He's in love with you," said Betsy, trying to keep the quaver out of her voice. John had shaken her more than she cared to show.

"But I can't let his loose tongue endanger my position with Wellborn, Hanson, and Smith."

"Well, then for heaven's sake, why do you tell him things you don't want repeated?"

"Because he's intensely interested in what I

do here, or pretends to be."

"Pretends?"

"Godwin is . . . perhaps 'used to be' is a better phrase. Godwin used to be a clever, charming, amusing, handsome, manipulative boy. It was fun letting him tease me into giving him things, and telling him the juicy tidbits I learn about my clients. He still uses many of his old tricks, but we both understand now that they are tricks, and it's more of a game. He's come a long way from his beginnings — did you know he was very poor?"

"No, he never talks to me about his past."

John nodded. "Good thing, probably. You'd be shocked and disgusted if you knew."

"Godwin's past is none of my business, is it? He is a talented and valuable employee, and has become a trusted friend."

John's eyes narrowed. "You don't mean that, not entirely, or you wouldn't be here to check up on the story he told you."

"I'm sure he repeated what you told him. I wanted to make sure you didn't tell him something that isn't true." She raised both hands. "Oh, I'm not accusing you of lying. But this is about murder, and I must check everything. With your education, you understand the importance of primary sources."

He cocked his head at her, then nodded once. "All right, I do. And perhaps it is a good thing for you to know not to trust him."

"Why shouldn't I?"

"Because there's a streak of insecurity and greed in Goddy. It comes from his early experiences. If something happened in your relationship that frightened him or made him feel insecure, he'd do whatever he felt necessary to save his own neck, even if it meant breaking yours."

"Is that why he breaks your confidences?" asked Betsy, anger flaring again, understanding suddenly who was the manipulative one in their relationship. "Because you deliberately make him feel insecure?"

"I've always treated him with every kindness," declared John. He looked away. "But you see how he repays me."

How could he speak of Goddy as if he were some kind of pet? Betsy sat down and tried to put a tone of sweet reason into her voice. "Godwin has never before told me about any of your cases, and I doubt if he ever will again. But this is important. A young man's life is at stake. Please, so long he has told me about the viatical, can you confirm the details as he explained them to me?"

He made eye contact and held it for several seconds. "All right, yes. I'm Ian Masterson's attorney. He came to me and I arranged a lump-sum payment to Robert McFey, in return for which Mr. Masterson was made beneficiary of an insurance policy on Mr. McFey's life."

183

"Thank you."

"But if you think that gives him a motive for murder, let me disabuse you of that notion. I can assure you, absolutely, that Mr. Masterson is in no need of the payout of that policy. If Mr. McFey lived to be a hundred, it would not have incommoded Mr. Masterson in the least." His look was intent, his tone sincere and confident.

Going down in the elevator a few minutes later, Betsy reflected that while she had lost a dandy suspect, she would no longer have to worry about Shelly dating a murderer.

Betsy had been pleased to find a parking spot on a downtown Minneapolis street, but the instant she unlocked the door, she wished she'd gone into a parking ramp. The car was like an oven inside, and the steering wheel was so hot it burned her fingers. She started the engine, turned the air-conditioning on high, and stood outside for a minute while things cooled off in there. She was parked near Mr. Nye's office, the great, green-glass IDS Tower, the one where Mary Tyler Moore was seen shopping on the old television show. There was even a bronze statue of Ms. Moore just a block away that captured her throwing her cap in the air. When that show was made, the IDS Tower was the only real skyscraper in Minneapolis; now it had a number of rivals. Betsy looked around while her car's air conditioner worked. There was something to be said for a skyline that managed to wait until American architects had outgrown their fondness for plain glass boxes — the newer towers were of brick or stone, with interesting cornices and toplines.

Coming back into the shop half an hour later, Betsy saw two customers and said to Godwin, "Could you show me how to fix the coffee urn? It's acting up again." Which was Betsy's way of getting Godwin out of earshot into the back room of the shop.

Godwin, knowing where she'd been, followed her warily. She closed the door behind them and said, "Godwin, I seem to do nothing but put my foot in it lately. First Jill, now you."

Godwin's wariness deepened to fear. "Why? Where did you — oh, my God, you went to see John, didn't you?"

"Yes. I felt I had to confirm that Ian Masterson bought that viatical. He did confirm it, but he says he told you about it in confidence."

"Oh, lordy, lordy, lordy!" sighed Godwin. "I wish I hadn't mentioned it!"

"How could you not, knowing how important it is to the case I'm investigating?"

Godwin turned away from Betsy, to lean against the door, hiding his face in his elbow. It was an exceedingly dramatic pose — Goddy was fond of dramatic gestures — but also a very sincere one. Over the last couple of years, the relationship between John and Godwin had become strained, and Godwin had often feared it was coming to a breach. "He expects me not to repeat his gossip. And I *don't!* I *never* did before!"

"Why does he tell you things he shouldn't?"

"I don't know. It makes him feel even bigger when he can dish the dirt about important clients. He knows you're looking into the Rob McFey murder, it was talking about you doing that that reminded him about the viatical. Sometimes I think he sets me up to do things that will make him angry!"

Betsy didn't doubt it. And now she had to add to his sorrows. "He ordered me to fire you."

Godwin smacked his hand against the door. "Oh, *no!* He's wanted me to quit for simply *ages,* he says it's making me too *serious!* Oh, this is terrible, I *adore* working here! Does he think working at Stitchville or Zandy's would be the *same?*" He sighed deeply, trying not to cry.

Betsy said, "I told him I wouldn't, of course."

Godwin peeped over his shoulder at her. "You did?"

"Of course. Goddy, I can't run the shop without you, surely you know that!"

He came away from the door to hug her. "Oh, you are the sweetest, the bestest, I just love you to death!"

"Now, now, settle down, or I might suspect you of heterosexual thoughts."

He giggled, but let go. Then he turned serious. "But what am I going to do about John?"

"Can I help? What do you want me to do?"

"Nothing. I mean, I'll have to figure out how to make up with him, and try to get things to be like they were before."

"Do you think you can do that without quitting this job?"

"I don't know. He can make things very hard if I don't."

"Well, I told him I'd fight any attempt on his part to make you quit."

"How can you fight him? What can you do?"

Betsy's chin came up, the way it had in John's office, the way it had on the trip home, when she'd come to a decision. "Can you stay after work tonight for, say, half an hour? I'll tell you then."

He looked at her, trying to read her expression. "I think you'll like it," she said. "At least, I hope you do."

"Does it involve a raise?"

"Well, yes, it does."

He beamed at her. "Well, all right! Sure I can stay awhile."

They went back out and found two customers waiting for them. They stood together at the checkout desk, talking like friends, their selections heaped on the desk.

They were from Canada, here for an Embroiderers' Guild of America meeting. They introduced themselves as Alice Morgan and Tara Dewdney. Alice had found a Christmas stocking kit she'd been looking for; what's more, it was in a sale bin, so she was very pleased. But Tara had come into a small inheritance. She had spent one portion of it buying tickets for herself and Alice to the conference, and another on a buying trip to Stitchville USA. She was in Crewel World for a final splurge before flying home.

"This is Becky," she said to Alice, introducing Betsy by the wrong name. But Tara was buying a color wheel and some other items that brought her total to over two hundred dollars. At that level of spending, Tara Dewdney could call Betsy Monkey-face if she liked. Perhaps Betsy's accountant would smile this month after all.

Chapter 11

Godwin shooed the last customer out right at five, and turned the needlepointed sign around to closed. The money was counted, the deposit slip made out, the coffee urn unplugged, emptied, and washed, stock replaced, the radio shut off, and all but one light extinguished.

They both stood a moment, looking around, going down the close-up list in their heads. This was Betsy's favorite time of day, and not just because another hard day at work was finished. The air in the shop seemed full of small vibrations and a very fine dust, as if a herd of horses had just gone through. Betsy felt as if she were exhaling slowly after having inhaled all day, and the shop was exhaling with her.

Though it was still bright daylight outside, in the shop with the lights off the glowing colors of the yarns were dulled and the shimmer of the flosses was gone, and the little herd of yarn baskets in the corner had blended into a mass of smooth wicker and fuzzy wool. Godwin sighed softly, changing gears himself, then turned toward Betsy, who was standing behind the big old checkout desk. "Well?" he said.

He'd been very patient all afternoon, disarming and amusing every customer who came his way with his usual gay-on-parade behavior, only very rarely looking at his watch and rolling his eyes at heaven for arranging such a pokey passage of time.

"Yes," said Betsy. "Let's sit down." She picked up a legal-size yellow notepad and made for the library table that filled the center of the room. She pulled out a chair and seated herself. She put some effort into not smiling; she wanted this to be a real surprise.

"All right," said Godwin, hurrying to take another chair.

"I had a talk with my financial advisor last night," began Betsy, speaking with some deliberation. She turned over the blank top page of the pad, revealing some notes on the second page. "He suggested several changes I need to make in my fiscal planning for the next few years."

"Oh, my *God,* he told you to declare *bankruptcy!*" shrieked Godwin in faux hysteria. "I *knew* we weren't making much *money* the last two months, but I *didn't* know it was as bad as all *that!*"

"Godwin, for heaven's sake!"

"Sorry," said Godwin, not very contritely. "But can't you talk any faster? Or just give me the summation? I'm simply dying of curiosity."

Betsy allowed her smile to appear, and accepting the challenge, she said rapidly, "All right, here's the bottom line: I propose to double your salary, offer you a benefit package like my own, and arrange for you to have power of attorney if something happens to me and I can't take care of things myself."

Godwin took in a great gulp of air and stopped there, staring at her for long enough that his complexion turned deep pink. His hands splayed on the table and then began to scramble as he struggled for control. He finally managed to exhale and draw another breath. *"Strewth!"* he exclaimed.

"Was that succinct enough for you?"

"Have *mercy!*" he gulped. "I guess it is! Why, this is so amazing! I — I —" A slow-going grin morphed his expression from amazement to delight. "John will just *shit!*"

"Good. I'll teach him to mess with my employees."

Godwin held out his arms, wrists together, then yanked them apart. "The golden handcuffs are *broken!*"

She patted the air with one hand. "Now, don't get too excited. Even on double your current salary, you won't be able to jet to New York on weekends to attend Broadway shows and dine at whichever restaurant is hottest at present."

"Salt," said Godwin absently.

"What?"

"Well, L'Impero, then. Does this mean I get to make more decisions about running the shop?"

"You already make decisions."

"But I mean like a, a *manager!* Could I be *Manager* of Crewel World?"

Betsy laughed. "Why stop there? Why not be Vice President in Charge of Operations?"

"Could I? Really? Could I?"

Caught up in his excitement, she laughed and said, "Why not?"

Godwin rose from the chair to dance in a series of curved-spine, arms-forward, Gene Kelly turns all the way around the table. He wound up standing behind the chair he'd occupied, one arm bent in front, the other up and out.

Betsy, still laughing, rose to give him a standing O, and he bowed deeply, then sat down. "What does an operations manager do?" he asked.

Betsy hesitated. Her main purpose had been to thwart John, and she had reacted impulsively in saying Godwin could be an officer of Crewel World, Inc. But Godwin was not just a golden, eager puppy, and she was not going to be like John, winning him with trifles, to betray him when it came to realities. "If you're serious, I'm prepared to give you real responsibility."

He grinned and spread his arms. "Lay it on me."

She reached into a coffee can in the center of the table that held scissors, rulers, crochet hooks, a pair of size eleven knitting needles, and an assortment of marking pens and pencils. She pulled out a pencil, turned over another page in the notebook, and wrote the numeral 1 on the top line. "All right, manager, you run the shop." She went back and wrote MANAGER on top of the page, then went to number 1, and numbered the rest as she wrote them down. "First, you set the hours we're open; second, you decide how much off the regular price we'll give for sales — and third, you can set the dates of sales. Fourth, we work together on ads, but you're in charge of ordering stock from now on. And you can set the work schedules, too — which means you can hire and fire part-timers as necessary." She dotted the last item with a firm mark and put the pencil down. "But run your decisions past me, at least at first, so I can approve them."

Godwin had been nodding eagerly, watching the list grow. "Yes, yes, I can handle all of that," he said. "Can I do a newsletter, too?"

"Come on, isn't this enough?"

"Please?"

"Goddy, newsletters are a lot of work. It's easy to do one or two, or even three, but then they turn into a real chore. I helped put out a monthly one for a book club a long time ago, and I came to hate that deadline. Trust me, you will, too."

"Yes, but Stitchville has a newsletter, so it's not like it's impossible. Susan Greening Davis says they're important, and since they go only to customers who want them, they aren't wasted like newspaper ads can be. And they're cheaper than any other kind of advertising except a sign in the window."

Susan Greening Davis was a needlework shop maven, appearing at conventions and markets and putting out her own newsletter full of advice and suggestions. Betsy subscribed to it, but Godwin also read it, and he was always trying to get Betsy to use more of her ideas.

"They're way, way more work than you think, Goddy."

"I'm up for it! You wouldn't believe how much material I've already got. Please, I've always wanted to do one, I have a computer at home with a newsletter program." He raised his right hand. "I *swear*, you won't have to lift a finger, I'll do *all* the work."

"Okay, all right," yielded Betsy, but then she picked up and pointed the pencil at Godwin as if it were a pistol and warned him, "If you come to me *one time* for help, that will be the last issue."

"Yes! Yes! Yes! Vice President *and* Editor in

Chief!" Godwin pumped a fist in the air while she wrote "7. Newsletter" on the list. He shifted mood instantly to worry, "What shall I call it?"

He looked at Betsy for advice, but she refused to be drawn. "It's your project, you name it."

"All right." He pressed a forefinger into his cheek, composing. Godwin was a really good actor; Betsy could almost see the green eyeshade and ink stains. *"Crewel World News? Stitchin' Print? A Stitch in Time?"* He looked over to see if Betsy had brightened at any of these.

She hadn't. "May we talk about some other things now?"

"Sure, like what?"

"Like the apology I owe you for not doing something like this a long time ago. Mr. Forseth was rather sharp to me about that. He says I should be more willing to respond generously to valuable employees." She went back a page in the notepad. "In fact, one thing he also suggested is that I take out 'valuable employee' insurance on you. Even though I told him that no amount of money would bring me a replacement with all the qualities you bring to Crewel World." Betsy felt her face grow hot.

Godwin swallowed hard and said carelessly, "Oh, I don't know. Donny DePere can stitch. And he's even more flamboyant than I am."

"Yes, but is he as handsome?"

Godwin smiled and preened just a little. "No." This broke the sentimental moment satisfactorily. Godwin frowned. "What did you mean about becoming incapacitated? Oh, my God, you're sick, aren't you?"

"No, no, of course not! But remember how I was in the hospital twice winter before last? Suppose I'd had to stay longer, or had to stop working for a long while? Who would have paid my bills, ordered more stock, arranged to have the parking lot plowed?"

"I suppose Shelly and I could have handled that."

"No, you couldn't. Neither of you are legally able to sign checks or withdraw funds from my bank account. That's what this is about. Mr. Forseth is drawing up a legal document called a 'springing durable power of attorney,' and that means if I become incapacitated, you'd be able to do those things. In fact, if I'm in a mysterious coma due to ingestion of an unnamed drug, or chained to a wall in the farthest reaches of a secret dungeon constructed by the maniacal Doctor Dread, you could even make decisions about my other holdings."

"Hey, what else are you investigating?" asked Godwin, alarmed.

"Nothing, nothing," she replied. "The only way I can talk about such things is by making a joke of them. But you know what I mean. If I get run over by Lars's Stanley Steamer, or fall through the ice on Lake Minnetonka . . ."

"All right, I get it," Godwin said, nodding. "If I might be allowed a serious remark, I'm honored you think I can handle things like that. But why me? Why not Shelly?"

"Because while she knows quite a bit about running Crewel World, she can only work regular hours here in the summer. You know how it should be run even better than Shelly does. Or me, for that matter." She looked around the shop, at the six door-like flats on one wall that held painted needlepoint canvases, and the white dresser near the door on whose mirror were taped announcements of classes and needlework events. "I wouldn't have this place if you hadn't been there from the start for me."

He looked around, too, at the box shelves with their burdens of books, magazines, and needlework gadgets. "That's true," he said, not kidding. "But I don't know much about the other things. I suppose I could collect the rents. I've been a tenant enough times to have a little understanding of how that works. But what about the other stuff? Like New York Motto?"

"What about it?"

"I don't know how it works."

"Frankly, I don't understand it very well, either. They buy bankruptcy estates, and have a semisecret way of finding out about them. Every so often I get a phone call or an e-mail advising me that X amount of dollars is needed, or that X amount of dollars is being forwarded to me. So far, more has come in than gone out. In fact, it paid off my car and it helped buy the new roof. Goddy, will you formally advise me that you accept my offer?"

"What, write you a letter?"

"I'll write you one and you reply. But just for now, to make it real, say you accept in so many words."

"Okay. I formally accept your offer to become Vice President in Charge of Operations of Crewel World, Incorporated, and Editor in Chief of its newsletter. Since it's two titles, shouldn't you triple my pay?"

She laughed. "Not until we double our profits."

"All right, then how about a pension plan?"

"All right. I'll come halfway to matching any money you put into a special savings or investment account for your retirement." She wrote that down so she'd remember to put it in her letter to him. It was a perfectly safe offer; Godwin was the eternal grasshopper.

"Done." He grimaced suddenly and she realized he was trying not to cry.

"Tears on this occasion are entirely suitable," she said.

"Oh, Betsy! You don't know, you don't know!" A tear escaped, rolled down the side of his nose, and crossed his upper lip, where it was captured by a nimble tongue.

"What don't I know?"

"How scared I've been. John has been so mean to me lately, and I've been behaving badly because I'm scared. I keep waiting for the axe to fall, and waiting, and *waiting,* so I've been pushing his buttons, just to get the damn thing over with. Now . . ." He blinked rapidly. "Now I can be myself again, because I've got my own feet on solid ground."

"Oh, Goddy, you make me feel so guilty for not doing this sooner!"

"No, never feel guilty! You were working your own way through some bad things. That divorce and your sister, and trying to learn how to own your own business and manage your money — it hasn't been easy."

"No, it hasn't. But I was lucky to have some good friends to show me the way." She reached out and took one of his hands. It was warm and grasped back firmly, and they sat like that for a minute.

He said at last, "Well, it's nice that you've learned enough so that the store and the building can pay both our ways now."

She gave her head a wry twist. "Not quite. The money from Crewel World will pay only my employees' salaries. I have a money market account that pays my salary and helps with other bills. The rents I collect are paying the mortgage, taxes, and some of the upkeep on the building. The money I have in stocks and bonds doesn't need much tending."

"Did you take a bath on the stock market?"

Betsy nodded. "I thought Margot's holdings were way too conservative, so I moved quite a bit into tech stocks."

"Ouch."

"Indeed. But I know better now, and the market has started to climb back."

"John got out in time. Inside information, probably."

Betsy frowned at him. "You're not serious!"

Godwin shrugged. "I don't know if I am or not. He had some kind of information, I know that; he was on the phone for most of a Saturday afternoon and on Monday he placed a lot of orders to sell. And less than a week later, *le deluge*."

"Goddy, is he some kind of crook?"

"No, no. Well, not really. I mean, if you play golf with someone and that person mentions that an uncle has told his children to sell, is that insider trading?"

Betsy shrugged. "I don't know. I understand that even people in the investment business, including the enforcement end, don't know what the term means, exactly. Are you going home now to tell John it's over?"

Godwin shrugged and then huddled a bit inside his shirt. "I may not have to. I may go home and find all my things out in the gutter again."

"If you do, pick up what you need and come back here. You can stay in my guest room. Unless you'd rather stay at Shelly's house like last time."

"I don't know if Shelly wants company."

"Why wouldn't she?"

"She's dating Ian Masterson, you know."

"Yes, she told me all about it."

"Well," sighed Godwin, and he stood. "I'd better go see how bad it is with John."

"Call me and let me know. At least you're not going in unarmed, Mr. Vice President."

Chapter 12

Ian woke from a lovely dream without knowing why, to crisp sheets (funny, he didn't remember changing them) and sunlight sieved through miniblinds. That was definitely wrong; he had heavy drapes in his bedroom to keep the sun from waking him. And the mattress was too firm. And there was a faint scent of perfume.

It had not been a dream.

Or perhaps it still was.

The cell phone rang — again, he realized. Not a dream, then; cell phones didn't ring in one's dreams. That meant — that he'd better get the phone. He reached for it on the unfamiliar bedside table.

"Uh-huh?" he said in a sleep-thickened voice.

"Hmmmm?" murmured a voice beside him. He glanced over. Yes, she had been real, too. Delightful!

A voice from the cell phone said, "Ian?"

"Yes, this is Ian Masterson," he said.

"Ian, this is Skye."

"Who?"

Impatiently, "Skye McFey."

His heart clenched painfully. "Skye, my dear, how sorry I am for you!"

"That's all right, I'm fine, I'm really just fine," said Skye. Which wasn't true, the tone of her voice was so altered he would not have recognized it if she hadn't identified herself.

"Who's it?" asked a sleepy voice from the other side of the bed.

"It's not important, go back to sleep," he said, and to the caller, "Can you hold on for just a minute? I want to go into another room."

"Do you have company?"

"No, I'm in someone else's house." He rose from the bed and walked quietly into the living room. He closed the bedroom door and said, still quietly, "How are you, my dear?"

Sky said, "I need your help."

"Of course, if I can."

"Mommy showed me Pop's will, and he left all his art to me."

"Good for you! That's fortunate, and very appropriate. You're the one member of his family best able to appreciate his work. He loved you for many reasons, but that one was special."

"I know, I know," said the voice wretchedly. "But I wasn't wrong, or was I? You really did think he was good, that he should get into a gallery to start building a national reputation."

"Yes, I thought that — and it was true. But my dear, he's past all that now, on this plane, anyway."

"He's past it on *any* plane!" she replied, her voice harsh with anger. "Dead's dead."

He felt suddenly sad and old. "Oh, poor Skye, how awful to believe that! But true or not, don't you see? Fame doesn't matter anymore."

"Of course it does! Oh, not to him! But I want people to remember my father as the great artist he was! That means we need to build his reputation! You *have* to help me! You promised my father you would help him!"

She was excited and wretched at once; he couldn't deal with her in this state, not on the phone. He said, "I remember my promise. And I keep my promises, to the best of my ability. What is it you want me to do?"

"First of all, we have to stop Mommy."

His stomach lurched. "Why, what has she done?"

"She told me she's going over to Pop's place to organize an estate sale."

"Why do we have to stop her?"

"Because she's going to have like a garage sale!"

"How do you know that?"

"Because she said she'd give me the proceeds."

"I don't understand, I should think you'd

be happy about that," said Ian, bewildered.

"Don't you get it? She'd never give me thousands of dollars! So that means she's not expecting to get more than a couple hundred, and *that* means a dollar apiece for everything! Don't you see? She'll sell the lion for a dollar and the sea birds for fifty cents and his practice pieces for kindling!"

He said quickly, "She wouldn't!" Then, "Surely she knows better. Why would she spoil your inheritance like that?"

"Because she's still mad at him for selling Information Please."

"Oh. Oh, yes, of course. I see. Do you know how much material there is?"

"Quite a bit, if you count his practice pieces."

"I remember him telling me he destroyed his practice pieces."

"The *clay* ones he did," she said with exaggerated patience. "He dumped them back into the clay barrel. And the really bad wooden ones, he broke those. But some, they're almost done, and some are just pieces, like a paw or a head. I suppose most of them aren't worth anything, but I remember that one that's just the face of a fox, it's beautiful, and I bet we could get three hundred dollars for it if we put it up on a wire spoke and found a pretty base for it."

He'd seen that mask; he didn't think it was a practice piece but a finished one. He asked,

"Are there a lot of those practice pieces?"

"Sure. Pop did practice pieces of almost all his stuff, even those silly animals that look like cartoons. He always started in clay, then did them in wood. And then he wouldn't be satisfied and he'd start over. But sometimes he kept the practice wooden ones, because sometimes he could rework them and sell them."

Again his heart was squeezed. There were two of him, one very amusing — and a very cruel one. "That's interesting, that he did practice pieces of the caricatures. I thought he just did them quickly, like doodling."

"Is that what they are, caricatures? I called them cartoons, they made me laugh. But speaking of them, that reminds me: We *have* to get there ahead of Mommy. I think there are two or three versions of that cartoon, I mean caricature, the one he did of her as a Doberman pinscher. If she finds that, she'll go postal and not hold even a garage sale but a big weenie roast, studio and all."

He found himself trying to make a fist of his burned hand and gritted his teeth in pain. "When did she say she's going over?"

"Monday or Tuesday. Today's Saturday and I'm going to be busy tomorrow, so we'd better get our butts in gear today."

"Yes, you're right. Okay, let me think. You said someone has already collected all your father's work into his studio?"

"If you mean the stuff from the art fair, someone brought that back, yes. I have two pieces in my bedroom which I'll bring along, but everything else should be there; he didn't have anything out on consignment. We'll need a good-size chunk of time, because after you take a look, then you have to go talk to Mommy."

"Why do you even think she'll listen to me?"

"Because you're rich, and to Mommy, that makes you important! It'll be easy, just tell her they're worth a *whole lot* of money. I'm sure Pop told you money is like her god. He told me that often enough."

Ian smiled, a bit tightly. "Yes, he mentioned that."

"It should be easy to convince her there's a lot of money at stake, because there is. Then you can help us organize a real auction, something we can advertise, maybe get a gallery interested, maybe even someone from a museum."

"I don't know —"

"Yes, you do know. But first you have to go see what's there."

"Yes, all right, all right," he said and sighed heavily. "But listen, why do you need to get involved? How about I come over to your place and get the key to the studio?"

"No, huh-uh, Pop left this stuff to me, so I have to be involved, it's my responsibility. So please, *please* come over real soon, and take me with you."

He sighed again, this time in surrender. "Yes, all right. What time is it, anyway?" He held his watch up to one eye. "My God, it's seven o'clock in the morning!"

"I know, and I'm sorry," she said. "I waited as long as I could."

He said, jocularly but sincerely exasperated, "Dear Skye, you will never become a true artist until you learn to stay up late and sleep in!"

"I know, I know, but I can't help it; the sun comes up and I get up. Anyway, you're up and out."

He started to reply, but stopped himself. He didn't want to let her know he'd spent the night here. She dressed like a goth, but her soul was still innocent, he was sure. Well, probably. Or mostly. He said instead, "Yes, that's true. But I haven't had my morning coffee yet. Let me see what I've agreed to do this day, and what I have to do to break loose a big-enough chunk to comply with your request. I shall call you back in, say, two hours."

"Make it ninety minutes. And I knew I could count on you! Thanks, Ian. Bye."

He closed his phone and scratched his head hard with the other hand, trying to stir up some circulation. He really didn't want to drive all the way over to the McFey house in

Maple Plain, then all the way in to Golden Valley, look at Robbie's work — a damnable task, especially with this frantic child-woman peering over his shoulder — then drive all the way back out again. On the other hand, Skye was right, he had to see what was there. Now.

He wondered how angry Pam was. And if some of that anger was directed at him. How much did she know about his encouraging Robbie to follow his dream? He might not be able to talk any sense into her. But what might she do if he didn't try? Burn everything? Or hold a garage sale and sell that lovely fox mask for fifty cents to one of those magpie people?

Magpie people — good phrase to describe those creatures who flocked to garage and estate sales in search of something shiny to carry home.

His massaging fingers slowed as his muse continued, Who are those people anyway? What were they after? What must their own homes look like? Like a magpie's nest, obviously. He contemplated a piece of art that looked like a large, badly made bird's nest, do it in wire and sheet metal cut into bird feathers. Put in it a chipped vase in some impossible color, a velvet painting of Elvis, a string of Christmas tree lights with a bulb broken — everything would have those colored stick-on dots used to price garage sales items, of course — and let's see, a blender, one very used ice skate . . .

The door to the bedroom opened and Shelly came out. "Ian? Is something wrong?"

Her voice startled him out of his musing. "No, no, my love, I just had a phone call from someone who needs to see me."

"At seven o'clock in the morning?" Shelly's voice was creaky from sleep, and she yawned hugely, stretching her arms over her head. Ah, God willing, he would make a worshipful sculpture of that body!

He came to gather it into his arms. "No, she doesn't need to see me right away. Just later on." He kissed her bed-warmed neck.

"She?" The voice was quite awake now.

Damn all women! He released her. "Yes, a very lovely young woman who in a few months will enter the tenth grade."

"Oh. Wait, I thought you told me your younger daughter is in college."

"She is. This is the daughter of Robbie McFey, who wants me to help her sort out her father's artwork."

"Oh, that poor creature! But is she your responsibility? I mean, do you really have to go?"

"Yes, I absolutely, positively have to go. But before I do . . ." Wait, there was another appetite asking for attention. "Could I possibly get you to make a pot of coffee?"

"Would you like some pancakes and sausage to go with?"

"Woman, your price is above rubies. I shall have a quick shower and join you in the kitchen. May I borrow a plastic bag for my bandage?"

Betsy was in the shop. It was Saturday, a few minutes after ten. The shop had just opened, but it was already crowded. Women who worked office hours were the norm these days, and they had only weekends for the kind of slow, savoring shopping called for in a needlework store.

Betsy was helping a woman choose among several baby sampler patterns for a nephew-in-waiting. "He's due October ninth," the customer said, "so maybe something in autumn colors?"

"Well, I don't think I've ever seen a baby design in orange, red, and gold," Betsy said.

Shelly, eavesdropping, said, "We do have a clever one with an acorn and two trees." She quickly fingered through the square basket of birth and marriage samplers to find it. "See? There's no rule against changing the colors in any pattern. Substitute orange and brown, say Anchor 304 or maybe 925 and 901 or 374 for the two shades of green, do the lettering in 1015 — no, 1041."

The customer cocked her head and half closed one eye. "Do you know, I think that might work." She took the pattern and began to count how many stitches wide it was.

"Maybe on a natural linen, twenty-eight count, over two," she murmured.

"Mark your substitutions on the color key so you're consistent," Shelly reminded her. "The result will be a really unique gift."

The phone rang. Shelly turned, but Betsy was nearer, so she excused herself and picked up the cordless on the library table. "Crewel World, Betsy speaking, how may I help you?" she said.

"I repeat, you are the very best!" It was Godwin.

"Thank you very much. So John is happy for you?"

"Flattened is more like it! He was surprised when I told him last night, then he said he was pleased, then he went for a walk. He came home with *flowers* — he hasn't done that for ages! — and took me out to dinner and woke this morning a gentler, better man. I really think he was impressed that you trusted me with this responsibility. We had the most *interesting* conversation over breakfast! He thought you were trying to *break us up*, isn't that strange?"

"Why would I want to do that? And how could I possibly accomplish it?"

"By taking the *joie de vivre* out of me. Making me a regular nine-to-five adult."

"Goddy, I don't need a regular nine-to-five adult in the shop, I need the creative, amusing, charming you."

"You also need a knowledgeable, reliable executive, and that *never* used to be me. I think he understands that I can still be me, even if I have become a reliable corporate executive. But to make sure he understands, we're taking me, Vice President in Charge of Operations, out to buy that lavender silk shirt I saw at Abercrombie and Fitch last week. I may even buy a *tie!*" The thought of that sent him off again into gales of laughter.

"Enjoy," said Betsy.

"I will, I will!" said Godwin gaily and hung up.

Betsy was still smiling when the door went *Bing!* and she looked over to see Jill coming in.

Betsy nearly rushed over to greet her, but stopped herself in time. She tried out her most ordinary smile and said, "Well, hello, Jill. Is there something you're looking for? The trunk sale isn't until Wednesday."

Jill smiled. "I know. When's your day off next week?"

"Thursday, why?"

"Have you made any plans?"

"Not really. The car needs to be serviced, I thought I'd take it in. What, you need someone to go shopping with you?"

Jill approached, her face a blank mask. "You think you're so clever, don't you?" she said quietly.

Betsy, somewhat alarmed said, "Hardly ever. Why?"

"Lars told you about how we got caught in the department's no-fraternization rule, and you and Shelly — who also thinks she's clever — couldn't come up with a clever way to get around the rule." Jill could look almost as intimidating as Lars when she wanted to, and right now she was only inches from Betsy's face. "When it's a friend, the cleverness well runs dry, I guess."

Betsy's brain was scrabbling in its cage, seeking a way out. "Wh-what do you want me to do?"

"I want you to stand up for me at my wedding to Lars." Jill was speaking so quietly, Betsy got the sense of this mostly by reading Jill's lips.

"Sure, okay, I — *wait* a second! How can you — I mean, isn't it against regulations?"

Jill was suddenly smiling broadly. She put a finger over her mouth and Betsy realized she'd said that really loud. Shelly and several customers in the shop had turned to stare at them, all eyes and ears. Betsy whispered, "You mean on Thursday? How can you — I mean, I thought —"

"Never mind what you thought. Can you shake loose a couple of hours on Thursday, say around two?"

"Certainly." Suddenly Betsy was grinning, too, she couldn't help it. "Oh, Jill, congratulations!" And she couldn't help giving Jill a hug.

"That's enough, people are staring! I'll call you tomorrow." Jill turned and walked out.

Shelly was at Betsy's elbow a fraction of a second after the door closed. "What was that all about? What are you smiling at? What did Jill tell you?"

"Nothing important. Well, except our quarrel's over. And we're having a late lunch together on Thursday."

"Well, I could tell the fight was over, though I thought at first she was coming in to say something mean."

"So did I. But you know that weird sense of humor she has. I think it comes from trying to repress it, it jumps out at strange angles when it gets a chance."

"Maybe that's what it is. Do you know what she did to me? About two years ago she pulled me over, siren and lights and everything, and I was wondering what law I'd broken, but she just stood there at my car window talking about a new needlepoint stitch she was trying out and at the same time pretending to write me a ticket. Had her book out and everything. People going by were grinning at me, and I was so mad! She never cracked a smile until she got back in her car and drove past me with a chicken-eating grin. Honestly, I had people asking me for a month after that what I'd gotten a ticket for. You'd never know it looking at her that she's a practical joker. But isn't it great that she's not mad at you anymore? I'm so happy for both of you!" Shelly gave Betsy a hug, which Betsy returned, happy to hide her delighted grin in Shelly's shoulder until she could gain control over her silly mouth. A wedding!

Chapter 13

Ian and Skye walked into Rob McFey's Golden Valley apartment around ten-thirty. The air-conditioning was on full blast, so he was glad he'd worn his new long-sleeved green shirt; though pretty soon his toes, bare in their sandals, would feel a chill. Skye was in her goth uniform of black cotton shirt and immense-legged denim overalls that fully covered her bare feet. Her hair, Kool-Aid lime darkened with gel, bristled with a dozen six-inch spikes, and a silver knob glittered on one nostril.

Ian hesitated just inside the door. The little apartment had not yet taken on the abandoned feel it would have in another week or two; one might almost have expected to hear Robbie's cheery hail from another room. But of course . . . Ian sighed and started for the bedroom, which Robbie used as a studio. The sagging couch in the living room had sheets and blankets neatly folded at one end. Ian had been here before, though not so often as Skye, of course. But she gestured at him to lead while she followed in silence.

Ian opened the door to the studio and was

assaulted by a smell of sawdust and varnish. Harsh sunlight poured in through the dusty, uncurtained window. Robbie had installed three rows of shelves on the two long walls of the room and spaced his carvings along them. It was sad to see the amount of space left; it meant he'd sold a lot of his work, which meant there wasn't much left to sell at the much higher price his death could command. Some of the lack was filled by books on wood carving, and there was a lovely jointed artist's model of a horse, the equine equivalent of the more familiar human figure — that was Skye's, he suspected, knowing her fondness for drawing them. A neat stack of debarked hardwood in the far corner, chunks of varying sizes and irregular shapes, waited in vain for a knowing hand to disclose the animal in them.

Robbie had taken up the carpet, exposing the plywood floor. The reason was made clear by the scatter of sawdust and wood shavings a lazy broom had missed.

A little away from the window stood Robbie's work bench, a heavy wooden table with thick square legs. There was a wooden vise on one end of it, a leather strop hanging down in front. Beside it, on a metal stand, was a small bandsaw with sawdust heaped on and around it. Behind them, beside the window, was a shelf and a wooden rack holding knives, gouges, and chisels of many sizes, some with the patina that comes of long use.

A chisel and very small gouge were on the work bench, along with a jar of paste Robbie had made himself. He had told Ian it was just a blend of aluminum oxide and mineral oil, and it was in constant need to hone his carving blades. "A sharp knife makes a happy whittler," he'd said.

Centered on the table, where the sun could strike it hardest, was a skeletal sculpture done in wire, only partly filled out with clay. It was an animal of some sort — probably a bear, thought Ian. It was caught in a clumsy run, and its head was looking to one side, mouth open. Even in this sketchy stage of design, it was humorously evocative of frustration and anger; Ian thought it looked as if bees were after it.

As he approached, he saw several color photos clipped from magazines strewn on the bench, of black bears walking, climbing, waving hello. Another, bigger, photo of a bear hustling across a meadow, was stuck with a lump of clay to the shelf over the tool holders on the wall. On the shelf were grubby cans and jars of stains and varnishes and a bright silver can marked THINNER; beside it was a pint mayonnaise jar half full of brown liquid with four brush handles sticking out of it.

Ian paused to contemplate the wall. The

backlighting from the sunlight made interesting shadows. Something like this wall, done in old iron and stained aluminum . . . No, take the whole thing, table, saw, shelves, even the stacked wood —

Suddenly Skye brushed past him. She stopped at the table, hesitated, then touched the bear figure very lightly with her fingertips. "He was working on this on the last Friday of his life," she said in a rusty voice, and burst into tears.

Ian reached for her, but she ducked away with an almost angry squall, still crying. Hurt, he turned to look back at the wall with the door in it, which held a filing cabinet and a small mirror — used, Ian knew, to check the proportions of a carving. Holding art up to a mirror revealed errors by throwing the image into a new perspective.

On top of the filing cabinet was the magnificent lion carving. He went for a closer look and found himself trying to see from the placement of the legs if the antelope would move ahead before the lion finished his swipe. Damn, damn, *damn,* the old drunk had been good.

"I-Ian?" came a small voice. He turned. Skye's arms were spread beseechingly, and black eye makeup was running down her cheeks.

He knew he didn't have a handkerchief — he hadn't carried a handkerchief for years — but he fumbled in his pockets anyway, as he walked toward her.

She met him halfway, throwing her arms around his neck and wiping her face on the shoulder of his new green shirt. He sighed as inconspicuously as he could and held her until the renewed storm was over.

"There, now," he said gently, when she was reduced to occasional hiccups. "Feel better?"

"Y-yes, I guess so. Oh, Ian, he was so wonderful, and he was teaching me how to be an artist, too! I'm going to miss him forever!"

"Yes, sweetheart, I know. I'll miss him, too. What happened to him was grossly unfair."

"It wasn't unfair, it was *evil!* I hope the police put Pop's killer into jail for the rest of his life!"

"It would be less than he deserves for taking your pop away from you — and a good friend from me!" he said harshly. "But go gently, dear heart. Don't allow hatred to damage your soul. Whoever did this acted not out of wickedness, but most likely from a sudden burst of fear and greed."

"What do you mean, 'whoever did this'? The police have arrested that kid, he's in jail and everything!"

He took her by the shoulders and pushed her gently back so he could look at her puzzled, mascara-stained face.

"There are some people, mostly the kid's family, of course, but not entirely, who aren't convinced he did it."

"That's stupid! I mean, they practically caught him red-handed, didn't they? Who else *could* have done it?"

"That, my dear, is the question they are asking. Who else? I understand the police have talked to you, and your mother."

Skye nodded. "They've come out twice, actually. The second time they talked to Coy, too." She frowned. "Oh, you don't mean they think — well, that's crazy! Why would he — Oh. The money."

She looked frightened now, and he brought her back into an embrace so he wouldn't have to see what he was doing to her. "There, now, of course they're mistaken to think it was one of you. But you see, if they're still looking, then they're not sure. So let's put our thinking caps on, and try to think who else, if not that boy, *and* not any member of your family, might have done this."

She grew very still, and he began to think she was totally baffled, or at least waiting for him to go first. So he said, "There's me, of course."

That surprised her; he felt her start against him. "You? Why you?"

"Because I bought a viatical from Robbie. That means I gave him a sum of money and in return he made me beneficiary of his life insurance policy."

"Oh, *you're* the one!"

"What, you know about this?"

"Mama was just furious about it, until she found out it was the littler policy."

He snorted. "I see. Well, I don't think I could have afforded the bigger one."

Skye chuckled faintly.

He said, "So you see, we both have an interest in finding someone else who might have done this. You're sure there's no one else who was mad at your pop?"

She fell silent again for a few moments, but he could feel the tension in her shoulders while she thought hard. Then, as if coming to a decision rather than getting an idea, she pushed back from him to say, "I don't know if this is a good idea, but there's Banner Wilcox."

"Who's Banner Wilcox when he's at home?"

She smiled at this ancient witticism. "He was Pop's partner in Information Please."

"Oh, yes, I remember Robbie talking about him."

She nodded. "Yes. He was like a junior partner, which I used to think was strange because he's really old, almost sixty. He went to work for Makejoy, which is the company Pop sold out to, but then they went bankrupt and Banner was fired. And he was broke, because . . ." She had to think for a bit. "How did it work? Pop said they gave Banner some stock in Makejoy, too, and Banner bought more stock with his share of the buyout money. Yes, that's how it went. So when they went out of business, Banner lost everything. And he's too old to get another job as good as the one he had, which already wasn't as good as when he was Pop's partner. For about a month after that happened, he called Pop almost every day. Pop told us not to talk to Banner on the phone, because Banner was having a nervous breakdown and thought Pop did all this to him on purpose. Pop wanted to get an unlisted phone number, but Mommy said she needed to hear from her friends, and anyway Banner would stop calling once he cooled off."

"And did he?"

Skye shook her head. "No. Pop never said anything more about it, but I know Banner still called, at least once in a while, because once I answered the phone and it was him." She frowned. "No, it was twice, because the first time Pop was getting his car serviced, and the second time it was after Pop moved out. Coy told me that one time he answered the phone and Banner thought it was Pop, and Coy caught an earful. He said Banner used really filthy words. Coy laughed about it, but . . ."

"Yes, I see."

"When Pop moved out, he told us not to give Banner his address or phone number."

"Did you all obey this?"

"I did. When Banner talked to me that second time, he sounded like he always did, nice and polite. He asked for Pop's phone number, but I told him I couldn't tell him that."

"Did he get mad?"

"Nope, he just said 'All right,' and hung up."

"Did your mother and Coyne obey?"

"I think they did. But I don't know for sure. I mean Coy wouldn't, I'm sure . . . but Mommy was awful mad at Pop."

"If your mother didn't tell him, would Banner have any way of finding out Robbie would be at the Excelsior art fair?"

"No, I don't think so. They don't advertise the names of artists ahead of time, I know that. But Pop had told lots of people he'd be there. I don't know if Banner could've talked to any of them." She was looking rather pale. "Oh, Ian, do you think . . . ?"

"Probably not. I think it was probably that juvenile delinquent who was arrested to start with. But I also think it wouldn't hurt to have Mr. Wilcox questioned. I wonder if he's got an alibi. What do you know about him, Skye? Did you ever meet him, I mean before all this happened? Did he always have a bad temper?"

"Oh, I've met him lots of times. He and his wife used to come over to dinner and have us over to their house. I know they have two kids. Jennifer's almost finished with college, or maybe has finished now, and Jake is married and his wife has twins, they were so adorable. And no, Banner doesn't have a bad temper, or he didn't. That's why we're wrong to think Banner could have murdered Pop. I mean, Banner's sweet — kind of a wuss, really. When Coy said Banner sounded insanely angry, I couldn't believe it. He was always nice and quiet before."

"Then he probably got it out of his system with just yelling. When did he call last?"

"I don't know. Coy told me about the call back before Pop moved out. But Mommy mentioned not long ago that Banner had called her and said she told him that if he didn't stop it, she was going to get a, a cease and desist? Is that what's it's called, the legal paper?"

"A restraining order. When was this?"

Skye thought. "It was when we just finished final exams. That was the first week in June."

"And your father was killed the second weekend in June."

"But she didn't say anything about him screaming and yelling, so maybe he was getting over it," said Skye. She sniffled and wiped her nose with the back of one hand, and he smiled a little at her, a smile full of sympathy for her youth and ignorance.

He said, "Why don't you go wash your

face?" and gently rubbed one cheek with his thumb.

She reached up for his hand, and saw the black on it. This made her smile, too, and attempt a weak jest. "Phony advertising, they said this was waterproof. All right, excuse me."

While she was gone, he began looking at the art on the shelves. He paused for a moment to admire the sandpipers. What an amazing economy of line! Yet one could almost hear the shush of waves as the lively birds ran along the shore or prodded the wet sand for — what were they after, anyway? Bugs? Clams? Ian shrugged and moved on. Here were half a dozen of the little caricature pieces, all in a cluster. He selected the pair that showed a furious Doberman standing on its hind legs and wearing a very becoming dress with a suggestion of an elaborate necklace. Dobermans are slender dogs with delicate bones, and perhaps that was what made Robbie select that breed to represent his wife, who was, if Ian remembered correctly, fine-boned. The teeth in the pieces were not delicate, however, and the eyes were evil slashes. He looked among the others but couldn't find either of the two Robbie had done of him.

He went around the room again, looking at the practice pieces that took up two-thirds of a shelf. Some of them were definitely salable.

Maybe not the wolf's head with the lips pulled back but somehow not looking very fierce, but the lion's head in a ferocious snarl was great, and the raccoon head looking wise and amused, and maybe the empty turtle shell that was only half done, seeming to emerge in some natural process from the wood.

The last third of the shelf was taken up by the little caricatures. The nearly finished caricature of a plumber as a sleepy possum in overalls, with its tail around a plumber's helper, was cute and would certainly sell. And too bad there were only two of the attorney with the briefcase and the face of a weasel; Robbie had said he usually sold three or four of those a day.

In a cardboard box on the floor were a half-dozen finished and half-finished caricatures, all of them snapped in half — Robbie broke the ones he wasn't satisfied with. These weren't salable; Ian picked out two and put them in his pocket to keep for himself.

He searched the room thoroughly, opening the file cabinet drawers and even peeling the flexible cap off a five-gallon steel drum behind the work bench. He found it about half full of pale gray clay, the kind that hardens only when baked. On top he could recognize a fox's head, a powerfully muscled lion's shoulder, leg and broad paw set into the hindquarters of the fleeing antelope — apparently Robbie had meant at first for the lion to get his dinner. The rest all seemed to have blended down into unidentifiable hunks.

He was handling the fox's mask when Skye came back, face clean and spikes combed out of her hair — they had gotten bent when he held her during her weeping.

"If you tell me I look about twelve years old, I'll never speak to you again," she said. So he didn't.

"This can't be everything of your father's," he said.

"Sure it is." She looked around. "He's been selling quite a few, and I'm pretty sure this is all that he had left last time I saw him. No, wait, the snapping turtle is gone. He must've sold it on Saturday." She looked along the shelves quickly. "Oh, and he sold the cringing wolf, too. I never thought anyone would buy that, I mean, it had its tail between its legs and its head kind of twisted sideways and its tongue stuck out, like the wolf at the bottom of the pack does to the alpha wolf, ick. I told him people want their wolves howling or biting, but he liked it, and I guess someone else did, too."

"Is that all that's gone? How about the little caricatures?"

She went to look at them. "The German shepherd soldier is gone, and the turtle house painter, and the pig police officer — he sells

229

a lot of those, he can practically carve them with his eyes closed now — I mean . . ." She took a calming breath. "Why do you ask?"

"Well, he did a caricature of me as a peacock setting fire to my tail with a blowtorch," he said. "I found a broken practice piece, but not the finished one."

"That's because I have it." She was wearing those outsize jeans the kids liked, and her arm disappeared up to the elbow as she leaned sideways to reach into a pocket. It was a basswood carving not quite three inches tall. "It's so like you, Ian, proud and sometimes careless."

"I am *never* careless," he asserted, taking it from her. "I'm just not as much of a craftsman as some. I thought you only had two of your father's pieces."

She shrugged. "Okay, if you count these cartoon ones, I have three. Or four. Does it matter all that much?"

"When I am supposed to convince your mother there is enough of your father's *oeuvres* to hold a proper show and/or auction, then every piece counts."

"Well, you can have the peacock if you insist. And we forgot to bring in the two big ones. Want me to go get them?"

"I'll do it."

He went back out to his Miata in the parking lot. It was far and away the best-looking car there. Poor Robbie had really come down in the world. Ian remembered the big house and the SUV and Lincoln Town Car — Robbie had been driving a second-hand Kia, which wasn't here, he noted; and even it was nicer than most of the other cars around this apartment building.

He sighed, opened his trunk, and got out the two wood carvings. One was of two stallions fighting, a fiery and exciting piece, if a bit clichéd. The other was of a little hairy dog leaping in the air with a ball growing out of one side of his face. The dog, he knew, was "Spanky," who had been a much-loved tyrant in the McFey household back when the children were in grade school. Spanky had been one of Robbie's first efforts to put his figures into action poses. The anatomy was peculiar and the ball a mistake, but even in that early piece the vigor was remarkable, and according to Skye, Spanky used to snap sideways at the ball just as depicted. Ian had every intention of buying the Spanky carving and giving it to Skye. It meant too much to her to let it go into strangers' hands.

He went back into the building and down the echoing hall to Robbie's apartment.

"Now, do I have everything?"

"Well," she said grudgingly and went again into her pocket. There was plenty of room in there; Ian half expected her to bring out a life-size crow. But the fourth piece was another caricature, of a boy as a gawky giraffe in jeans and sweatshirt, with big, gentle eyes and a thick book labeled math. "He's not as pencil-necked as he was when Pop did this, and he's toughened up, too."

"Who is it supposed to be?"

"Coy," she said, surprised he didn't recognize him.

"I was Robbie's friend and yours, not your family's," he reminded her. "I don't think I've talked with Coyne more than twice."

"Oh, yeah. And this was done when Coy was twelve."

"Now I want you to look at every piece here and tell me what else is missing."

But she didn't think anything else was. They searched the rest of the apartment, which was relatively clean and furnished in Motel Six style. Ian could not have lived in this place for more than two days; he could have welded a couch with more style than what slumped against that wall. There were no other carvings, though on the wall over the graceless couch were three neatly framed pencil sketches, one of Robbie, one of France Avenue in Edina during their annual art fair, and one of the wood carving of Spanky. All were very competent, any flaws overcome by the passion of the artist for the subjects. Ian spent a few minutes looking at them — each was signed *Skye,* the letters twisted to form a little cloud.

"What are we looking for?" Skye complained impatiently, coming back from the bathroom. "I mean, is it one of those cartoon pieces or something bigger?"

"I don't know," Ian said. "Maybe we do have it all. I just want to make sure."

"I don't see how we could've missed anything. Is there enough to do a show with?"

He hesitated, then decided on candor. "There would be, if all the pieces were as extraordinary as the lion. But one marvelous piece doesn't make a show. I think we should see if a Minnesota gallery would handle them for us, or if they could join an auction of outdoor art. We could place a couple of ads and, if we're lucky, might easily realize twenty or twenty-five thousand dollars, perhaps more."

Her eyes shone. "That's pretty good, isn't it? You're being so good, helping me with this. Do you really think we can get twenty-five thousand dollars? Wouldn't that be great? Pop would be so proud!"

"That much?" said Pam McFey thoughtfully. "Really, I had no idea. He's been selling things at those silly street fairs, where things aren't generally that expensive. No wonder he wasn't making a decent living, if he was asking those kind of prices at a street fair."

"As you possibly know," said Ian, throwing

a repressive glance at Skye, who immediately put both hands over her mouth to show she would keep still, "he wasn't asking those kind of prices. We can, because he's gone and won't be doing any more work. And because some of his work is much better then he knew. I tried to tell him, and I've been working to arrange a show for him at my gallery. He was in the process of selecting some of his work to send them to look at. I have no doubt they would have accepted him, and worked with him to get the recognition he richly deserved. Who knows how far it might have gone? That's why this whole thing is a tragedy."

"I had no idea," Pam repeated. Her hand went to her throat, where the slim fingers gently touched a necklace of carved amber beads that looked too heavy for her slender neck.

"And although Marvin Gardens would not be interested in representing so few pieces from a deceased artist, I hope you will allow me to look into getting them into an art auction, or perhaps another gallery willing to take on such a sadly limited number of pieces."

"You think you can do that?"

"I'm sure I can make some kind of arrangement that will get you much more money than an estate sale would bring."

"What about the other things in his apartment? Clothes and furniture?"

"I'm no expert on that sort of thing, but I don't think there's anything else valuable in there. There might be a market for his newer tools, if we can attract the attention of other wood carvers. Certainly they would want the band saw, and probably the unused wood."

"Should they be included in an auction, then?"

"It depends on the kind of auction. Will you let me see what I can find out?"

"Thank you." Pam smiled just a little bit, and thawed enough to say, "You really are being very kind."

"Not at all." And as a reward for those words of praise, Ian gave her the two little Doberman caricatures. "I don't think we need to let anyone see these," he said.

"Yes," she said, and her fist closed so quickly over them he knew she had seen them before. The look she gave him was startlingly fierce, and it was only in retrospect that he realized she was angry because he had seen them.

Chapter 14

Sunday morning, Betsy went to the ten-thirty service at Trinity. She usually went to the first service at eight, having gotten back into her old habit of rising early, but was hoping to meet someone at the second.

It wasn't Father John Rettger, who was celebrant at both services. Short and white-haired, Father John was his usual careful self this morning — if he wasn't careful, he tended to wander unannounced into a non-standard communion service or start forgiving the congregation their sins before they admitted they had done things they ought not to have done and not done things they had ought. His sermon was lucid and learned, the congregation attentive — well, an ear-pulling contest broke out among three preteen boys, but their mother quelled it with a look and a couple of gestures. The hymns selected were comfortable; the small choir leading them was excellent. Besides the music — the first service was conducted in a sad silence — the other major difference at the second service was that the Lord's Prayer was the modern-language version, which

Betsy didn't realize but went along reciting the traditional one and wondering vaguely why she couldn't stay in chorus. The whole thing was over in about eighty minutes.

The reason Betsy didn't realize she was reciting the wrong prayer was the same reason she could not have told anyone anything about the music or the sermon one minute after the Dismissal. Because she, from her place near the back, had seen Jill sitting close to the front and fixed her attention on her, trying to find a way of drawing her attention without waving or making a noise. Lars wasn't with her; if he wasn't on duty, he was over at Saint Elwin's Lutheran.

Jill paused to talk to someone in the aisle before coming out, so Betsy went out into the big hall that the church backed into, turned, and waited. When she saw Jill, she raised her hand tentatively. But Jill saw her and changed directions to come to her.

"Have brunch with me?" asked Betsy.

"All right," said Jill.

"I'm buying, so you choose where."

"Waterfront Café," said Jill promptly. "And we're going dutch." They walked down the hill to Water Street and turned toward the lake. It was already a blazing-hot day, with only the faintest hint of a cooling breeze coming off the water.

There had been a rumor that the Waterfront Café was being sold to an Asian couple who wanted to turn it into a sushi bar. True or not, the town broke into laughter at the idea, so the owner, who really had wanted to retire, went back to frying eggs and making a very mild hamburger stew he called "chili."

"Two eggs over easy, bacon, whole wheat toast, coffee, large orange juice," ordered Jill, who had the metabolism of a weight lifter.

"English muffin, small grapefruit juice, tea," ordered Betsy, who didn't. But her ears perked up at the request for bacon; the Waterfront Café's serving of bacon was three strips, and Betsy thought perhaps she could acquire one.

When their orders came, Jill said, "So what's up?"

"What do you mean, what's up? You're getting married this week! Aren't you excited? Or nervous?"

"Not really," said Jill, cutting into her eggs with a fork.

"Well, you're the only woman on earth who wouldn't be. Or is there some kind of problem? Jill, are you sure this is what you want to do? I mean, if this is about the no-fraternization rule, couldn't you just get engaged? Wouldn't that solve the problem?"

"Yes, it would. But I'm worried they might change the rules again on us. I'm very sure about Lars being the right one for me. We've talked about getting married before; I was the one putting it off because I couldn't work patrol if I was pregnant. Now I'm a desk jockey, so that's all right. Besides, this Thursday thing isn't like really getting married. It won't be the real thing until we get Father John to bless us in church."

Betsy stared at her. "You don't mean this is some kind of fake marriage!"

"No, of course not. So far as the state of Minnesota is concerned, we'll be married. But I won't *feel* married until I walk down the aisle at Trinity."

Betsy didn't want to offend Jill by blurting out what she was thinking, so she busied herself with her muffin for a few moments until she could figure out how to edge her way into the topic. "Does Lars know about this?"

"Yes."

"What does he think about it?"

"Not much. Nor do I, when it comes to that. But at least we can date again."

Betsy still wanted to jump up and shout, "You can't do this to Lars!" Instead she grabbed her mug and took a mouthful of tea. It was far too hot; she hastily grabbed her water glass to suck up a piece of ice. It cooled her temper as well as her tongue. Around the ice she said, "He's a stronger man than I am, Gunga Din."

Jill laughed.

Betsy said, "When the blessing part happens, um, may I still be your maid of honor?"

Jill nodded. "Yes, of course." She ate more egg.

Betsy said, "May I?" and reached across the little table with her fork to lift up a slice of crisp bacon. "So meanwhile, as your almost-maid-of-honor, or is a divorcee a matron of honor? It doesn't matter, whichever, what do you want me to do?"

"Come to the Elks Club overlooking beautiful Lake Minnetonka at two p.m. on Thursday."

"Nothing else? No shower? No organizing the bridesmaids?"

"No. No shower, and you're the only attendant I want."

Betsy took a small bite of the bacon, savoring its rich, salty flavor. "All right. What shall I wear?"

Jill considered this while she put a dab of preserves on her toast. "Something kind of dressy. I'm wearing a new pastel silk suit."

"What color? So I don't clash."

"It's kind of an ice blue. Well, an ice blue-green, if you can imagine that."

Amazingly, Betsy could. "I saw a suit that color at Cynthia Rae's." Which was a specialty store right up Water Street.

Jill nodded. "That's where I got it."

"But you don't take extra-large dresses!"

"Sometimes I do. I'm tall and my shoulders are broad, so I'm hard to fit. I saw that suit in the window and I went in, and the smallest size she carries fit me just right." Jill smiled. "Sometimes it's fun to buy from the other end of the rack."

"Okay, I'll go look again at that suit in her window and find something that complements it."

"You don't have to buy something special."

"But I want to! This is a special occasion! I want it to look as if we put some thought into it! What else are you wearing?"

"Okay, then, I found a little white hat with a stiff little veil, and I'm wearing white shoes."

"White accessories, right. Except I don't think I'll wear a hat, unless you think I should."

Jill shrugged. "Suit yourself."

Betsy shook her head at Jill, who looked back calmly. Jill had a trick of absorbing anything thrust at her — whether anger, distrust, amusement, or as now, bafflement — and giving nothing back, disarming the emotion. But Betsy knew about the trick and held on to her feelings.

She said, "It's the police chief, isn't it? You're mad at him."

"No, he's not the one who wanted the policy set. In fact, he laughed when I told him what I wanted to do. He thinks it's a great joke on the people who like to set hard-and-fast rules."

"But I thought cops liked hard-and-fast rules."

"Have you ever talked your way out of a speeding ticket?"

"Sure, a couple of times, why? Oh. Yes, I see. But you really are going to marry Lars in church pretty soon? It would be too cruel to make him wait, you know. He's been very patient with you."

"I know." This was said quietly, but there was weight behind it. "It will definitely happen, and before too long. But this was too good a chance to pass up, so I had to take it. Lars understands, really he does." She ate more egg and asked, "How are things going with the McFey murder?"

"I'm stuck," said Betsy, glad Jill had brought it up, so she didn't have to. "Is there some way you can help me? Within the guidelines of the department, I mean."

Jill smiled. "Probably. You still think Mickey Sinclair didn't do it?"

"No. Well, maybe not. I thought I had a really good alternate suspect, but the motive I thought he had isn't there anymore."

"Who was your suspect?" Jill picked up a slice of bacon with her fingers and ate it in three bites.

"Ian Masterson. He's an artist who was helping McFey raise his standing by getting him into a gallery in Santa Fe. He also gave McFey sixty-five thousand dollars in return for being made beneficiary of McFey's hundred-thousand-dollar insurance policy. McFey was supposed to be dying, did you know that?"

Jill nodded. "Yes, but he was disappointing people by not getting on with it. I don't understand about this motive Ian Masterson did or did not have. Was it not true about buying the policy?"

"It's true. It's called a viatical, buying the right to be made a beneficiary. But it turns out Ian Masterson is so rich that it didn't hurt him in the least to have to wait for his money." Betsy tried another sip of her tea, blowing first across the surface. "But who else was McFey disappointing by not dying? You said, 'people,' right?"

"Yes, I did. His wife and son were upset at McFey for quitting a career that was generating lots of money. He wasn't earning nearly as much at art fairs. They didn't mind at first, when they thought he had only a year or two to live. He had a second life insurance policy, worth a million and a half dollars."

"I see," said Betsy.

Jill nodded. "But then it turned out his hepatitis C wasn't going to kill him, so the policy wasn't going to be cashed in for a long while."

"Were they all right with that? I mean, were they happy to have him around longer than they thought — or were they disappointed at having to lower their standard of living?"

"Pam McFey was right at home in that big house with all the trappings of wealth, and dropping the name of Northwestern University among her friends, where her son Coyne is a junior. But now the big house is for sale, and Coyne is looking for a job to pay his college tuition. And neither of them has an alibi worth anything. The daughter of the house does have a solid alibi." She told the story of the two interviews with the McFey family. "Mike said at first it would be stupid to rely on a tardy realtor for an alibi, but when he talked to the realtor, she said that Pam told her not to come before noon."

Betsy pursed her lips and thought before she spoke. "Is there any way I can learn about this except by talking to you?"

"Well, you could talk to Mike Malloy, but I don't think he'll tell you anything." Her mouth twitched. "I appreciate your concern for my loose lips, by the way." She took a drink of her coffee, which she'd doctored with sugar and half-and-half.

"How about Morrie?" asked Betsy. "Maybe he could talk to Mike or someone else in the department."

"Maybe, but he's a civilian now. It's different once you retire."

"Really? Well, I suppose it would be. Do you think the McFey family would talk to me?"

"I don't know. The girl might. Her name is

Skye, and she's fifteen."

"Jill, having been burnt badly because you talked to me about this case before, why are you still willing to talk to me now?"

"The problem wasn't my talking to you, it was you repeating some of it as gossip to people who had no business knowing about it. I don't think you'll make that mistake again."

Betsy smiled. "I certainly won't."

"On the other hand, you have a talent for solving this kind of crime; that's why I want to keep you advised of what we find out on the official end. I trust you will continue to let us in on anything interesting you find out, and not do something silly like agreeing to meet a suspect in some lonely place."

"No fear of that." Betsy did not want her own corpse to be the focus of a murder investigation. Godwin could jolly well wait for his chance to run Crewel World, Inc.

She asked, "Who do you think killed Rob McFey?"

Jill shrugged. "Mike is sure it's Mickey Sinclair, Mickey left his fingerprints on McFey's cash box and a footprint at the scene. You've got an uphill battle on your hands, that's for sure."

"So why are you helping me try to prove he's innocent?"

"Because you have a good batting record in that sort of thing. And because when a cop helps send a man to prison and finds out ten years into the sentence that the man didn't do it, it can do terrible things to his peace of mind."

"It would upset Mike?" asked Betsy.

"It would upset me," replied Jill.

Godwin came into Crewel World on Monday morning in a new lavender silk shirt and tie, which looked stunning with his purple linen trousers and white sport coat. He carried a soft white leather briefcase and, catching Betsy's amazed, admiring, amused look, paused to lift one trouser leg to show off the purple and white saddle shoe. His socks, of course, were white cotton, knit with his own hands; the dye in colored socks irritated his feet.

"You look wonderful!" she exclaimed.

"You are too gorgeous!" agreed Shelly. "Where on earth did you find that briefcase?"

Godwin laughed. "Would you believe it once belonged to John? He says an old boyfriend bought it for him back when he first got his degree. He wouldn't dream of carrying it, of course."

"Why not? I think it's cool. What's in it?"

Godwin said loftily, "The same thing that most executives carry in their briefcases: a copy of the *Wall Street Journal* and my lunch. Oh, and this." He handed Shelly a single sheet of legal-size paper, then went to hang up the jacket and tuck the briefcase away in the back room.

He came back to find Shelly reading Volume One, Number One of *Hasta la Stitches.*

She waved the paper at him. "What is this? What does it mean?"

Betsy said, "It's a Crewel World newsletter Goddy is going to put out."

Godwin said, "My Spanish isn't very good, but *hasta la vista* means until I see you again. So I figure *Hasta la Stitches* should mean something like until I stitch again. So the name means, this will keep you occupied between stitching."

Shelly was reading swiftly down the double columns of type. "Oh, wow, too cool!" She turned it over. "Oh, look, here's a counted pattern! It's an ear of corn . . ." She turned, frowning at Godwin. "Why an ear of corn?"

"To put on your barbecue apron, of course. I'm thinking people will have time to finish it before the first sweet corn arrives." He said to Betsy, "We ordered too much waste canvas last time, and to put this onto an apron they'll need a piece around six inches by four inches. Bigger if they want to put some cute slogan with it, like KISS THE COOK, or REAL MEN COOK."

Waste canvas is a heavily starched even-weave meant to be basted onto a sweatshirt or jeans or any other ordinary fabric. Then a counted cross-stitch pattern is done on the clothing with the waste threads as a guide. When washed, waste canvas threads became thin and can be pulled from under the stitches.

Betsy nodded approval. "That's the way, Goddy."

He continued, "Maybe we should make it HEART THE COOK, or I HEART TO GRILL, and suggest that instead of a stitched heart they should use a button or charm. I know we have a lot of heart buttons."

"Cle-*ver!*" Shelly said, adding, "Hey, the pattern colors are given only in Anchor."

"I know," said Godwin. "I wrote down the DMC equivalents in case anyone asks, but I didn't put them in the newsletter." DMC floss was sold in discount stores at prices Crewel World could not afford to match; Anchor flosses were sold only in independent needlework shops. Godwin was anxious to get as much of a return for Crewel World as possible.

Shelly said, "These aren't hard to translate anyway: I know that Anchor 226, 227, and 228 are greens that match DMC 700, 701 and 702. I assume the other numbers are yellows."

"Show-off!"

"Here, let me see it," said Betsy, and Shelly handed over the newsletter. "I like the pattern," Betsy said. She turned the sheet over and sat down to read it.

There had been an article in last December's "Nuts About Needlework," an online newsletter for needlepointers. It had some great tips for correcting mistakes in color on needlepoint canvases that didn't call for the stitcher to frog whole sections. Betsy had read it there, having had that very problem not long before — and here it was again. "Godwin, did you get permission to reprint this?"

"Yes, of course," he said. "In fact, when I e-mailed them about it, they told me I could take all the helpful hints I wanted from their newsletters, so long as I gave credit."

Betsy had already seen that he credited the original author of the article, Janet Perry. She looked down at the bottom of the article, and sure enough, he'd put a note: *Want more of this kind of stuff?* Contact Nuts-About-Needlepoint-subscribe@yahoogroups.com *to subscribe*.

"Well, that's all right, then." She held out the newsletter at arm's length. "You know this layout is pretty nifty; I like the two columns."

"Thanks," said Godwin with a lofty air. "Photocopy ready and everything."

"But you put only one T in 'newsletter.' And you spelled 'foreground' without an E. And 'aspects' is not spelled with a Z."

"Those are typos," said Godwin. "Mostly. Does 'foreground' really have an E in it?"

Shelly said, "I'll proofread for you, Goddy, if you like."

Betsy looked at her. "He wants to bring one out every other month. Are you going to have time when school is in session to proofread this?"

"Two sides of a single sheet of paper? Piece of cake."

"Two sides of a legal-size sheet of paper."

"Piece of cake," insisted Shelly.

Betsy handed the sheet to her. "Be sure your name goes on under Goddy's, so they'll know who to blame if you don't fix every mistake. I'll put our mailing list on a disk for you, Goddy, so you can run a set of labels."

"I'll pick it up when I come to Char's Hardanger class tonight," said Godwin. "Could you also put the schedule of classes on the disk? There's a space I left in the newsletter for that."

Shelly said, "I thought that was for the address of the customer."

"But envelopes are classier," said Godwin.

"And more expensive than the dabs of tape it takes to close the folds tight before mailing them."

"Oh." He looked at Betsy, who nodded. "All right. I'll see if I can rearrange things to put the schedule in and still leave room for mailing addresses." He looked over his copy-ready efforts like an author who had just been told his favorite scene in a manuscript has to come out.

Chapter 15

Monday evening, another Hardanger class. Betsy had managed to finish the first pattern, but the new pattern Char Norton handed around was bigger and more complex. Betsy took it with such an unhappy sigh that Char said, "Betsy, I don't think you're having a good time in this class."

Betsy replied candidly, "I'm not. I guess there are areas of needlework that are still beyond my little skills."

Godwin said stoutly, "What 'little skills'? Your needlepoint is as good as almost anyone's, and you're an excellent knitter — you've learned some stitches it took me *years* to master."

"Yes, but I *like* knitting. It's . . . soothing. My mind seems to open to big thoughts when I'm into the rhythm of knitting."

There was a murmur of understanding around the table.

"But you don't like Hardanger," said Char.

"It's not that I don't like it," said Betsy slowly, feeling her way. "It's that . . . Well, all right, I don't like it. There's no wiggle room in Hardanger; you have to do it exactly right or it doesn't work."

Ivy said, a little surprised, "But that's why I like it. Every single stitch is important. It's, like, perfection. I can make this one thing absolutely perfect. When I snip and pull and it comes right out like it should, it's a good feeling."

Again a murmur of agreement.

Char said, "That's why I like it, too. Life is so messy, but here is one thing where I'm in control and I can do it exactly right." She smiled at Betsy. "It's all right. Needlework is a huge arena, and people have always played 'pick and choose.' Bobbin lace is another area where you have to be really careful, but I don't like bobbin lace."

"You can make a mistake and keep going in bobbin lace," reflected Bershada. "Of course, when you look at it later, it sticks out like a sore thumb."

"I don't like to crochet," confessed Shelly. "I don't know why, I just don't."

This set off a round-table discussion of needle lace, counted cross-stitch, bargello, cutwork, stumpwork, schwalm, crochet, crewel, knitting, needlepoint, and other forms of stitchery one or more of the students didn't get or even couldn't stand. Doris had the fewest, but that was because she had come to needlework late in life and hadn't tried as many as the others.

"Remember macramé?" asked Ivy.

"Remember it?" said Bershada with a sigh. "I still have an owl in my attic made of macramé!"

"Gosh, I did that owl, too," said Ivy. "I made him of white cotton twine, with brown beads for the eyes and a twig for his feet to hang on to."

"Twig? Twig?" said Bershada, laughing now. "I made mine of half-inch rope and he's got a big ol' *limb* off a tree in his claws!"

"I did that owl," said Margie. "Made him of string. I was in third grade and it was a Christmas present for my mother. She hung it in a tree in the backyard. Said it was to keep starlings away, but I think she was hoping it would rot faster in the outdoors."

Everyone laughed, and Char said, "So okay, macramé was one thing we all liked."

"Not me," said Godwin. "I was still just a twinkle in my daddy's eye when you all were doing macramé."

"Hush, baby, Char's making a point," said Bershada.

"The point is," said Char, "we don't want to run Betsy out of the class, but on the other hand we don't want to make her miserable. What do you want to do, Betsy? Is there something else I can teach you?"

"Do you know how to do other kinds of cutwork?"

"Other kinds than what?"

"Than Hardanger."

"Hardanger isn't cutwork."

"Sure it is. Isn't it? I mean, you surround areas of fabric with stitching and you cut out the areas. That's cutwork, right?"

Char gestured. "No, Hardanger is drawn-thread work. Drawn thread is about symmetry. Hardanger has to be symmetrical, every kloster has to line up, or you can't pull the threads. Cutwork is about . . ." She thought for a moment. "Curves. Outlines. And though you wouldn't think it, cutwork is the ancestor of lace."

Bershada said, "It is? I thought Hardanger was!"

Char shook her head. "Hardanger is its own self, not ancestor or descendant. It was invented in Norway."

Shelly asked, "Well, where did cutwork come from?"

"Cutwork was invented in Italy, though its ancestors were forms of embroidery that came from the Orient by way of ancient Greece or Egypt. It was done on linen with linen threads, back before they had dyes that really took, so both cloth and floss were the natural tans of linen. That's why purists like me still prefer it done color on color." Char counted on her fingers. "First there was cutwork; and then Richelieu, where they cut so much away they had to invent stabilizing bars across the open areas so the pattern would hold its shape; then *punto tagliato,*

255

where they filled some of the open areas with patterns made of thread; and then *punto in aria,* 'stitching in the air,' when they realized they didn't need to stitch on the fabric at all, but just used it to hold down the corners of a pattern they made entirely in thread."

"Are we here to stitch or take a class in history?" interrupted Bershada.

"Sorry," said Char, turning pink. "I forget that for you all this is a hobby. For me it's my life."

"Trust me, it's our lives, too," said Godwin. "When I think of all the other places I could be . . ."

"But you'd far, far rather be here," said Bershada. "Me, too."

Betsy said, "Char, you know how to do cutwork, right?"

"Yes. In fact, I brought a pattern to show." She produced a square of white cloth on which was printed the outlines of a squared wreath of flowers. "This is the top of a pillow, like for a ring bearer. You trace these petal and leaf shapes by stitching around the edges. Then you cut it out of the cloth and appliqué it to the silk cloth of your pillow." She was holding the cutwork pattern out, and Betsy took it. Char continued, "Cutwork can be symmetrical or not. It doesn't matter, so long as the areas you want to cut out are surrounded by solid lines of buttonhole stitching. That is a relatively easy pattern —

some are more complex."

"I think it's attractive," said Betsy, tracing the lines with her forefinger. The flowers and leaves outlined an empty square. "I can see this cut out and appliquéd around the neck of a black dress, can't you? Lay it over the shoulders and across the back and front." She picked it up and held it out, head cocked, eyes half closed as she visualized it on a dress upstairs in her closet. She turned the fabric around so the others could see the pattern.

"Ooooh, yes," said Bershada, "that *would* be pretty."

"Which did you like in high school?" asked Shelly. "Algebra or geometry?"

"Why?" asked Betsy, surprised at this sudden change of subject.

"Because almost everyone liked one but not the other. I liked algebra."

"Me, too," said Char, and Margie nodded, also looking puzzled.

"No." Betsy shook her head. "I liked geometry."

"And I bet that's why you like cutwork rather than Hardanger. Your head can get around that kind of pattern better than this." She held out the new Hardanger pattern in its hoops.

"Have you tried cutwork, Shelly?" asked Betsy.

"No." Shelly shook her head. "I have three

pairs of my grandmother's cutwork pillow-cases, and that's all I need of cutwork. You can have too much of it, in my opinion."

Betsy smiled. Shelly had to rotate her finished counted cross-stitch projects to give them all a chance to be displayed on the walls of her house. Yet she was working on at least three at present, had two being finished by a framer, owned dozens of unworked patterns — and was always on the lookout for more.

Bershada said, "I tried it, but it was too much work. The buttonhole stitch isn't my favorite."

"But that's the stitch we're doing here!" said Betsy.

"No, the kloster stitch isn't the same as buttonhole; plus we change direction by ninety degrees every five stitches. Cutwork is following a line that curves forever — and I hate going around curves with that sad buttonhole stitch."

But Betsy remembered doing curves in a decorative buttonhole stitch back when all she did was embroidery, and how it was interesting to follow the curves. So while everyone else settled into making kloster blocks, Betsy took a sharp needle from the packet of them on the table and spent the rest of the session rediscovering the buttonhole stitch.

After the class broke up, Char again remained behind. "Any progress to report?" she asked. "I only ask because Faith called me. She said she wasn't sure what you were doing and she didn't want to bother you if you were busy and . . ." That trailed off.

"And she realized she and Greg didn't make a very good impression?" asked Betsy.

Char nodded, shamed. "The girls were angry and Faith was scared and Greg was being Greg."

Betsy said, "I almost walked away from this. Mickey is not exactly the shining ornament of his generation, and he's a liar besides, which makes him hard to work with. Or for. But I have been looking around, and there are some possibilities. I think it's possible, for example, that someone else murdered Rob McFey and Mickey simply came along after and took the money."

Char beamed. "So you are looking into it!"

"Yes. There are some people who are not unhappy that Rob is dead."

"Who?" Char asked at once.

"I don't want to name anyone, because I have no proof." But she was thinking of Ian.

"I hope you keep looking until you find the proof. Oh, Betsy, if you could just bring that boy home! The scare he's been given will straighten him out for certain!"

Betsy wasn't at all sure of that, but she just nodded and sent Char away happy.

After the class Betsy went upstairs and

changed into her pajamas. She had thought to make an early evening of it, but remembered she had some shop business to take care of. She pulled on a robe and went into the other bedroom to open her business accounts program on her computer. She hadn't realized there was so much paperwork to do — but she'd been neglecting it to sleuth. She entered the latest time-card hours, then told the program about Godwin's new wages. She was only halfway through entering a stack of sales records when the doorbell rang.

She had invested in an intercom system for her upstairs tenants, one of whom was herself, so she went to the little hallway that led to her front door and pressed a button.

"Who is it?" she asked.

"Ian Masterson," came the prompt reply.

"Me, too — Shelly," said another voice.

Frowning, Betsy pressed the release button, which made a loud buzz she could hear from all the way downstairs. She opened the door to her apartment and watched as their heads appeared in the stairwell. Shelly was looking important and excited, Ian sober and uncertain.

They came up into the big hallway that was divided by the staircase and turned toward Betsy's door. Shelly was in a flowing, flower-print, sleeveless dress with a deep scoop neckline — the breasts on display made Betsy realize, with a little shock, that

Shelly probably had a sex life. Ian wore another pair of too-short trousers and a bright blue Hawaiian shirt.

"Come in," said Betsy, stepping back and holding the door open. "Excuse the way I look." The robe she wore was a big, long flannel number with broad vertical stripes of gray and maroon, the very opposite of Shelly's outfit.

"You look very 'at home,'" said Ian kindly.

The hallway was short but narrow. A doorway on the left led into the galley kitchen; visible beyond it was the dining nook with its round table and prettily curtained window. Betsy noticed Ian's nosy interest and was glad the table was cleared and its bouquet of silk flowers in place.

The living room was low-ceilinged, which gave it a snug feel. The curtains on the double front window were chintz. One of their reds was the same shade as the dark red carpet. Betsy had replaced her sister's original love seat with a couch upholstered in light gray, but had kept the very comfortable upholstered chair and footstool. A magnifying light on a wheeled pedestal was beside the chair and on the other side was a large fabric bag in a wooden frame that held Betsy's latest counted cross-stitch work.

Ian stood a moment or two, just looking around with his artist's eye, nodding at the lighted cabinet with its books, Bose audio

261

system, and the Lladro figurines Betsy's sister had collected. "This feels like my aunt's condo in Ohio, even though hers looks nothing like this."

Shelly giggled and said, "How can it feel the same if it doesn't look the same?"

"They're both — cozy," said Ian. "You just know a pampered cat lives here, the bathroom smells of perfumed soap, and there's a cookie jar in the kitchen."

Betsy said, "Your aunt and I have been living parallel lives, I guess."

"Oh, you and her and lots of people. Nice people. Backbone of our culture. It's people like you who give bohemians like me the security to live as we like. If everyone lived the way I do, the country would collapse into chaos."

Shelly laughed. "He's right, Betsy. You should see his place, heaps of dust everywhere, nothing in the fridge but three cans of beer and a very old pizza." She looked at him admiringly. "But his art is wonderful."

"Here, sit down," said Betsy, remembering her manners. "May I get you something? Iced tea? Coffee?"

"No, we just had a late supper," said Shelly, and she smiled at something. Lovers can be tedious, but Shelly didn't go with the moment, no rapturous sighs or blowing of kisses.

Ian took a seat on the couch, still looking

around, amused and sharp-eyed. He patted the back of the couch and Shelly sat down next to him, smiling at Betsy.

"What brings you here?" asked Betsy, who had work to do before her evening was over.

Shelly was instantly serious. "Ian told me something that I think you should know." Ian made a gesture as if to disagree, but she waved it off, saying to him, "Now, we agreed. I told you how Betsy does this thing where she finds out someone who everyone thinks committed a crime, didn't; and she does it by finding out who did. She thinks Mickey Sinclair didn't kill Robert McFey, and you know something that may help her investigate."

Ian looked at her for a long moment, then at Betsy. "All right, I did hear something." He drew a sigh. "Do you know the McFey family?"

"Not really," said Betsy, sitting down in the comfortable chair, prepared to listen.

"Well, there's Robbie's widow, her name is Pam. And there are two children; the older is in college, his name is Coyne, and the younger is a girl, Skye. Skye was very close to her father, and he left her all his unsold artwork in his will. She wanted me to help her arrange a sale, so we went over to Robbie's apartment this past Sunday. She was upset because the police came twice to talk to her family and seem to think that if the teenager they've arrested proves to be innocent, then Pam or Coyne make excellent replacement suspects."

"Not Skye?"

"No, she was swimming with friends when it happened. Anyway she was very close to her father, she wouldn't have harmed him. But she's very upset that the police are looking at her mother and brother. She told me that if the police need another suspect, they should be looking at Banner Wilcox, who was Robbie's partner in his advertising business."

"Why does she say that?" asked Betsy.

"Because Banner took a real bath in the breakup of the business. And he was, according to Skye, pretty damned mad about it. He used to phone Robbie at home and shout threats and obscenities to the point where Pam took out an order of protection. According to Skye, Pam said Banner was having a nervous breakdown. Once Coyne picked up the phone when it rang, and Banner thought it was Robbie and ranted at him. Coyne told Skye about it. Said he threatened Robbie's life."

"Was Banner serious about the threat?"

"I don't know — this is third-hand, after all. And I've never met Banner Wilcox. But Skye said that when Robbie moved out, he told everyone not to give his new address or phone number to Banner."

Betsy thought this over for a while. Then she asked, "How old is Skye?"

Ian said, "Fifteen."

"Is she the sort to exaggerate?"

"I don't think so. I do know she's an artist in her own right, with an artist's honest soul — you know, tell the truth and damn the consequences."

"What do you know about Banner Wilcox?"

"Only what she told me. Robbie never mentioned him that I can remember. Skye's known him for years, and thought he was a gentle person. 'Wuss' is the term she used, actually." Ian smiled and shook his head at the term.

"So what do you make of all this?"

The grin vanished. "Well, it occurs to me that if I was a successful businessman and had it all taken away from me, I'd be damn angry. Banner lost his career, his executive job, his retirement account . . . Oh, yes, that's another detail: Skye said Banner was persuaded to invest in the company that bought Information Please, and then that company went belly up. What she didn't say was that Banner might be right to blame Robbie for all this."

"Do you think Banner was right?"

Ian hesitated. "Robbie was a good friend," he hedged, after a few moments.

Betsy persisted. "Do you think it possible

he lied to Banner about the terms of the sale, or about the company he sold out to?"

"No," he said. Then he twisted his head sideways and pursed his lips. "Not deliberately," he amended. Shelly put a hand on his knee, and when he looked at her, she nodded encouragingly. He shrugged and said, "He didn't like advertising. He thought he was going to die doing a job he hated. He was drinking more than he should, which distorts judgment. I don't think he would lie to Banner on purpose, but he would probably make the deal look as good as he could so Banner would go along."

"That would explain why Banner invested in the new owner," noted Betsy.

"Yes, and why, when the company went out of business, he blamed Robbie."

"Is there a reason why none of the McFeys have told the police about this person?"

Ian looked uncomfortable. "I don't know that they haven't," he said.

"I do know they haven't," said Betsy.

"Maybe they didn't ask," suggested Shelly. "You know Mike, not the sharpest hook in the tacklebox."

Betsy nodded. Mike was sure he already had the murderer safe in custody down at Juvenile Detention. He'd gone to see the McFeys only because Jill persuaded him to.

"All the same," she said, "I'd prefer not to be the one bringing this to Mike." She looked at Ian. "I think you should advise the family to tell Sergeant Malloy about this."

After they left, Betsy went back to entering data into her computer. But she found herself impatient with all the numbers — numbers weren't like words; "lfoss" was obviously a typo for floss, while 743 was as good a number as 437. Except, of course, it wasn't. Accounting numbers had to be correct in a cruel and mindless sort of way, no inattention or creativity allowed. Like Hardanger. Worse, in fact; incorrect numbers could lead to bankruptcy or even trouble with the IRS. Was Ian in trouble with the IRS? Why was she thinking that? Her fingers came away from the keyboard. She didn't like Ian, did she?

She considered the man, his keen, amused eyes, his smug smile. No, not smug, something else. Lacking in sympathy? That was closer. Self-centered — that was it. He was like many artists, totally in thrall to his muse. Everything must get out of the way when Ian wanted to create. Like Rob McFey. Yes. When you thought about it, it was surprising those two were friends, because each was so focused on his art there was little time or room to consider the other's wants or needs.

Except Ian did consider the needs of other artists. He gave money, arranged for viaticals or mortgages in support of them. Had Rob McFey ever done anything like that? She felt a dash of anger at Rob, who had allowed his partner in business to be ruined, and ignored the needs of his family, too, all because he was desperately desirous of carving wood into shapes. Beautiful shapes, of course.

What was it about artists, who seemed so brimful of feeling, so in touch with their childlike hearts — and so ruthless in pursuit of their heart's desire?

Was that why she didn't like Ian? Because he went after Shelly ruthlessly, and it wasn't because he loved her but because she thrilled his muse? And would the resulting work of art be worth her broken heart? She had seen Rob's art. It was very beautiful. Was Ian's art beautiful? Or was he, despite Shelly's protests to the contrary, a *poseur?*

That was an even uglier thought. She determinedly pulled her attention away from it, and finished her bookkeeping.

But when she was done, she didn't shut down her computer, but sat thinking some more.

Rob's work was wonderful, almost lyrical. Ian, working in a much harsher medium, must hear a harder music. Or was it something decidedly unmusical? She logged on to the Internet, did a Google search for Ian Masterson, and was directed to his site. There wasn't much of a biography, just a mention of a degree in fine arts from the University of Minnesota and two adult children. There were a lot of pictures of his work. His early pieces were folk art, passionate but hardly talented, consisting of sheet iron hammered, bolted, and welded into hollow shapes. The effect was of aliens' discarded and rusty suits of armor. Then came the big beams or girders, some several stories high, Ian himself a small figure standing by one of them. Then, in another total change of pace, came his newest works, metal cut into clumsy strips or chunks and welded together into mere suggestions of human shapes. But here was a powerful step upward, onto a new plane. The first set of his works had been amusing, the second derivative. But here was *Art,* unmistakably. An angry child with a raised fist, its strips of descending metal plates suggesting rags; the head of a frightened man, all wide-open, screaming mouth; a sad woman whose huge tears were like a flow of lava. Amazing how a seemingly careless crooked twist to a mouth, the way the weight was distributed on the unequal legs, the awkward droop of hair on a forehead, all evoked a powerful emotional response in the viewer — and these were only photographs. What must they be like when seen in person? Betsy clicked out of the site and went to bed, awed and reflective.

Chapter 16

It was late Tuesday morning. Malloy was alone in the small, two-man office trying to put together a progress report on the McFey case. His partner was out talking to the Leipolds about a chronic shoplifting problem in their store, though how they could tell items had gone missing in the dense maze of secondhand books, wind socks, souvenir T-shirts, lamp shades, antique toys, fishermen's maps, and comic postcards, Mike couldn't imagine.

His phone rang twice, a sign of an internal call. "Malloy," he said on picking it up.

"Mike, Skye McFey is here to see you." It was Sergeant Cross.

"She say what she wants?"

"To talk to you."

Mike looked at the sprawl of papers on his desk: forensic reports, autopsy reports, interview and interrogation reports, a drawing, forensic sketches, and worst of all, photographs of the crime scene. He said, "Give me two minutes, then send her down."

"Right."

Malloy sorted the papers into three piles,

stacked them with the photographs on top, and put them in a file folder, which he slid into a desk drawer. He'd barely finished when there came a single rap on the open door and he looked up to see the teen in a long, slinky-but-raggedy black dress held together with safety pins. And black army boots. She'd been sent down the hall alone — the station was small, finding his office wasn't hard.

He studied her briefly. Her spiked hair was an angry red on the left side and a totally wrong shade of fuchsia on the right. There was a tiny silver ring in one nostril. Her expression behind the black eye shadow and brown lipstick was resolute. He remembered the preppy clothes on her brother and the pretty dress and elaborate jewelry her mother wore and decided here was rebellion in full bloom.

"Miss McFey?" he asked, rising.

"Yes," she said quietly, but not shyly.

"Come in," he said. "Take a seat." There was a green metal chair with a padded green seat beside his desk, which he indicated with a wave of his hand.

She marched bravely into the room, her lace-up boots thumping on the linoleum floor. It was nearly ninety degrees outside, with the humidity way up there; her feet must be soggy with sweat. Kids today were out of their minds, in Malloy's seldom-humble opinion.

271

She took the chair. "You're the one who talked to my mother and brother last week," she said.

"Yes. Your mother said I could talk to you if I wanted to, but only in her presence. Does she know you're here?"

"Like I told Sergeant Cross, she drove me to Excelsior, but she thinks I came to have lunch with my friend Madison and then go to a movie with her. I didn't tell Mommy that I want to talk to you. She's picking me up in three hours, that's enough time to do all that and talk to you, too. You aren't going to call her, are you? I don't want you to."

"Why not?"

"Because she doesn't want me talking to the police. But this isn't about her, or Coy, so it's all right, isn't it?"

"What do you want to talk to me about?"

"A man named Banner Wilcox. He was very angry with my father."

Right after Skye left, Sergeant Cross stuck her head into his office. She noted the resuming sprawl of paper, the drawing, sketches, and photos on his desk, and started to say something but wisely said instead, "Did Skye McFey have anything to say?"

"She says we should look at Banner Wilcox instead of her brother as a suspect."

"And Banner Wilcox is — ?"

"According to Skye, her father's old business partner. He took a bath when the business was sold and he was mad as hell at McFey. Skye says Wilcox called McFey almost daily to rant and make threats."

"And where was Mr. Wilcox when the murder went down?"

"At church, he says. But who cares?"

Jill blinked at him in surprise. "What do you mean?"

"I think someone sicced Skye on me about Banner."

"Her mother."

"Huh-uh, Pam McFey's far too cool a head."

"Her brother?"

Mike nodded, satisfied that Jill had seconded his own opinion. "Who lied to me about his trip to seek work at a car dealership? Coyne McFey. The boy's afraid I'll find out he lied and arrest him."

"You gonna go talk to him?"

"No need to. Take a look at this." He turned the drawing toward her.

She came to the desk to look. It was on soft twenty by twenty-four paper, done in black crayon. "It's from that lady at the art fair, the caricaturist," said Mike. "When it started to rain on Sunday, customers dried up." He paused to admire that oxymoron, then continued, "She was on the side of the field near the bandshell, so to keep her drawing hand warm, she did this."

The sketch was of people standing out of the rain in the bandshell. There were ten or twelve of them, and near the front was a sullen-faced young man. His expression made him stand out from the others even though they were a diverse bunch, from the soccer mom in front to the old hippie in back. And he also looked very much like Mickey Sinclair.

"Is this admissible as evidence?" asked Jill.

"I am going to ask the county attorney that. But also, get a load of this." He handed her two sheets of paper stapled together. "It's from BCA: The blood on the shoes we retrieved from the Dumpster is Robert McFey's, and the DNA inside the shoes makes them Mickey's." He smiled a very cool smile. "This is as close to open and shut as we can get without an eyewitness to the actual murder. A new ten-dollar bill in Mickey's bedroom had McFey's thumbprint on it, the cash box had Mickey's fingerprints on it, there is a footprint at the scene that came from a shoe we can absolutely tie to Mickey. I'd say the only person who could remain convinced he didn't do it is his mother."

"What about Betsy Devonshire? Last I heard, she's still trying to prove he didn't do it."

"Why should I care about Betsy Devonshire's opinion, when I have fingerprints, footprints, and blood evidence? I've got an iron-clad, rock-solid case, so there's no reason to try to build a second one."

It had been a busy morning, but things had slowed down, and Betsy was thinking about lunch. Godwin had the day off so Shelly was working. Shelly hummed as she bustled about, her eyes bright and her movements brisk. She had hinted a time or two that she wanted to gush about Ian, but Betsy had headed that off. Between one thing and another, she hadn't seen Morrie for four days and was in no mood to hear how fulfilled and happy Shelly was.

But with no customers present, all the stock in order, empty spaces on spinner racks refilled, orders for new stock placed, every flat surface dusted, and a different, more-pleasant radio station found, Betsy couldn't think of anything else for Shelly to do.

She was about to allow her to gush away when the door went *Bing!* and Betsy looked up to see a teenager in a black evening dress and Kool-Aid hair come in. Betsy had never seen her before, even walking around town. There was a city bus that ran from Minneapolis out here; perhaps she had come out on that.

"May I help you?" asked Betsy.

"Is one of you named Betsy?" asked the girl.

"I am."

"I'm Skye McFey and a police officer named Jill Cross told me to come and talk to you."

A few minutes later Shelly was headed next door to Sol's Deli for lunch with instructions to bring back a chef salad, hold the cheese, and poppy seed dressing on the side.

"Now," said Betsy, after seating Skye at the little round table in the back area of the shop, "why did Jill ask you to come and talk with me?"

"Because of Banner Wilcox, who used to be my father's partner in the ad agency, and who was mad when Pop sold out."

"Do you know if the police have talked to him?"

"I was just over there, and I talked with Sergeant Malloy about him. He seemed interested and wrote things down."

"Hmmm. Can you wait right here a minute?"

"Sure."

Betsy went to the library table in the front of the store, where she used the cordless phone to call Jill at the police station. "Is it all right to ask if Mike Malloy has gone to talk to Banner Wilcox?"

"Skye did come to see you, then," said Jill.

"She's here now."

"I can tell you that Mike spoke briefly with Mr. Wilcox on the phone, but isn't interested in going any further. He's satisfied that he's got enough to convict Mickey Sinclair."

"Oh? What does he — no, that's not a good question, is it?"

Jill smiled; Betsy could hear it in her voice. "No, not a good question. Go talk to the child."

So Betsy went back to talk to Skye. "Do you have to ask her if you can talk to me?" asked Skye.

"Not always, but in this case, yes. You see, interfering with a police investigation is illegal."

"You mean Sergeant Malloy? He thinks Coy did it."

"No, he thinks Mickey Sinclair did it."

"Then why did he come out and scare Coy and Mommy half to death?"

"Because sometimes cases fall apart, and he doesn't want to have to start over from scratch on a case that is several weeks old. Or older, if it goes to trial and Mickey is found not guilty."

"I think Mickey did it."

"So why are you here to tell me about Banner Wilcox?"

Skye crossed her arms and tried to look huffy, then sighed and uncrossed them again. "For the same reason, I guess. Because if it turns out Mickey didn't do it, they may come after Coy, and I don't want my brother to go to jail. Because he didn't do it, either."

"You're sure?"

Skye went white. "My brother may be a jerk, but he wouldn't kill his own father! So it *has* to be Mickey. Unless it's Banner Wilcox."

"Do you know Mickey?"

"Kind of. We're in the same school. When he comes to school. And he hangs with a different crowd than me; all of them are criminals. He steals stuff and he smokes marijuana like *all* the time. So I don't know why you're trying to help him. And anyhow, if you don't think Mickey did it, who do you think?"

"I don't know. That's why I'm asking questions. For example, why did Banner Wilcox have a motive to kill your father?"

Skye swallowed hard and said, "Could you not say it like that? Killed my father? I feel all icky when I think about someone killing my father, especially Banner." Her voice rose high. "Banner's always been nice, and it's bad enough he's, my daddy's dead."

Betsy reached out to touch the girl on her shoulder. "I'm really sorry. It must be terrible for you."

Skye only nodded, no longer able to speak.

Betsy said, "May I get you something to drink? We have bottled water, coffee, and several kinds of tea."

Skye made an effort. "Water," she said in a shaky voice.

Betsy took her time getting a bottle of water out of the little refrigerator and pouring it into two foam cups. She berated herself for being so focused on her sleuthing she missed the obvious signs of Skye's suffering. Skye had loved her father, with whom she shared an artistic soul and who had been taken from her in a very ugly way — and now suspicion was falling on her mother and her one sibling. Betsy resolved to treat her with more respect.

When she got back to the table, Skye had taken hold of her emotions. "Thanks," she said in a near-normal voice, taking the cup of water. She took a quick swallow and said, "I'm okay now. You can ask me anything."

"Skye, I am very impressed that you would make this effort to help your family. I know this is a difficult thing for you to do."

"It's okay, I want to help if I can. What do you want to know?"

"Tell me about Banner Wilcox."

"Well, he was my father's partner in Information Please. He didn't want Pop to sell it, but Pop thought he was dying and he wanted to spend his last year carving animals and selling them. Pop told Banner that the company he was selling to —"

Betsy interrupted, "Excuse me, but if they were partners, how did your father sell it over Banner's objections?"

"Pop was the senior partner. It was like two-thirds and one-third. Besides, Pop told Banner it was a great deal, that the alternative was to wait till he died, when the sharks would close in. What he meant was, Banner didn't have Pop's sales sense and he might mess up trying to run the company alone. Banner was nice; he wasn't a hard-nose like Pop could be. And Pop told Banner that Makejoy, the company making the offer, was solid and growing. So Banner went along. And Makejoy gave him a job, only it wasn't as good a job as he'd had with Pop, and he didn't get along with the new bosses. And then he got downsized. He'd put most of his share of the money he got from selling into Makejoy, so he still thought he was all right — but then Makejoy went broke. So he was really screwed and he was really, really mad. He used to call our house and yell. One time he went off on Coy, because he thought it was Pop answering the phone, and Coy said he was like insane. He threatened to kill Pop."

"How did your father take this? Was he frightened?"

Skye shook her head. "I don't think so. He was upset, but it was about Banner, not himself. He really liked Banner. We all liked him."

"If your father was a hard-nosed business man earning good money, it's interesting that he should want to throw all that away to become an artist earning very little."

Skye sat still for a few moments, but she

was only gathering her strength, and choosing among memories to relate. "Pop started carving before I was born, before Coy was born, I think. He said it relaxed him, which I thought was funny, because he'd get really intense about it. But now I know what he meant, because I get intense about drawing, and it's like everything else goes away, all my problems, all my sadness, even my good things. Nothing matters but getting the way light lays on a horse's face just right."

She paused to think some more. "My mother's okay, mostly. It's just that she likes having lots of money. I think she pushed Pop into advertising so he'd make a good salary. What's interesting, now I think about it, is that he went along. I think he must have loved her very much." She sniffed lightly and folded her lips in, biting them to regain control. "But then, when . . . when we thought he was dying, she let him do what he really wanted. And once he found out how good he was, nothing in the world would make him go back to advertising, even when he found out he wasn't dying after all."

Skye nearly broke down at this point, but Betsy, while filled with distress, took a page from Jill's book, and only sat quietly. Skye doggedly pulled herself back together and went on, "Pop had a friend named Ian Masterson, he's a famous artist, and Ian was going to help Pop get his work for sale in a big, important gallery. Then everyone would see that Pop was also a great artist."

"Have you met Ian Masterson yourself?"

Skye suddenly bloomed into a smile. "Oh, yes, lots of times. He's like if your grandpa was a king, so he's famous but he's like a normal person to talk to. Strong and bossy, but nice. He . . ." She hesitated, then made up her mind and went on, "It was his idea that I should tell the police about Banner, because I told him — Ian — about how Banner said he wanted to kill my father." She reached for her water, but changed her mind. Her face was sad.

The door to the shop went *Bing!* Betsy stood, but it was only Shelly, back with Betsy's salad.

She came between the box shelves and was pulled up short by the look on Skye's face. "What's the matter here?" she asked.

Skye turned to her and demanded, "Is it true this person helps people the police think killed someone?"

Shelly smiled. "Yes, she does. She's very good at it."

"But she's trying to help Mickey Sinclair."

"Yes. His family asked me to."

"But he really did it, you know. It wasn't Banner, it couldn't be Banner! He's too nice!" Skye was near tears.

Shelly said, "Are you sure of that?"

"I've known him since I was a little baby! I

don't want him to go to jail!"

"Of course you don't. But think about it; Mickey's family doesn't want him to go to jail either."

"But he's such a criminal!"

"Perhaps. But people always stick up for their family."

Betsy, inspired, said, "Yes, they do, just as you are doing now, trying to help your mother and your brother."

Skye frowned. "Is it really the same thing? Me trying to help Coy and them trying to help Mickey?"

Shelly said, "Yes, almost exactly the same. And if your brother and your mother — and even Banner Wilcox — didn't do this terrible thing, Betsy will find that out, too."

Skye settled back in her chair and thought that over. Shelly and Betsy let her take her time. At last Skye said, "Okay, you can go talk to him." She gave his phone number as well as an address in Edina.

Betsy said, "Thank you. Have you had lunch, Skye?"

"I was supposed to have it with a friend, but it's too late now."

"Would you like my salad? I can go next door for another one. Meanwhile, Shelly can keep you company. Right, Shelly?"

Shelly smiled and said, "Of course."

"Okay. Thanks."

Betsy smiled, and went next door for another salad, which she ate slowly. When she came back to the shop, she found Shelly and Skye looking at Halloween patterns. She stayed out of their way until Skye left a few minutes later.

"That is one mixed-up kid," said Shelly. "She's almost crazy with grief over her father, and her mother is *not* helping. And *you're* not any better, Miss Snoop."

Betsy sighed. "I know. That's why I aimed her at you. She was about to walk out on me because she's so distressed at having to make me suspect Banner Wilcox of murder. She may become angry at Ian for putting the idea in her head."

"How do you know he did that?"

"Well, I don't. But it was her confiding in him that opened this particular can of worms, don't you think?"

"Oh, I suppose so. But she's not mad at him now. We mostly talked about Ian Masterson, how nice he is, what a great artist he is. But she's hurting badly right now, poor kid."

"Is she going to be all right, Shelly? What do you think of her? I know you specialize in elementary-age kids, but she's not all that far out of elementary school, is she?"

"Hah, in some respects she's forty years old!" Shelly added, more seriously, "I've hardly ever seen a kid more in need of a sympathetic shoulder. Ian can talk to her better than I can, about art anyway, but I can fill in around the edges. Which I am glad to do."

"What about her mother? What will she think of you taking on this burden?"

"It's not a burden, and I don't think her mother will mind."

"Shelly . . . thanks."

They settled into one of those afternoons that makes a shop owner despair. Not even a passerby stopped long enough to look in their window. Betsy got her cutwork pattern out, and the ball of Number Five thread, and continued tracing the lines with buttonhole stitch.

When she'd first learned it, it had been called the blanket stitch. Blanket or button-hole, it was a series of vertical stitches with a raised edge, like a row of capital T's whose crossbars overlap: **TTTTTT**. It wasn't hard to learn, but it took a bit of concentration at first to make every stitch identical, especially when working around curves.

Shelly kept coming by the desk, pausing to look at what Betsy was doing, and when Betsy refused to look up, sighing and going on. She had a project of her own to work on, and even got it out, but kept putting it down to sigh and look significantly at Betsy.

Who finally said, "Is there something you want to talk about, Shelly?"

"Who, me?" said Shelly, laughing.

"Well, all right," said Betsy, pretending to take her at her word, and returning to work on her project.

"Oh, okay, if you're going to twist my arm, then sure, I'll talk about him." Shelly put her work away and came to the desk.

"Who?" asked Betsy.

"The man I am seriously thinking of falling in love with."

"I thought you were already in love with Ian."

Shelly started to say something else, but paused. "Have you ever experienced love at first sight?"

"No."

"Then it's hard to explain. It's not really love, because it's not based on anything."

"Sure it is. It's based on looks, isn't it?"

"No, not the way you think, because once before when it happened to me, the guy wasn't good looking at all. It's more like . . . like recognition. It's enough to make you believe in reincarnation, truly it is, because you see this person and it's as if you've been waiting for years, maybe all your life, for him to come back. Even though you've never seen him before. It's like, somewhere in your heart you recognize him and you can't imagine why you didn't realize he wasn't around, that you've been longing for him without knowing it, and here he is at last."

"Sounds spooky," said Betsy.

"It isn't, it's like at last the world has come around right, and everything's okay. You didn't know before anything was wrong, but now you realize it's all been wrong until now. The bad part is, any complications, like he's married or he's a criminal or he's a drug addict, don't really matter. They're things you're sure you can fix. It's only later, when he's gone, that you look back and seriously wonder if for a little while you were insane. *That* part is scary. I've been lucky; this is my third trip on the twinkie-mobile, and none of my fellow passengers have been carrying serious baggage."

" 'Twinkie-mobile?' "

"Don't you remember that TV show 'Barney Miller'?"

"Sure — oh, Ron Harris, who had all those euphemisms for Bellevue and the wagon that took you there!" Betsy laughed. "So when you fell in love, it was a mutual thing?"

"Not always. Well, hardly ever. Once, actually."

"Is this the one time?"

"No, the one was my first husband. This one's infatuated."

"Shelly . . ."

"I know, I know. But infatuation can lead to love. And I've intrigued the artist in him. He wants to make a kinetic sculpture of me."

"What's a kinetic sculpture?"

"I'm not sure. It moves — he says he loves

the way I walk." Shelly demonstrated her walk, mugging elaborately over her shoulder as she went between the box shelves into the back of the store. She did a model's turn. "What do you think? Am I poetry in motion?"

"You move smoothly, I can see that." And she did, she was graceful as a dancer. As Shelly came back, Betsy continued, "What's he like as an artist? I mean, do you really think he's an artist, or is he a *poseur?*"

"We had a conversation about that. I like your word, *poseur,* better than mine, *pretender* — but he's not either; he really is an artist. He's starting to influence me, the way he looks at everything, really everything, as a possible work of art. He got all interested in the light on the irises in Mrs. Elmo's backyard, how the eye perceives shape and how distorted from reality perspective can be. So I told him about Marc Saastad's patterns of roses and irises, and how he indicates shadows with color changes, and I almost had him persuaded to try a counted cross-stitch pattern. I guess you had to be there, but it was really amazing. I love the way his mind works, always aware of the play of light on textured surfaces. It must be like hearing music *all the time.*"

Betsy said, "I had a friend who was a writer, and she said a part of her is always standing off to one side, taking notes."

"He says to be a successful artist he has to stay in touch with his inner child."

"I've heard that. Ever notice how often their inner child is a brat?"

Shelly winced. "*Touché!* Though his doesn't seem to be altogether a brat. It's more like taking a three-year-old for a walk. It's a way to see with new eyes how wonderful the familiar is."

"Speaking of new and familiar, this favor Ian did for Rob McFey, giving him money for his insurance policy, is this something he's done before?"

Shelly turned serious. "I asked him about that. And he says he's always tried to spread the wealth around when he can, but nowadays he mostly gives money to foundations that aid artists. He says he used to make loans but he hardly ever got it back. And they'd just waste it, anyhow. Artists, he says, are rarely able to manage money. He includes himself in that — he has an attorney handling his money."

"So why did he give money to Rob McFey?"

"Rob wasn't stupid about money — and anyway, he didn't give him money, he bought a viatical. He's done things like that before. Once, when an artist didn't have any insurance, he gave him a kind of mortgage. It was another welding artist. He says that's where he got his oxyacetylene torch. The artist died in a fire in his studio that was attached to his house and all Ian got was the torch and a heap of ashes."

"When was this?"

"I don't know. From the way he talked about it, he gave him the money three or four years ago. The artist died in a fire soon after."

"Was this welding artist on the verge of becoming famous, like Rob McFey?"

Shelly shook her head — then did a perfect double take. "What, you think Ian murders artists he thinks might become rivals?"

Betsy raised both hands in protest. Put baldly like that, it did seem ludicrous. "No, of course not! I'm just trying to collect as much information as I can. Somewhere in all this mess, there's a clue I'm probably missing."

"Oh. Okay." She thought. "I don't think he was about to become famous — this other welding artist. I'd never heard of him, anyway. He told me the guy's name. Begins with an O. Benedict O. Gregory O? A Pope's name," she said, and thought some more. "His last name was Omar. No, Oscar. Well, something like that." She shook her head.

"Does Ian ever talk about why he does welded-metal sculpture? I mean, as opposed to clay, or stone."

"He can do clay, and stone. But he told me he likes the primal appeal of metal, its ability to take on any shape. He says most of the art we're making today will rot or fade or fall apart, but metal won't. He says metal is . . . alchemical. He says it's like wizardry. You take copper and tin and melt them together to get bronze, which isn't what you'd expect. It's a whole different metal, not like either of them. And copper and zinc make brass, which is even more different."

Betsy said, "Wait a minute, I want to hear about Ian, not get a lecture on metal alloys."

"Well, it's kind of to the point," said Shelly. "Ian says people used to think metal workers were in league with the devil, you know, because they could handle white-hot iron and not get burned to death. And I think he kind of likes that idea, that his work is dangerous, both really and spiritually. He quotes this poem by Kipling: 'Iron, cold iron, is master of them all.' Meaning master of metals."

Betsy recited, " 'Gold is for the mistress, Silver for the maid, Copper for the craftsman, cunning at his trade.' "

"Yes," nodded Shelly, "that's the poem, about the baron sitting in his hall. He gets all moved and excited about steel. He does this thing with the surface, gives it a patina, so it turns colors."

Betsy said, "I thought those big steel beams were painted."

"They were. But he hasn't done the big steel beams in years. He does these smaller things — well, comparatively smaller. I saw a model of the tree piece, it was kind of like an Ent from *Lord of the Rings*, old and noble and sad. He said inspiration smote him hard and he did about six of these figures all in a rush. His gallery got all excited so he did two more not quite so fast — and he's not satisfied with the later ones. He says that well was shallow and went dry, and now he wants to move on. But his gallery wants more of them. He's working on one, it looks like an old man with a lantern, and he doesn't like it very much, either. The Ent one turned up at a major auction and sold for over three times what the gallery price was, which was sixty-five thousand dollars. He's getting reviewed by important critics and museums are interested." Shelly's voice had softened with awe. "His gallery keeps raising its prices, now they're into the higher six figures, and they've still sold all but one. But he insists this lantern man will be the last. I told him he can work on whatever he wants to part of the time but he should definitely go with the flow and make more of the ones that really sell. Do you think I was wrong? I mean, there's this artist thing about inspiration, but how can he just shrug off eight hundred thousand dollars?"

Betsy lifted her hands. "You know him better than I do. Is he more after money than he is being true to his art?"

Shelly thought that over. "You know, I can't tell. Sometimes I think it's being rich and famous he likes, and other times, I think he'd live in an unheated basement rather than give up his welder."

"So long as he has a welder, he won't freeze," said Betsy with a wink.

But Shelly was too involved in talking about Ian to get the joke. "I told him, if he's out of inspirations he could maybe go back to the first ones and just do variations on them. There's a screaming little girl that's very powerful, I saw a picture of it on his website. He could do that child as a boy, for example."

"Isn't that cheating, to do something over again?"

"I don't think so. That artist who just paints his canvases all one color does that over and over. And museums just keep buying them. But . . ." She sighed. "Ian doesn't want to prostitute his art — that's what he calls it. He says he wants to move on to the next level."

"A kinetic sculpture of you."

"Well . . . Well, yes, that's right, isn't it? I wonder what it will look like?" Shelly did a few waltz steps, arms up and around an imaginary partner. "I shall inspire him to new heights."

Bing! A customer came in, and Shelly fell back to earth to help her find a wedding sampler. Betsy went back to stitching.

Now that she'd reeducated her fingers and was satisfied she could maintain a high level of sameness in the stitches, she could relax and get into the movement. As with knitting, the repetition took only a fraction of her concentration and the rest of her mind began to stroll through the furniture of this murder case. It studied the shapes and decided what went with what — and found a lot was missing.

For example, she didn't know much about the actual murder. Perhaps she should talk to Deb Hart, who had run the Art on the Lake fair for many years. Deb might know if there had been any previous trouble at Rob McFey's booth. For example, Sunday was the second day of the art fair. Had there been any trouble on Saturday? Had Banner Wilcox come by to make threats? Had Rob told anyone he was expecting trouble?

And was Banner really a nice little man, full of sound and fury but ineffective in action?

What was the relationship between Ian Masterson and Rob McFey? By Shelly's description, Ian was indeed well on his way to becoming an Important Artist, so how come he stayed friends with Rob after he realized Rob wasn't able to help him with publicity? Nice that he had, of course, because he was able to help Rob by buying that viatical —

and could afford to wait for the payoff. Had someone helped Ian when he was starting out, so that he thought it worth his while to do the same for others? Kind of nice to know he wasn't entirely self-centered, that he was a man who, having attained a high plateau, reached down to help others in their struggle to climb up.

Unfortunate that Rob McFey hadn't lived to realize his own dream of fame.

Or had he been happy where he was, selling at art fairs? Betsy, through her volunteer work at Excelsior's art fair, knew there were many who were content to travel from fair to fair, rubbing elbows with the general public, making them happy to take home something to ornament their houses.

Of course, Irene Potter, Excelsior's zaniest stitching artist, wasn't one of them. She had thought she would like selling at the fair, but she had only the smallest understanding of how other people's minds worked, and was always surprised by their vagaries. She was, however, so prodigiously talented with her needlework, that soon her contact with everyday people anxious — or not (and that was always to her amusingly great surprise) — to buy her work would be minimal. But Betsy was glad she was at this last fair, because her telling Betsy what she had seen that Sunday morning was very helpful.

It supported her theory that Mickey

Sinclair had come upon the murder scene right after it had happened, and had taken the money from the cash box left helpfully visible. And if that was so, maybe he had come there so promptly he had seen something useful. Or someone. She would have to go see him again and ask.

Once she started considering, there were a lot of questions she needed to ask. This case was like the cutwork she was trying to master, full of holes. Bad choice of comparison, she thought with a grimace, remembering how Rob McFey had died.

Tomorrow was her day off, but the major restocking of her refrigerator and linen closet she had planned would have to wait. It was time to go talk to people.

Chapter 17

After the shop closed, Betsy phoned the Wilcox home. Wilcox was puzzled when she said she wasn't with the police but wanted to talk to him about Rob McFey's murder anyway.

"Why, what's your interest in this? Are you a reporter?" His voice was pleasant but high-pitched.

"No, sir, I'm doing an investigation on my own, as a private citizen. I talked with Skye McFey today, and —"

"How is Skye?" he interrupted, sounding concerned.

"She's sad about her father, of course, but otherwise seems to be coping."

"Poor kid. She was her daddy's little girl, and he was crazy about her."

"Yes, I've gathered that. She's an intelligent young woman. She said I should talk to you, and I wonder what you're doing tomorrow."

"Well, ordinarily I might say it's none of your business what I'm doing tomorrow." Betsy crossed her fingers. "But since Skye said I should talk to you, all right. Still, tomorrow I've got three job interviews, the first one around ten and the last around three. How about day after tomorrow?"

"No, tomorrow would be best. May I take you to lunch?"

"No, I'll be on the road at lunchtime. But say, how about breakfast?"

"All right, where should we meet?"

"No, you come over to my house."

Betsy hesitated. "Well, I'd be all right with that but I wouldn't want to make extra trouble for your wife."

He replied, with a smile in his voice, "It won't put Peg out; I cook breakfast most mornings. Are you lactose intolerant? I make a mean pancake."

"No," said Betsy. "And I love pancakes."

So around seven the next morning, Betsy came into the sweet-smelling kitchen of a little white house in Edina. Banner was a trim, short man, seriously balding, with pale blue eyes behind rimless eyeglasses. He had a spatula in one hand and an apron protecting his good charcoal gray slacks. He wore a T-shirt, and Betsy noted there were no love handles.

He greeted her in his light, Father Mulcahy voice and led her into the kitchen. His wife was standing near a French window, a cup of coffee in her hand. She was a tiny creature, with graying blond hair cropped very short, and very pretty blue eyes.

"Hello, Ms. Devonshire," she said in a

voice made more pleasant by a Georgia drawl. "I'm Peggy Wilcox."

The kitchen had recently been expanded; it was bigger than the living room. It had stainless steel appliances, quarrystone counters, and a tile floor — a he-man kitchen. It smelled deliciously of coffee, pancakes, and spiced apples.

Banner seated Betsy at an oak breakfast bar and presented her with a plate of hot pancakes pulled from the warming oven and gave her a choice of syrups or apples cooked with cinnamon. Betsy chose the latter.

Peggy sat down to a quarter of a pancake and reached across to fill the cup waiting by Betsy's plate. "I'll just finish up and leave you two alone." She took a bite, drained her cup, and with an enigmatic glance at her husband, went away.

Banner piled a great heap of pancakes onto his plate and, when he came to the table, poured lots of blueberry syrup on them. He filled his cup from the pot on the table, added sugar and cream, and sat down. "I'm gifted with a pretty active metabolism," he said, gesturing at the plate. "I was the skinniest kid in my class right through college, even though I ate everything I could sink my teeth into." He cut into his pancakes with his fork and took a big mouthful.

Betsy cut off a bite and sank her teeth into a lightweight sweetness of apples and pastry.

She chewed, swallowed, and said, "Gosh!" Then, "Have you always liked to cook?"

He grinned, showing blue teeth, and said, "No, but if I wanted something good, I had to make it myself. Peg is a terrific wife everywhere but in the kitchen."

Betsy tasted her coffee, which proved to be industrial strength, but not bitter. "I told you I was investigating Rob McFey's murder," she said. "And I want to ask you about him."

He cut viciously into his stack, saying, "I wanted to kill him." He glanced at her, saw her raised eyebrows. He nodded sharply and continued, "I even bought a gun. If someone hadn't got there ahead of me, I might have. That bastard, excuse my French, ruined me."

"Were you on bad terms before he sold Information Please?"

"Hell, no! We were good friends for years, we'd started about the same time at Barton-Bailey and worked accounts together. It was his idea to start our own company, but I was glad to go along. I was management and accounting, he was sales and design. We had six employees and were looking for a seventh. The company was strong, we had some really satisfied accounts and were about to pick up another one, when he got sick. And all of a sudden he wasn't interested anymore. It was like, 'You know, I never liked this business.'" Banner said that in a slow, thoughtful, mocking voice. "I couldn't believe it. He

worked harder than anyone else, even me —
and I *did* like the business."

"I understand he drank a lot."

"Well, yes. Yes, he did. But he'd always
done that, even back at B and B. I never saw
him under the table, or even drunk enough
that I was afraid to let him drive home by
himself. He had what my father used to call
a hollow leg — he could drink a great deal
and not show any effect. He was a great
salesman, everyone looked forward to his pre-
sentations. He'd have clients and staff
laughing like maniacs. Everyone liked him. I
liked him — hell, I *loved* him. He took me
places I never thought we could go. We were
a success, a big, fat success. Then —" He
snapped his fingers. "He didn't like advertising anymore, he'd never liked advertising,
he wanted to carve statues out of wood and
sell them at street fairs like a goddam
hippie."

"He thought he was dying and wanted to
follow his dream."

Banner nodded and ate more pancake. "I
know, I know," he said to his plate, shrug-
ging. "But so what? If I found out I was
dying tomorrow — well, right now it
wouldn't be the great tragedy I would've
thought it was back when I was vice president of Information Please. But still, I would
remember my responsibilities, to my family
and fellow workers." He swallowed, looked a

bit distant for a moment, then recalled himself with another little shrug. "It was a sad day when we got the news. Poor Rob, I thought, what a tragedy. He's just hitting his stride with the company. We'd gone public, you know, and our stock was up a few points damn near every day the market was open. We'd been getting offers from Makejoy and ignoring them, but Rob got sick and suddenly things were different. He went to talk to them and came back all enthusiastic about how great they were, what a great offer they were making, how well we'd do if we accepted their offer. And I, like the gullible idiot I can be at times, believed him." His voice turned bitter. "I got screwed. I had put all my eggs into the Information Please basket, and it worked extremely well for me. So I transferred them to Makejoy — and lost it all." He took a deep breath, let it loose, and took a drink of coffee.

"So you were angry."

"Aren't you listening? I repeat, I was so mad I wanted to kill him." He drew another long breath. "I decided I *was* going to kill him."

Betsy, startled, said, "Did you say — what?"

"I mean it, I had made up my mind. Skye told me he was going to be at the Excelsior art fair, and I loaded my gun."

"And — so, did you?" Betsy hoped she

didn't sound as frightened as she felt, sitting alone in the kitchen with this man.

"No, I didn't. Peg found the gun and hid it on me."

Betsy released the breath she didn't know she'd been holding, and blurted, "God bless Peg!"

"Amen," he replied. "But I only say that now. Back then, I was furious, because I really meant to blow that bastard to hell. But I couldn't find the gun. I couldn't believe she'd do that to me, keep me from committing justice on Rob. That's how I thought of it, y'know, not committing murder, but committing justice."

"So what did you do?"

"I went to Excelsior. I went into the park and I walked by his booth about three times, gave him the evil eye. He only saw me once, and the jerk actually smiled and waved at me. Then I came home."

"What time of day did you see him?"

"About two, I think."

Betsy frowned. "No, no, he was dead by then."

"No, he wasn't. He was killed on Sunday, I went down there on Saturday."

"Oh. Oh! Where were you Sunday?"

He had been about to take a drink of coffee, but froze, and then put it down again and turned a megawatt smile on her. "So *that's* what this is about, huh? On Sunday I was in church, trying to get sorry for hating him so much. I thought I'd failed, but my first reaction when I heard he was dead was, 'Oh, my God, how dreadful.' "

"What time was church?"

The smile did not dim. "Nine a.m., lasted forty minutes, with a coffee hour after."

"Did anyone see you?"

"Lots of people. Friends, many of them. I can make you a list, if you want."

A little after ten, Betsy walked three blocks up Water Street from Lake Street to Deb Hart's artist supply store. The sky was overcast in a glaring white, the air hot, motionless, oppressive with humidity. Betsy walked slowly, trying not to work up a sweat, trying not to be both disappointed and relieved that Banner Wilcox wasn't guilty of murder.

Artworks was in a twin-shop, single-story building. On the corner, an old gas station had been converted to a small office building. Next to it was a tiny park in front of a parking lot, where a farmers' market was held on Thursdays. This arrangement left the side of Artworks exposed to view. On it was a mural in Impressionist style. It depicted an artist painting a pond covered with water lilies — Monet, of course! The mural was done in cool purples, blues, and greens, and looked very inviting. Betsy, imagining cool things, told herself that one day she'd go

wading in that pond looking for Impression-
istic frogs and turtles. That thought made
her smile. She had a special fondness for
frogs and turtles, and had made a number of
them live an unhappy week or two as cap-
tives during her childhood.

The front window of the store had a large
artist's mannequin in wood and wire, the
hands suggested by mitten-shaped pieces, the
face a flat blank. Today it was dressed in a
child's straw hat and carrying a seashore
bucket. Betsy went into the little entryway
and turned left — turning right would have
led her into Cynthia Rae's dress shop.

Deb stood behind the counter that ran half
the length of her store. She was consulting
with a man who had brought in some water-
color paintings he wanted framed — the wall
behind the counter held hundreds of frame
corners.

Deb was about five feet two, though the
way she carried herself made her look taller.
Her eyes were hooded but friendly, and there
was an alertness about her that spoke of energy and concentration. Her honey blond hair
was pulled back into the long single braid
that was her trademark.

Her tone with the customer was just a little
too patient, as if she was trying to be kind to
someone who was not as bright or energetic
as she was. Betsy recalled, with a pang, that
exact tone used on her while she was trying

to get up to speed with the other committee members planning the art fair. She hadn't recognized it back then, and thought the customer it was now being applied to probably didn't recognize it used on him, either.

Deb nodded at Betsy, a request to wait, and Betsy nodded back. She took a walk through the shop — the art fair planning meetings had all taken place at Excelsior's Elementary School library, and she hadn't been in the shop before. The aisles were narrow and had slanted shelves of painting and drawing supplies for an artist at any level working in anything from pencil to oils. In back there were light tables, Sculpey clay, and a wonderful wood-and-wire model of a horse in the same style as the artist's mannequin in the window. Betsy stopped to admire it, and then began moving the legs through the canter — that's what these models were for, to hold action positions — until Deb's voice called from up front. "Betsy, is there something I can help you find?"

"No, no. I just have some questions for you." Betsy hurried back up front. "It's about the murder at the fair."

Deb frowned very slightly — all her emotions tended to be performed in small motions. "What about it?"

"I'm doing an investigation. It's something I do, helping people falsely accused of a crime."

Deb nodded; apparently someone had told her about Betsy's peculiar hobby. "Are you talking about Mickey Sinclair?"

"Yes."

"But he really did murder Mr. McFey, don't you know that? The police have him in jail for it."

"Even so, I think perhaps he isn't guilty."

"Well, if it wasn't Mickey Sinclair, who do you think did it?"

"I'm trying to find that out. I've been asking questions, but so far the leads I've gotten either don't work out or are pretty vague. For example, I have a report that there was a quarrel at the McFey booth before Mickey Sinclair approached it. Did you hear anything about that?"

There was a pause while Deb went back through her memories of the fair. But at last she shook her head. "Just from one person, and she wasn't one of my people. And because of what happened, I'm sure I'd remember if someone else told me about that. Why, did you overhear it?"

"No." Betsy shook her head. "I was at the fair from very early Sunday morning, but I was stuck in the concession stand all day, too far from Mr. McFey's booth to hear anything."

"All day? That was too bad! Didn't someone relieve you for lunch or a break?"

"No. Everyone's schedule got messed up by

the investigation. It was all right, though; someone brought me lunch and took over long enough for a couple of trips to the rest room." Betsy chuckled. "You did tell us we could have all the free pop we wanted, right? I made quite a dent in the Diet Coke and Seven-Up."

"You were only supposed to work there till noon, you know. We'll have to talk about that at the wind-up meeting next week."

"Oh, please, don't mention it! I was fine, really I was! And people kept me informed, and sometimes stayed with me for a while. Remember, it rained quite a bit, so the crowds weren't bad. I never felt tired or over-whelmed."

But Deb wasn't comforted. She liked her art fair to run smoothly, for everyone to get a proper break, for no one to work more hours than they'd volunteered for. And — though it wasn't something she specifically wished for in advance — for all the artists to leave alive and well.

Betsy said, "So I was wondering if you saw or heard anything, or if anyone told you something about what happened that morning. I've already talked to Irene Potter."

Deb smiled faintly. "Yes, Irene came in here on Monday to tell me all about it, too. I think everyone in town has heard Irene's story. But I can't tell you much. The police called me to the booth to see if I could identify the dead man, and I could."

"Had you been to his booth before?"

"I went up and down the aisles a lot on Saturday, but didn't do more than ask him, like I did everyone, if everything was all right. It was another member of the committee who recommended him for an artist's award." The award was given to ten artists. They were presented a ribbon marked AWARD OF EXCELLENCE to display, and a more substantial award in the form of a purchase of his or her art. These pieces were later auctioned, the funds going into an arts scholarship fund.

"Who bought the piece from him?"

"I did, first thing on Sunday. Mr. McFey had just arrived, and he was setting his display of carvings out front. He had some nice pieces — you sat in on the jury committee meetings, didn't you?"

Betsy nodded. "Yes. I will never forget that one of the lion. But his prices were kind of high."

Deb nodded. "Much higher than average for an art fair. I was sure that this would be his only time at the fair — anyone who wanted some of his work was going to have to pay an even higher price at a gallery next year."

"What did you buy from him for the award?" asked Betsy.

"One of his little caricature carvings. I

thought about the rapper snapping turtle, but it was kind of politically incorrect, and rather vicious-looking. So I bought the weasel lawyer. He's vicious, too, but funny."

"Rapper snapper? Weasel lawyer?" repeated Betsy.

"Sure, you said you saw the slides." The Art by the Lake fair was a juried event, meaning that the fair committee had to look at a slide show of the work of any artist applying to sell at the fair. It took a long time, and Betsy's brain was thoroughly overwhelmed before the end. "I'm sorry, all I remember is the lion."

Deb said, "They were about three inches high, carved in basswood. They were like cartoon animals with human occupations, a fireman, a nurse, a plumber."

But Betsy could only shake her head.

"Want to see them? We haven't sent the slides back yet." Deb reached under the counter and pulled out a box full of slide holders. She ran her fingers along them, backed up, went forward again, and at last found what she was looking for, drawing out a flexible, clear-plastic slide holder with four slides in it.

She handed it to Betsy, reached again, couldn't find whatever it was, stooped out of sight, and came up again with one of those small, box-like slide viewers. Betsy pulled out the first slide, put it into the viewer, and held it up to her eyes.

Pressing down on the slide made a light inside the box come on. Suddenly she was looking at a row of four wooden carvings standing on what looked like a butcher block table. A ruler lay in front of them to give an idea of scale.

First on the left was a comical little possum standing on his hind legs, wearing a tiny set of coveralls, carrying a toolbox, his tail wrapped around a plumber's helper. The piece was unpainted and the knife marks were clear, but it was nicely done, down to the dull, sleepy look on his face. Next to him was a grinning raccoon, his bandit's mask blackened and further underlined by the big sack he carried on his back. The end of his tail came out from under the sack, its rings indicated with more blacking, done in paint or ink. The sack bulged and something like a knob on a stick stuck out of the top — a cudgel, perhaps. Next to the burglar was a pig in a cop's uniform, his fat face a study in smugness as he wrote in his ticket book with a thick pencil held in one cloven hoof. And last was the legal weasel, standing upright, one paw in the air, its angry mouth open to display tiny, sharp teeth. To explain what it represented, it was standing on a thick book on which Betsy could just make out the upside-down letters **L A W.**

"I'd say this man had issues," said Betsy

with a smile, handing the box back to Deb.

"Yes, but not all of the pieces were insulting." She took the slide out and replaced it in the holder. "I remember a Saint Bernard nurse and a seagull as a pilot, though now I think about it, it was probably an albatross — they're the great fliers of the avian world. And he must have been able to do them really fast, because on Sunday I saw he'd been working on one of a border collie with the hair on its back made into one long braid." She smiled and touched her forehead with her fingertips, as if saluting an applauding audience.

Betsy laughed, then pointed at the slide holder and said, "So some of them, at least, were real people."

"I suspect all of them were at least suggested by someone he knew. Never aggravate an artist or a writer, lest you be immortalized unflatteringly. But they were clever and well done, these little carvings, as well as funny; I would have put him up for approval just on the basis of them. But it's his big carvings that were really admirable. The world is the poorer because their maker is gone."

Betsy asked, "What do you know about the maker? As a person, I mean."

"Not much," said Deb, frowning just a little. "I had never met Mr. McFey before this year's fair. I only talked with him briefly." She hesitated, then said very quietly.

"He smelled of alcohol, even early Sunday morning. He didn't slur his words or anything, so I didn't mention it to anyone. But I thought I'd better keep an eye on him, because he was working with his knives. He'd set up a table and was the 'Artist at Work.' We have a demonstration area where artists can show off their process, but he was doing this in his booth. It was okay, a good sales technique, actually; people would stop to watch, and of course be more likely to buy. On Saturday I noticed he was working on one of those little comic animals, probably the one of me. They work up fast, because basswood is soft, not like the hardwoods he did his big pieces in."

"I wish I'd gotten to see them," said Betsy.

"Hah, I wish I'd bought his sea otter, I could've maxed out a credit card if I wanted to. Can't do it now; what's left is all there will ever be, and it will cost the price of a car to buy that piece, probably. I wonder which gallery will win the fight to take his work on consignment?"

Betsy said, "His daughter will be happy about that; she inherited his work. But I'm looking for suspects, and the place to find them is at points of friction. Is there a lot of rivalry and resentment among artists who do and do not get booth space? Are there quarrels and resentments over placement of booths, or . . . I don't know, whatever?"

Deb smiled. "If someone was to get murdered over choosing or placement, it would be me, or my committee. We're the gatekeepers, after all."

"Have you or any committee member ever been threatened?"

"With legal action, yes. And shouted at, even cursed. But we've never had a death threat. After all, one way to ensure you don't get a place at all is to make the gatekeepers scared of you. Besides, there's always next year. Quarrels happen among artists at the fair, but it's over things like encroachments — we nearly had a fistfight one year when someone set up his booth an inch and a half over the line onto someone else's space." She held up a thumb and forefinger to show the little bit of territory involved. "We even got a complaint about the kites this year, because the artist flying them encroached the *air space* over someone else's booth." She was grinning now, but sobered a bit to hold up a hand and tick off items on her fingers: "We got a complaint because we couldn't supply workers to help carry art into the grounds; because we couldn't help set up booths; and from one real pip, because we refused to sell for him while he went strolling around to look at what everyone else was selling."

Betsy shook her head. "Amazing. Was that last one Rob McFey? Or was he the person

314

encroaching? Or encroached upon?"

"No. Never heard a complaint out of him, or about him."

Betsy thought a moment, then asked, "Did you ever meet a friend of his named Ian Masterson?"

"You mean Ian Masterson the welding artist?"

"Yes."

"Was Mr. Masterson a friend of Mr. McFey's?" Deb's eyebrows lifted just a touch, a subtle sign she was impressed.

"Yes, he was. Or he told me he was. Do you know him?"

"Very slightly. He never sold at art fairs that I know of, but I've seen him at museum events. He's nice, and only eccentric enough to let you know he's an artist. So you've met him?"

"Yes. What's your impression of him?"

"Very, very charming. He comes across as good-humored, articulate, and intelligent, which make for a winning combination. I've heard he's good with customers, gallery owners, and the media. Not bad looking, either, which also helps. I have heard that he enjoys being famous. I have also heard that he's generous with time and money, especially to other artists" — she paused and raised a thin eyebrow — "provided they aren't into metalwork."

Betsy nodded. "He helped Rob McFey out,

I know that. I got to know Ian because he came to talk to me about Rob. He said Rob was a good friend and he wanted to give me any information he could in my investigation of the murder. He mentioned that McFey was a serious drinker. Do you know if Ian is, too?"

Deb shrugged meagerly. "No. I've only met him a couple of times, and he seemed sober both times. Of course, it would take a real effort to get drunk on wine, especially the lousy stuff museums serve to members at events."

Twin Cities museums gave special showings to members when a new exhibit opened. If the artist was living, she or he was often present. Betsy rarely had time to attend these events, and considered her memberships to be a form of giving.

"When was the last time you saw him?"

"Back in November. I've been too busy with my store and with planning the art fair to do anything since. Honestly, we get more applications every year, some from people who should know better."

A customer came into the shop right then, an obese man with a sharp voice and a lot of questions about oil paints. Betsy stood aside while Deb dealt with him.

Betsy recalled with a smile one artist who'd applied unsuccessfully for a booth at Excelsior whose art consisted of paper clips rebent into odd shapes then stuck into corks; there had been an occasional bead slid onto one, apparently to show the metal had been twisted in a fit of creativity. He hadn't been allowed to sell at the fair. And no makers of grapevine wreaths, Styrofoam Christmas tree ornaments, and other craft items got so far as the jury. The application process weeded crafts out very firmly.

Not that there was anything wrong with Styrofoam Christmas tree ornaments; Betsy had bought several for her tree last year. But there are classes of art, a ranking that begins with "original paintings" sold in motel rooms on weekends ("nothing over fifty dollars"), stepping up to craft days at malls, then art and craft fairs, art fairs, juried art fairs, then into art galleries and art auctions, and then the really important works that go to museums and, when sold, are at places like Sotheby's.

Betsy had been impressed at the efficiency of Deb Hart's direction of her fair, and the committee's work overall. At the first meeting for this year's art fair, last November, Deb had handed out a schedule of all the meetings, each with its agenda, and to Betsy's amazement, each meeting thereafter began on time, lasted only as long as scheduled, and completed its agenda. By the time the fair began, Betsy was ready to vote Deb into any political office she cared to run for, up to and including President of the United States. She had her cabinet already around her, experienced, hardworking, efficient.

When Deb finished with the customer, Betsy asked, "Do you know anyone I can talk to about how art works?"

Deb smiled. "How art works?"

"Yes. How does someone make money, real money, in art? I don't mean sellers, I mean artists. How does an artist get a name? Why, for example, is Ian Masterson rich and famous, while Rob McFey wasn't?"

"For one thing, Rob McFey did outdoor art — realistic wildlife art, which has its own admirers, but isn't considered important. And he hadn't been trying for as long, or as hard, as Ian. Does this have something to do with his murder?"

"I really have no idea. I'm floundering around, looking for something to take hold of. I'm so doggone ignorant about professional artists that I might be missing something."

Deb thought, then gave an almost invisible shrug before saying, "Well, you could talk to a friend of mine. He owns a gallery in Uptown and he's worked on a few public art committees. When do you want to talk to him?"

"Soon. Today, if possible."

"All right, I'll call him."

Chapter 18

At noon Betsy was shaking the hand of Peter Stephenson, a tall, affable man with naturally golden-blond hair and narrow blue eyes. They met at an Indian restaurant in the Uptown section of Minneapolis, an area rich in exotic cafés, art galleries, antique shops, and art movie houses.

The restaurant served buffet style. After they had filled their plates, Betsy, having said that she had received an invitation to serve on the board of the Modern Art Museum of Minneapolis — which was sort of true, someone had felt her out about it, but he'd lost interest before she got to tell him she was flattered but couldn't possibly serve — said, "Deb Hart told me you've worked on committees that select public art. Is that the art you find in parks?"

"No, it's the art in corporate landscapes. Typically, corporate art is part of the permit process. Corporations seeking to build or expand have to agree to spend a percentage of their investment in public art. They turn the money over to, say, Public Art Saint Paul, which actually selects the art. Often the art is by a local artist — an art instructor at Macalester University and his wife are two of the top public artists in the country. They do stone as well as welding and ironwork. But Ian Masterson was also building a name in that sort of thing himself, before he turned to smaller pieces."

"Is Ian's work still around the Twin Cities?"

"Yes, at Sweetwater and Minnesota Mills. He did one beside a reflecting pond that's rather good."

"Now I know there's important art, like Rembrandt, or Van Gogh, and that important art isn't the same thing as successful art, like what's his name, Kinkaid. And there's outdoor art, which isn't the same thing as art that sits in a garden or beside an office building, but paintings or statues of ducks or deer. What I don't understand is how someone becomes an 'important' artist. And why it sometimes — I mean some important art . . ." She paused, not wanting to say something to make him angry or feel insulted.

"Isn't very attractive?" he said with a smile.

"Well, maybe I don't understand it," she confessed.

"That's a good attitude," he said with a nod, stirring a bit of white rice into his curry. "What makes important art is the opinion of important museums and/or galleries. There's a certain amount of incest among them — they listen to one another's opinions, and they speak in a language that sounds like ordinary English but has very different meanings. Too often this makes members of the general public flatly denounce what they find ugly or incomprehensible. Unfortunately" — he shrugged — "such remarks usually only display their ignorance."

"So the art experts are correct when they discount the sneers of the ignorant — and the screams of the taxpayer who is subsidizing the museum?"

He smiled and gestured with his fork. "Frankly? Not always. Part of the problem is that beauty is near the bottom of the list of what makes a work of art important. But a bigger part is that the screaming people are often right: It's not only that much of what is considered important is ugly, it's that some of it isn't really art."

Betsy tasted her curry and immediately reached for the flatbread to soothe her burning mouth. "So how do you tell? Or perhaps more importantly, how does something awful get selected by a museum or gallery, or get put in a public place?" she asked.

"There is a short list of galleries who have a great deal of influence on who is named important. And certain museums, the Getty in Los Angeles and the Museum of Modern Art in New York City, for example, and certain museums abroad, are very influential.

But public art is another thing, and not the same as important art, though there can be overlap, like the Picasso in Daley Plaza, Chicago. Public art is chosen by committees, who may or may not be art experts."

"I would have thought the committees would be composed of gallery owners or museum curators."

He nodded at that, and took another bite. This gave him a few moments to think before he continued. "Sometimes they are. But more frequently, public art committees are composed of good, sincere people who want to be artists, who know the language, have the ego, know the names, but have little or no taste. That's why they will buy a wonderful and costly Chihuly chandelier for an orchestra hall being restored to its Victorian Gothic splendor. They are more interested in showing that they know about Chihuly than in buying something they think will look good there, or that fits with the architectural style of the place. Other members may express concern, but don't trust their own taste and so they go along with those who argue strongly that a certain artist or architect is a good choice." Stevenson smiled and pointed his fork at Betsy. "And of course, there is always that member under the spell of an artist who thinks the phrase 'art is in the eye of the beholder' means he should give a poke in that eye."

Betsy chuckled as she mixed a bit of chutney into her curry before taking another bite. "But that makes it sound so chancy. As if no one really knows. It's like the Episcopal Church, of which I am a member, which teaches that a new theory of religion is proved by whether it's still held as true a hundred or more years after it's proposed as dogma."

Stevenson nodded. "I'm afraid that's approximately correct. You might also think of it as like the fable of the emperor's new clothes, only with nobody to be the child's voice crying the truth. There are charlatans in this business who stand to make a lot of money if they can convince the right people that a certain artist is doing important work."

"But why don't the honest critics speak up?"

"For complicated reasons. Let me give you one example of how it happens — mind you, this is a made-up example, not a thinly disguised story of something I know actually happened, all right?"

"All right."

"A woman, let's call her Mary Smith, is extraordinarily pretty and not at all stupid, but the daughter of a farmer who didn't finish high school, and she graduates from a consolidated high school far from a big city. She is sent to the state college, where she meets and marries John Doe, the college football star, whose father owns a small manufacturing company. The company has come up with a product that does well. John Doe goes into his father's business and improves the product, and finds more and better ones, and so builds the company into something large and important. Mr. and Mrs. Doe become very wealthy.

"Once their only child is in school, Mary does a lot of volunteer work for garden clubs, hospitals, charities, and so forth. Her husband can be relied upon for major donations to worthy causes. Naturally, she comes to head many committees. She travels a lot and dresses expensively, buying clothes in New York and Los Angeles, even Paris and Rome. She begins to think she belongs to a 'community' that is much more sophisticated and stylish than her home city. She becomes bolder and more confident as time goes by, and starts appearing at concerts or plays in some outrageous outfit she presents as very high style, and gets a reputation for artistic taste. She begins to think Duluth is unsophisticated and would like to relocate to one coast or the other, but her husband is busier than ever growing his company, so they stay where they are. She cultivates friends in Duluth who admire her, who really think she is an expert in the sophisticated world of the arts. She has met movie stars, Broadway actors — she once had a conversation with Andy Warhol.

"So naturally she and a couple of her very dear friends are named to a committee that will select a design for a new museum. She persuades the committee to approach one or more famous architects for a proposal. One famous name, looking over the request, feels a certain contempt for Duluth, it being in the more distant reaches of flyover land, but he needs a new yacht or *pied-à-terre* in Costa del Sol, so he opens a drawer and pulls out a failed design, something found unworthy of Manhattan or San Francisco.

"Mary Doe is so thrilled to get an actual proposal from a famous name that she really talks up the design. Her friends support her. The committee nominates it as a finalist. The drawing is put in the newspaper. The public reacts badly, of course — but what did you expect from these unsophisticated rubes? An art critic for the newspaper decides to support the design, though he personally doesn't like it. Why? First, he is in awe of the designer. Second, he is in awe of Mary Doe. Third, the public never likes anything new and avant garde, and he does not wish to be thought as backward as they. Fourth, he has about as much aesthetic sense as Mary — but even if he knows that, so what? Aesthetic beauty, remember, is passé. This design is as ugly as it is impractical, so it must be the very latest thing. Fifth, like Mary, he wants Duluth to earn a place on the map, and a museum designed by a famous architect is one way to do it.

"After his brilliant column in support, the city's political class caves — what else can they do? They authorize the money, the committee offers the designer his price, and the designer concludes that the people in Duluth are as ignorant as he suspected. He cashes the check and doesn't come to the groundbreaking or the opening. And so something really dreadful comes to pass, and it's not really anyone's fault. Also, it is everyone's fault."

"You make it sound inevitable."

"It's only nearly inevitable. That child is out there, and one day his voice will be heard. Some of us will leave town in disgrace." He smiled again. "Others can't wait."

They ate in a depressed silence for a while. Then Betsy asked, "Do you know Ian Masterson?"

He said, "Are you going to ask me if he's an important artist, a real artist, or one living in fear of the child's asking about his lack of clothing?"

"Well . . . yes."

"Why do you want to know?"

Betsy said, "I've met him, and he seems very nice, and very sincere about his art. From what I've seen of it on his website, his latest work seems strange but powerful. He's dating an employee of mine, who is very impressed with him. And, he seems to be very concerned about the murder of Robert McFey."

Stephenson frowned. "McFey? I don't think I've heard of him."

"He was a wood carver. He was murdered at the Art on the Lake fair in Excelsior."

"Oh, yes. Was that his name? An ugly thing to happen. But why is Ian Masterson concerned about the murder of this . . . rather ordinary artist?"

"Ian was a friend of Mr. McFey's, arranging for him to get money to live on, trying to get his gallery to represent him. I understand Ian has helped other artists, which is very generous of him."

"Artists like this McFey person or artists who actually might become important?"

Betsy held her breath for a few moments, until her temper cooled a bit. To speak dismissively of Rob McFey after the lecture he'd just given on charlatans, fakers, and children crying unheard in the wilderness disclosed a level of sophistication she hoped she never rose to.

"I don't know. Probably mostly on the McFey level."

"That was very generous of him." Stephenson finished his curry with deliberation, put his fork down on his plate, and said, "All right, in my opinion, Masterson is the real thing, well on his way to becoming an important artist."

"Is he making a lot of money with his art?"

"A fair amount, yes. But that's not always the mark of someone who will become important. Artists whose work today sells for millions often died in obscure poverty. For artists breaking new ground, that's practically a requirement."

"Yes, of course."

"Masterson started out like a lot of artists, trying different techniques, different approaches. He did some interesting work with stone and wood, then started welding metal shapes. But his early metalwork didn't last, mostly because he did his own welding and he wasn't that good at it. Which is probably just as well, it wasn't very good art, either. So he decided to start over, and get into great big pieces, made of the kind of beams you build skyscrapers out of. Most of it is still around — one reason, possibly" — he smiled — "is that you hire a foundry to put the pieces together, rather than do them yourself. He liked broadly simple shapes . . ." Stephenson sketched what looked to Betsy like an A or an N in the air with his hands. "Then painted them in primary colors. Not exactly original, but he made a splash with a couple of colorful interviews. Then he announced he wanted to cross Minnesota with a row of these big sculptures and he wanted — no, he *demanded* — millions of dollars to do it. He got really passionate, he said that if every child in Minnesota were to contribute a dollar, it would pay for the project." Stephenson smiled. "He said it as if he sincerely thought that the children of Minnesota would be honored to cough up a dollar apiece to cross Minnesota with these objects. He showed drawings — he called them 'crosses,' and since he was crossing the state with crosses, he came up with the name 'Double Cross.' "

Betsy laughed in surprise, and Stephenson nodded significantly. He went on, "The pieces looked less like crosses than immense jacks, like from the children's game, you know? Thirty feet high, they were. And he sounded as if he had most of the land rented and permits in place to complete the project, though he admitted he'd probably have trouble getting permission to cut a swath through downtown Grand Forks.

"Well, people took him seriously — some thought that it was a ridiculous waste of land and money, but he gathered a number of supporters who got angry at those who laughed at this amazing artist's vision. And he double-crossed both of them. It turned out his art project wasn't the giant crosses but a project to show two things: that some people will support any kind of art that ordinary people don't understand, and that people who reflexively sneer at public art don't understand what it's about."

Betsy said, "The voice of the child!"

Stephenson stared at her. "By gum!" he said and grinned. "But it was also a brilliant way to make himself known. And by the time the joke got out, he was famous. He was asked to put one of his 'crosses across Minnesota' in the Minneapolis Sculpture Garden." Stephenson was grinning now in fond remembrance.

"But he's doing something different now."

Stephenson nodded. "It doesn't take long to reach saturation with structures this size, and he very wisely got into something quite different. Much more subtle, complex, and interesting. Fantastic in execution, and a totally new direction. And because he already has a recognizable name, he's doing extremely well."

Betsy nodded. "I agree, it's really different from those girders. Were you surprised?"

"Ah. Interesting question. I suppose I was. But not greatly. Artists have been known to change direction, though often it's an evolutionary thing. But he changed rather abruptly from his original work, too. I don't know him well, I've only met him a few times. He's an interesting character, a self-seller with a great line. His big pieces were good — individual and strong. But not subtle, not . . . intellectual. This new stuff was intelligent *and* indi-

330

vidual. I wasn't blown away, because I didn't know him well enough to have carved my opinion of his abilities in stone. But it's nice to find a new artist who is versatile as well as good."

"I've heard he's now looking to go in still another direction. He's talking about kinetic sculpture."

Stephenson's eyebrows lifted. "Really. He hasn't done a great many of these new pieces, and to change again, so soon, might not be a good idea."

"Should I warn him of that?"

He actually blushed, and lifted both hands to ward off the idea. "No, no, no. I wouldn't presume to advise an artist of his caliber not to follow a new idea."

Betsy smiled at his discomfiture. "Artists don't strike me as particularly sensitive."

"Some are, some aren't. I don't know which he is, and it certainly isn't in my interest to find out."

"Thank you. You've reassured me about him. May I ask another question about art in general?"

"Certainly."

"Is there anything you can say about artists that is true of all of them?"

He smiled. "You do ask interesting questions." He thought for a bit. "All right, this may sound contradictory, but I think it's true nonetheless. Once artists get an idea, it overwhelms them and everything else in their life becomes secondary. You can rush into the studio of an artist at work shouting that his place is on fire, and you'll get, 'Uh-huh, uh-huh, be with you in a minute.' " Stephenson nodded his head, his eyes distant, hands holding an imaginary brush and palette. "On the other hand, they are very distractible. You are going with one to a fair, a play, picnic. You're in the mood to make love or serve a meal and she's right there with you until suddenly her eye is caught by some notion and she's off with her muse, sifting sand through her fingers, staring at birds in flight, muttering to herself and making a sketch on the back of an envelope. And you might as well repack the basket or put your clothes back on, because you've lost her for the next little while."

Betsy laughed. "I've seen stitching designers — even stitchers — who get like that."

Stephenson nodded. "I'll stand by my statement, but of course it's not exclusive to artists. I get like that myself when I'm restoring old silver, totally lost in the project."

Betsy said, "All right, another question: Is there something absolutely forbidden to artists? You hear of drunken artists, lazy artists, lecherous artists, unfaithful artists, cruel artists, even insane artists, all of them famous, even revered. Is there something an artist can do that puts him or her beyond the pale?"

"Now that's a tough one," said Stephenson. He rubbed his chin with a forefinger, pulled an earlobe, blinked, and frowned. Suddenly a triumphant smile appeared on his face. "Okay, one thing," he announced. "You can't steal another artist's work. You can be derivative — with the critics falling over one another to say who or what you're being derivative of, they love to find connections like that — but you can't directly copy another artist's work and say it's your own."

Betsy said, "So those exact copies of famous paintings that you can buy aren't really art. For example, I am totally in love with Impressionist art, especially Manet and Van Gogh. But there is no way I could possibly afford an original, and posters just don't do it for me. I'm looking to connect with one of those studios that will paint a copy for me down to the last brush stroke. Is that wrong of me?"

He shook his head. "No, of course not. But you're right, that isn't really art. They're replicas, copies, fakes. The first criterion for art is originality. And it has to be work done by the artist who signs it. All the same, you have good taste and there's no reason you shouldn't have a really good replica for your home."

Stephenson looked at his watch and made an exclamation. He made a hasty apology and left while Betsy paid the bill. On the drive home, she thought over that conversation. Theft was the unforgivable sin. The image of the raccoon burglar Deb had showed her appeared at the front of her mind and asked for some consideration. What was it Deb had said? Don't annoy an artist or a writer; they may immortalize you unflatteringly. Had someone stolen something from Rob McFey?

Chapter 19

The weather broke at last; Betsy woke the next morning to the sound of thunder. The storm didn't last long — before Betsy pulled an English muffin from her toaster, the rain-laden clouds had sailed away across the lake, leaving the town refreshed, the dust washed away, the trees and hedges looking new-made, the air sweet and cool.

But the sky remained a pale gray runneled with darker shades. A brisk breeze tumbled droplets of water off the leaves and eaves, a process that continued until pedestrians realized it wasn't leftovers but more rain.

Betsy, knowing she was going late to lunch, ate a hearty breakfast. She put an egg, scrambled with green pepper and onion, onto the muffin and nuked a strip of bacon in the microwave. She drank a big glass of grapefruit juice and a cup of English breakfast tea with sugar and milk.

"Ah," she said on rising from the table to put her cup, plate and glass into the sink. "Come on, Sophie, let's get downstairs; we've got a lot to do this morning."

An order she had placed with Tapestry

Tent had come in yesterday. She took a few minutes to look over the painted canvases by Liz, delighted that the patterns were even more beautiful than she'd hoped. But now she had to find room for them. One would go in the window for a few days as advertisement — but which one?

An hour later, she was pinning a big painted canvas stocking of Santa with a dark and weather-beaten face, a wreath of holly for the hatband of his cowboy hat, and silver concho buttons on his denim jacket. A stitcher could work on that at a picnic without feeling the wrench that came from working on something out of season — which stitchers were always doing, as elaborate projects like this often took six months or a year of work to complete. She made a mental note to find a source for silver conchos in case the buyer wanted to put them over the painted ones.

Godwin came in dressed entirely in pale tan — except for his white socks, of course.

"Another new outfit?" said Betsy, looking him over.

"John is being rather kind to me lately," said the young man smugly.

"Well, it's about time," said Betsy.

"You're looking very spiffy yourself," said Godwin, cocking his head sideways at her.

"Thank you." Betsy, afraid she wouldn't have time to go upstairs and change, had put on her matron-of-honor suit this morning. It was a deep spice color that looked good on her. And she'd taken some time with her hair as well.

"What's the occasion? A supper date with Morrie?"

"No, I'm meeting Jill at the Elks Club for a late lunch."

"What, they have a new dress code?"

"No, it's . . . kind of a celebration."

Godwin frowned at her. "Uh-huuuuh," he said, drawing the second syllable out long and doubtfully. "Come on, tell Uncle Goddy all about it," he coaxed.

"Remember what happened the last time I broke a confidence that involved Jill?"

"Oops," said Godwin, and he turned back to unboxing and sorting an order of Kreinik threads without another word.

The morning fled swiftly, and Godwin remained good. When someone asked him if he knew what Betsy was dressed up for, he looked around at Betsy as if noticing for the first time how fancy her suit was, then said, "Beats me," in a tone of studied indifference.

Betsy prepared to leave shortly after one. She said to Godwin, "Because you were so good, I'm going to warn you that I'll come back from this lunch with some very interesting news."

"About Jill?" he asked, his eyes hopeful.

But Betsy had learned her lesson and only left it at that.

The ceremony was performed in a small meeting room at the club, with — surprise! — Mike Malloy standing up for Lars. The judge had a kind, smiling voice and used a standard service from a small book. Jill and Lars took one another without a quiver or hesitation. When the judge said, "You may kiss the bride," Lars did so with so much circumspection that one might have thought it perfunctory if one didn't know the couple were not normally so pink or bright-eyed.

Betsy took a couple of pictures with her new digital camera, and then they went to lunch. Well, first Betsy and Jill retired to the rest room, where Jill took off her hat but not her corsage of small lilies and tiny orchids.

Betsy took her courage in both hands and dared to ask, "Jill, is there some special reason, other than being mad at the rules, that you're getting not-quite-married right now, today, to Lars?"

Jill took more time than necessary to dry her hands, and then said, with a sigh, "You're getting better and better at reading motives, you know that?"

"Then why don't I have the slightest idea what you're up to?"

"But you know there's something up, and that's more than even Lars knows. Let me tell you something that happened a couple of weeks ago. Lars was at home letting the steam out of his Stanley when he heard a call go out about a prowler — he has a radio in his garage tuned to police calls, did you know that?"

"No," said Betsy, smiling, "but I'm not surprised."

"Anyway, the location was about five hundred yards from his place out on Saint Alban's Bay Road, and he's been to the address three times in the last month on a domestic. The woman is trying to divorce her husband, who keeps coming over to break windows and generally make her life miserable. But it's been escalating; last time he burned down her garage. So of course it was important that we get there fast. And Lars decided that since he was so near, he'd go. He was on his way up the road when he thought maybe he'd better call in to say what he was doing — and the battery on his cell phone was run down. But did he turn back? Not him. And I almost shot him."

She said this so quietly, so matter of factly, that Betsy almost missed it. *"What?!"*

"I almost shot him."

Though Jill tried to repeat it in the same tone, this time there was a very slight tremble in her voice. "Do you want to tell me about it?" asked Betsy.

"Jim was out on a call, Frank was on patrol, and Mike was fishing up in Alex. We called other jurisdictions and were getting arrival times of ten and fifteen minutes. And

Lars hadn't called in, so we didn't know he was on his way over there. The woman was screaming into the 911 operator's ear that he had a gun. So I grabbed a vest and said I'd go. I had to use my own car, so there was no siren to scare him off. I pulled up on the shoulder of Saint Alban's by their driveway and started up it. And I heard someone crashing through the woods off to the left, headed toward the house. I started angling toward him, and saw someone with what I thought was a gun in his hand. I braced" — Jill illustrated by holding both hands clasped in front of her — "and I was ready to shout and, if he turned toward me, shoot, when I got a whiff of kerosene and that nasty boiler oil." Jill lowered her arms. "I went to an arson fire set in a garage one time. It smelled something like that. He smelled something like that. Actually, *I've* smelled something like that, after being out for a ride with Lars." Her voice changed timbre. "It was Lars and — well, I had to go down on one knee to keep from falling on my face. If Lars hadn't gone over there straight from messing around with that stupid steam car, I might have shot the man I love."

"Oh, *Jill!*" said Betsy.

Jill nodded, and Betsy saw there were tears in her eyes. "Then and there, I decided something had to be done. I don't want one of us to die without leaving the other a

340

widow." With an effort, she managed not to let a sob escape. "Is that stupid, or what?"

Betsy came to Jill and put a hand on her arm. She wanted badly to embrace her, but Jill wasn't a hugger. She felt an enormous pity for this woman who so suppressed her feelings that they could only come out sideways like that. And at the exact same time an enormous pride in Jill, who made her way deftly through the land mines of her life without screaming about how victimized she was.

"That's the least stupid thing I've heard in a long time," Betsy said. "And I'm so glad you thought of this solution to the no-frat rule!"

Jill reached over to touch Betsy's hand. Her shiny-new, broad gold wedding ring gleamed on one finger. "Thank you," she said. "Now we'd better get back out there."

Betsy had the chicken salad for lunch. Lars, puffed up like a blowfish, could not take his eyes off Jill. And Jill glowed like a candle under his regard. Betsy thought that Father John had better find a hole in his calendar soon.

Mike, sitting next to Betsy, said, "How's the investigation going? Circling in on anyone?"

He said it lightly, but the fact that he asked made Betsy ask in return, "Are you maybe not so sure it's Mickey Sinclair anymore?"

"I am sure," he said with a short nod. "He's a punk from way back, and he needs to do some hard time."

"I can't disagree with you," said Betsy. "He's a liar with a bad attitude and a larcenous soul. But I don't think he's a murderer. Have you talked with him lately?"

"No. I think his attorney is working on him to cop some kind of plea. It won't work; this isn't some jerkoff who got killed. And it happened in the course of another crime, a felony, which bumps it up to murder one."

"I think the murder had already happened when Mick came along."

"Oh, yeah? Two separate criminals happening along at the same time?"

"Things like that happen. How many times have the police arrived at a disaster and had to run off the thieves busy picking the pockets of the victims?"

"Yeah, but they're just amateur thieves, taking advantage of an opportunity. Like when the back door of an armored truck opens up and twenty-dollar bills go scattering along the freeway. Some gather them up and turn them in, some don't stop, and some think of them as a bonus for being in the right place at the right time. Professional thieves will make an opportunity."

"Still, it takes a certain hard-heartedness to go poking through a dead man's pockets, surely," said Betsy.

"Oh, I agree that's different, going through a dead man's pockets."

Betsy nodded. "Okay, but stealing is stealing; it's only a matter of degree."

Mike nodded back. "And nerve. Me, I'm too busy trying to hang on to my dinner when I come across something gross to think about dipping into a pocket."

Betsy looked across the table at Lars and Jill, lost in their own conversation. How nice to think that something gross was averted in their case. And led directly to this very pleasant occasion.

"Lars," she said, and he looked over at her, eyebrows raised in inquiry. "Did you drive out here in your Stanley?"

"Yep," he said. "Gonna take my bride for a ride."

Jill smiled at Betsy. She hadn't liked the machine when Lars first bought it, but Betsy knew now she would never again complain about its peculiar ways and bad smells.

Back at the shop, Godwin was waiting with six customers, all of them agog for the news. Betsy, glad she wasn't going to disappoint them, laughed at their eagerness and said, "Officer Lars Larson and Sergeant Jill Cross were married today. They are very happy, and I'm happy for them."

Godwin gaped satisfactorily, and most of the customers cheered — one or two didn't

343

know the happy couple. They all slowly cleared out, revealing Shelly waiting impatiently. It was not a day she was scheduled to work, and she didn't have any needlework materials in her hand she wanted to buy. "I'm not telling you anything more about the wedding," warned Betsy.

Shelly laughed. "No, I want to show you something." She dipped into her purse and came up with some computer printouts of photos taken with a digital camera. "Here, look at this."

Obediently, Betsy took the sheets and looked at them. They appeared to be of a very large puppet made of sheet metal suspended on wire cables. The figure was of a nude woman, her figure voluptuous, her pose graceful. A length of very thin material had been wrapped across her breasts and around her upper thighs. A gentle breeze must have been blowing, since a streamer of the fabric was lifted into a graceful line.

The second picture was taken from a slightly different angle — no, it was the same angle, but *the figure had moved.* The pose was more sensual. Betsy looked inquiringly at Shelly, who nodded vigorously. "Isn't he wonderful?" Shelly said.

Betsy looked again at the photos. "He did say he wanted to make a kinetic sculpture. Is this it?"

"More like a study or a model," said

Shelly. "The final piece will be jointed differently, and about ten feet tall. It's supposed to hang outside so the wind can make it change poses. What do you think?"

Betsy thought she knew Shelly, but the Shelly she thought she knew couldn't possibly be pleased to think the general public would someday be staring at her naked self doing a bit of dirty dancing. But it was not her place to say so. "It's . . . interesting," said Betsy, the standard Minnesota reply to a question one didn't want to answer honestly.

"Look at the next one," said Shelly.

On the next sheet was a picture more like the sculptures Betsy had seen on Ian's website. It was of an old man peering forward, as if straining to see. His ancient skin had as many folds as the loincloth he wore. He held a lantern high in one hand. The patina had come out wrong, thought Betsy. Instead of an effect as of light coming from the lantern, it was as if the lantern had spilled soot all over the old man on that side.

Betsy studied it for a minute. "It's really nice," she said. And it was, but it was somehow different from the ones she'd seen on the website. The figure was more explicit, somehow. Apparently Ian's excitement over the kinetic sculpture had started him thinking differently about his style. It more nearly resembled the veiled dancer than it did the angry child.

"There's not a strong expression on the face of the man," said Shelly.

"Well, yes, now you point it out," said Betsy. The man looked lost, or maybe just sad, it was hard to tell. And that was the big thing that was wrong with it; the other sculptures expressed powerful, unmistakable emotions.

"Ian's not satisfied with this," said Shelly, coming to look over Betsy's shoulder. "But they're really anxious for it, so he's shipping it off today."

"It will be interesting to see if this commands as big a price as the others."

"Well, why shouldn't it?" asked Shelly, surprised.

"Yes, why shouldn't it?" echoed Betsy. Shelly nodded, satisfied, and went back to admiring the photos of the kinetic sculpture. But Betsy was thoughtful for the rest of the afternoon.

Chapter 20

Mickey's attorney called the next morning to say the boy had been moved to adult jail. Mr. Wannamaker was going to see him, and Mickey had asked to see Betsy. Did she care to come along?

Betsy did indeed. Godwin sighed and pretended to be overburdened at being left alone in the shop, but his hurt feelings were suspiciously easy to soothe with a promise to let him know what the Sinclair boy had to say for himself.

Mickey was looking a lot less sullen than he had the last time. In fact, he had that starey look of someone who has lost everything in a tornado or revolution. Adult jail is not a pleasant place to be. He sat in the plastic chair across from his attorney and Betsy and said — to her, not to him, "Please, help me."

Betsy said, "I absolutely can't do that unless you stop lying to me."

"I'm not lying . . ." he began with a whine, but she gestured at him to stop it.

"You were in the park. You and your friends Thief and Noose went there to look for something to steal. You wanted to sell it so you could buy marijuana."

Mickey's attorney said warningly, "I am not hearing any of this."

"Of course not," said Betsy. To Mickey, she went on, "You separated in the park, and not long after, you called Thief's cell phone from home to tell him you had copped some money and for him to bring Noose over."

"No, you're wrong, I never —" began Mickey, but Betsy was rising to her feet and he stopped.

"If you tell me again you weren't in the park, I am going to leave, and I won't be back."

Mickey looked at his attorney for advice, but Mr. Wannamaker had gone into resting mode behind his expensive eyeglasses and didn't even return the look. Mickey opened his mouth and closed it as he thought of various lies he might try, only to discard them unvoiced. Finally he shrugged and said sullenly to his hands on the table, "All right, I was in the park."

"And you took the money from the cash box in Mr. McFey's booth."

Very quietly, almost with relief, "Yes." Betsy sat down and Mickey raised his eyes and started, "But . . ." He stopped, with a desperate look that said that even though he was going to tell the truth, she wouldn't believe him.

"But Mr. McFey was already dead when you got there," she said.

His whole face lit up. "*Yes!* I thought nobody was in there. I didn't see him until I was already in the booth and, and, I looked down and I was standing in blood." His face echoed the sickening distress he must have felt at the time. "It was all over the place, like a mud puddle, only . . . And I didn't know what to do. There was this dead guy, and I didn't do it. I mean, he was really dead. I would've yelled for help, if I'd thought . . ." His eyes slid sideways, a sign he was edging away from fact. Then they came back, and he continued, "But he wasn't moving or breathing or anything. And, and, well, there was this money, and I needed the money."

"So you took it," said Betsy.

"Well, it was like, I mean, he's dead, he don't need it anymore, right?" He took a breath and said all in a rush, "So okay, I took it and I tried to wipe my shoe off in the booth but it wouldn't come off so I ran through the rain outside but the grass didn't brush it off, it was still there, it even spread up on the shoelaces somehow. So I took them off and I threw them in this big trash bin behind the guy selling pork chops." He paused long enough to swallow, relieved at having gotten past the really bad part. In fact, he waxed indignant. "Who knew they'd find them? What kind of cop goes digging in the garbage, anyhow?" He waned a little under her sardonic look.

"Anyway, I went home and I called Thief and he came over with Noose and I told them where I got it, and they didn't believe me, that I saw a dead man. I was like, well, catch the news on TV, homies. And Thief went, maybe it's true, there was cops and the fire department at the park. I gave them each twenty dollars, which they took, no problem, and they left." The habitual whine came back. "And I just got the rest hid in my closet when the doorbell rings and it was the cops. I didn't even get to spend any of it."

Betsy said, "I believe you."

"Thank you," he said, chin up, as if he'd done a noble act.

"Now, think hard: Did you see or hear anyone as you came up to the booth initially?"

He frowned at her, reluctant to revisit the event. But after a pause while he thought, he said, "No. Probably not. I don't know. I was walking kind of slow, you know, just looking around . . ." He humped his shoulders up and down, nodding, an innocent kid taking an innocent stroll.

"Uh-huh," said Betsy.

"Okay, okay. But wait, I must not've seen anyone. 'Cause if I would've, I wouldn't've gone in the booth."

★ ★ ★

At home that night, Morrie and Betsy had a quiet dinner. Morrie, a retired police detective, was tall and thin, with a long, narrow jaw and kind eyes. She told him about seeing the Sinclair boy.

"You think he's telling the truth now?" Morrie asked.

"Yes. He is not a sweet, innocent child, even his parents know that. But now I'm certain he did not murder Rob McFey."

"Why did you doubt it in the first place? The evidence was strong. And it's gotten stronger."

"Well, for one thing, when I offered to believe he didn't do it the first time I saw him, it was like striking a match in the dark. His eyes fairly blazed at me, and not with surprise, but with hope."

Morrie nodded, but it was with a cop's "just the facts" skepticism.

"Well, that's not all, of course. But once that seed of doubt was planted, it made it possible to realize that the evidence Mike had was flawed. For example, I heard 'fingerprints on the cash box, fingerprints on the cash box' but never anything about fingerprints on the knife. So I thought maybe there aren't any fingerprints on the knife. Mike did let you look at the file, didn't he?" Though retired from the police department, Morrie maintained his relationships with various members of local constabularies, and so was sometimes able to help Betsy find things out.

"Not he. I am retired and therefore no better than any civilian." He smiled into her disappointed eyes and said, "But Jill did. And yes, the knife handle was wiped clean."

"I thought so," she said, with satisfaction.

"So he wiped one but not the other. So what?"

"Now, I have never killed anyone, but it seems to me that if I stabbed someone, especially out of fear, the first thing I'd do is drop the knife. And then, if I recovered enough to decide to steal the money I came for in the first place, and if I remembered to wipe my fingerprints off the cash box, that would remind me to wipe the knife off, too."

"Maybe he went to wipe the knife first, and was interrupted by someone coming along and didn't have time to wipe the cash box as well," suggested Morrie.

"Maybe, but if I had the cash box in my hand and suddenly remembered about fingerprints, I'd wipe the thing that reminded me first."

"Still."

"Yes, all right, maybe he put the money in his pocket and went to wipe the knife blade first. He's not the bright and well-organized type." She wiped her own fingers on a napkin. "So you're thinking that if Mickey is guilty, then the order of the crime was that he went for the cash box first because Rob McFey wasn't there."

"Yes, and Mr. McFey came back and caught him at it."

"Okay, suppose. He's got the money and is thinking about wiping the cash box when Mr. McFey comes in. And he panics and grabs a knife and stabs him."

"Yes, that sounds right."

"And then he wipes the knife — but not the cash box."

"Maybe someone came along about then and frightened him off."

"Maybe. But if the murder was done in a fit of panic," said Betsy, "then it would be more likely he'd drop the knife and run, and there would be fingerprints on the knife. Or having dropped the knife in horror, he then recovered enough to rob the cash box and, being a cool customer, wipe it down — in which case, he'd remember to go back and wipe the knife off as well. But then there'd be no prints on either the box *or* the knife handle. I dunno, it seems more likely to me that, if there were prints on only one item, they'd be on the knife, not the cash box."

"Maybe he was interrupted a second time, by someone coming by."

"Yes," said Betsy. "Yes, that could be."

"Or maybe he was wearing gloves."

"Then there wouldn't be fingerprints at all. Both Irene Potter and I remember him skulking around with what seemed intent Sunday morning. But he wasn't wearing gloves."

"Well, of course not," said Morrie, amused. "They were in a pocket. And he took them off to get the money out, because it's hard to do fine motor movements while wearing gloves."

"So he didn't wear them while rifling the cash box, but when Rob came in and caught him, he put them on hastily before picking up the knife and stabbing him."

"That is a rather difficult scenario to imagine, isn't it? So all right, he went in there wearing gloves, and McFey came in, so he stabbed him. Then he took them off to rifle the cash box, and didn't think to wipe his prints off before running away."

"Well, maybe," conceded Betsy. "But then where are the gloves? If he wore them to stab Mr. McFey, then he would have thrown them into the Dumpster with his shoes, wouldn't he?"

"Hmmmm," said Morrie.

"And if he was thoughtful enough to bring gloves along, why did he have to use one of Rob's own knives?"

"Because he's a thief, not a murderer. The gloves were an attempt not to leave finger-prints on the cash box, not to avoid finger-prints on a murder weapon. Or maybe he did have a knife in a pocket, but when he saw

Rob's knife right there so handy, a knife that couldn't be traced back to him, why, he just used it instead."

"I doubt if Mickey's bright enough to think of all that, especially when there's an open cash box within reach. When I talked to him today, there was something about him that just yelled that he was telling the truth at last. I really don't think he did it."

"All right, here's the big question: Who?"

"Yes, that is the big question. I thought it might be a man named Banner Wilcox, but he's got a wonderful alibi: standing in a church hall full of people he knows, having coffee after service." Betsy fell silent. She absently forked up another bite of lasagna, even though she was always promising herself she was going to stop eating as soon as she wasn't hungry anymore.

"Penny?" said Morrie.

"Hmm?" She swallowed, saw where her hand was, and put the fork down.

"For that thought you're having."

"Oh, there's this local man who's getting to be an important artist. He's eccentric in a very charming way — Shelly's dating him and is very taken — and he does some interesting things with metal. He's also generous, especially to struggling artists, loaning them money. He bought a viatical from the man who was murdered at the Art in the Park fair, Rob McFey."

She paused but Morrie only nodded, his light blue eyes keenly interested. "I know about viaticals," he said. "I've often thought they'd make a wonderful motive for murder."

"Yes, I did, too, when I heard about this one. But it turns out Ian wasn't anxious about the money. Still, I wonder if he ever forgives a loan. There was another artist who died in a fire — it wasn't arson," she said, "the fire wasn't suspicious or anything. But Ian said he had given the guy some money and got a mortgage on the guy's house, which burned down. All he got out of it, he said, was an oxyacetylene torch and some scrap metal. But there's something about that whole deal that makes my brain itch. I wish I knew what it was."

"What could it be?"

"I don't know, that's what bothers me. I wonder if the land the house and studio stood on went to Ian, too, or if the mortgage was just on the building. I wonder who has the land now. I wonder if Rob McFey knew the dead man's heir, if there was one. I wonder if there isn't some kind of broker out there, putting artists with money together with artists who need it."

"You wonder some strange things, Kukla," he said.

"I know," she sighed. "And I'm like a computer whose hard disk is damaged. I think there's an idea in there somewhere, but I can't get at it. And I can't get it off my mind. I'm sorry, I'm turning into bad company. Could you either go home or sit here and read while I go Google something?"

He looked at her, his expression sympathetic. "Do you want me to go home?"

She smiled at him. "No. But I don't know how long this will take."

"May I sit behind you and make encouraging noises?"

"Sure. You may even see something I've been missing." So they went into the spare bedroom that was also Betsy's office. She sat down at the desk and booted up.

She decided that she first needed to know was more about the artist who had died in the fire. What was his name? Oscar or Omar, or something like that, Shelly had said. First name Benedict or Gregory. Google.com was amazing; she asked for obituaries in Minnesota nine to twelve years ago and it promptly linked her to newspaper archives and several genealogical sites. But she couldn't find any dead man with a surname Oscar or Omar, or anyone dead during that time whose first name was Gregory or Benedict.

"How could Shelly confuse Benedict with Gregory?" Morrie asked.

"Well, she said it was some Pope's name."

"Probably not Pius," said Morrie.

Betsy snorted in amusement. "Or John or John Paul, she'd remember those," she said.

"Gregory and Benedict were not only Popes, they're saints," Morrie pointed out. "How many other Popes are also saints?"

"I'll ask Google."

The list was surprisingly short. "Sylvester, I'll bet," said Betsy. And sure enough, one Sylvester Osman died in a fire near Farmington in Dakota county, south of the Cities, four years ago. The fire was caused by faulty wiring. A fireman had broken his hand fighting it. A poke into genealogy records indicated Sylvester Osman's cousin, Wilmar Osman, inherited the land and sold it to a developer.

"So what does all that prove?" asked Morrie, tickling the back of Betsy's neck with his breath.

She drew up her shoulders and he sat back. "I don't know," she said. "But I'm sure there's something in here that's important." She thought hard. "But I just don't see it. Maybe the itch will go away if I ignore it. No, no, there's something . . . Nuts, my head is stuffed with cotton, hay, and rags."

"Then tell it to go to Hartford, Hereford, and Hampshire," he said, recognizing the reference. "Come out to the kitchen and serve that dessert you promised me."

"All right."

She got the ambrosia out of the refrigerator, a stirred-up mix of Jell-O, grapes, chunks of mandarin orange, pecans, and

Kool Whip. But she didn't talk much while they ate it; she was feeling tired and distracted. She put the bowls in the sink and sent Morrie home so she could go to bed.

At three she jumped awake with the tail end of a bad dream drifting inexorably away before she could catch hold of it. It had featured angry people marching at her, kerchiefs around their faces, fists upraised, shouting something . . . U.S. Out of Mexico? Something impossible like that. What did it mean? She shook her head and lay back down. But convinced there was a clue in that dream, she couldn't get back to sleep; so she got up and went into the living room, sat down, and took out her cutwork. Buttonholing around the endless curves of leaves and petals soothed her ruffled mind, but it didn't give her any fresh ideas. She finished the second side of the pattern and decided she would put tiny seed pearls in the centers of the flowers. But she couldn't find the little packet of them, and so gave up and went back to bed.

Chapter 21

But while Betsy slept, some part of her brain must have kept working, because when she woke next morning, it was with a clear head and some urgent questions. After she had brushed her teeth and fed the cat, she dug out the papers from her volunteer work on Art on the Lake, and phoned Deb Hart.

Deb's first reaction was a slightly grumpy, "What? What?" Because it was barely six-thirty. Then, when Betsy explained, there came a more conciliatory, "Well, yes, I suppose it could be. In fact, now you ask me, yes, I think so. But how strange. Okay, I'd put off sending the slides back another day."

Betsy didn't explain, but thanked her, then phoned Shelly at home. "I know you're working here today, but this can't wait. Are you and Skye still getting along?"

"Of course we are. In fact, I've agreed she can come over once a week, more often if her mother gets difficult. Honestly, that woman! But Skye's really a sweet child under all that goth nonsense. I like her a lot."

"What has she told you about Ian and Rob?"

There was a pause on the other end of the line. "That's a funny question."

"I know, and I'm sorry, but it's kind of important."

"All right. He was a friend of her father's, and Skye adored her father, poor thing. Ian is a famous artist and his show of interest in her father was very flattering. She wants to study art and she's proud to know him."

"Is Ian arranging to sell her father's carvings?"

"Oh, that. Yes. He's talking to his studio in Santa Fe about it, Marvin Gardens. But it takes a while to work that out, you know. And anyway, they might not do it, even as a favor. So Ian is also looking into getting Robbie's work into an art auction, one that's well publicized."

That sounded more like something Shelly knew directly from Ian, rather than something Skye had told her. "Does Skye have any of her father's work, or did she turn everything over to Ian?"

Another hesitation. "Well, Ian said he needed everything, to make up as big a collection as possible . . ."

Betsy bit her top lip to keep silent, and after a wait, Shelly conceded, "But she did keep a couple of pieces. She doesn't want Ian to know."

"Was one the peacock setting fire to its own tail with a blowtorch?"

"No . . ." Shelly suddenly giggled. "Oh, gosh, that *has* to be Ian, right? She didn't mention that one, I guess because she knows I'm kind of funny about Ian."

"Yes," said Betsy.

"Well, she doesn't have that piece. A peacock, setting fire to its own tail, what a riot!" Shelly laughed.

"So that isn't one of the pieces Skye has?" persisted Betsy.

"No. She's shown me what she has. In fact, they're here; they are just little things, but she's afraid her mother might take them away from her." Shelly described them. "The gawky giraffe is her brother, of course."

Betsy, relieved she wouldn't have to ask Skye for them, asked Shelly to bring them with her when she came to work.

"But she doesn't want anyone to know about them."

"I'm not going to keep them. And I'm not going to tell her mother about them. Shelly, it's important."

Shelly came in a little before ten with the pieces wrapped in several layers of Kleenex. "What's this all about?" she asked as Betsy uncovered them. But her face showed she was halfway to suspecting, and Betsy made her sit down with a cup of tea while she explained.

"No," said Shelly flatly when Betsy had finished. "You are *so* wrong, Betsy, you are going to be sorry you even thought about that, I promise you."

"I'll be relieved to discover that, believe me. But it fits, don't you see? It fits."

"So what are you going to do?"

"First, call Sergeant Malloy. Then I think . . . No, first of all, could you call Ian, and see if he'll come to lunch? Then we'll call Mike."

"What about Skye?"

"Not yet. We'll talk to her after we talk to Ian."

"All right."

Ian said he had some phone work to do, but could come in for a late lunch. Shelly, hanging up, her face a study in grief, said, "I really think you should let me talk to Skye now. I don't want to spring this on her without any warning."

But Betsy was adamant. "Not yet," she said. "Please, not yet."

Ian turned up late, claiming to be hungry as a wolf after a hard winter. "I understand I'm taking you both to lunch, is that right?" he said, indicating with one raised eyebrow and peculiarly direct look all sorts of possibilities in that question.

"Perhaps we should ask Shelly if she minds if I come along," said Betsy, with a very direct look at Shelly.

Ian glanced at Shelly, a teasing smile on his lips, then saw her distress and immediately shifted his tone. "Do you really mind, sweetheart?" he asked, his voice now only friendly. He reached out to Shelly, who came immediately to hug him.

He looked down at her, surprised. "I didn't know you were the jealous type," he murmured. "It's kind of sweet, if you are."

"Of course I'm not," she said into his shirt. But the frown didn't go away.

"A headache, maybe?" He stroked her forehead with a forefinger.

"A little one, I guess," she said, and pushed away from him. "Let's go."

"Of course." He turned to open the door for them.

Sol's Deli was a few steps away and they went in silence. Again he held the door and they went in ahead. It was nearly two, so there were no customers lined up at the slant-fronted counter.

Inside, there were two small, marble-topped tables with wire-backed chairs. The one nearer the door was occupied by a man in a suit and a police officer in uniform.

"Hi, Mike," said Betsy, nodding as she went past. Shelly didn't say anything; Ian nodded briefly.

Malloy acknowledged them with a little wave and went back to his sandwich, a thick mix of cheeses and processed meats. The uniformed cop had a meatball sandwich.

Betsy ordered a salad, as it was easier to

talk around that. Shelly ordered a bowl of chicken noodle soup.

"I'll have your turkey sandwich, extra meat, and extra mayo," said Ian. He glanced at Shelly and added, "No onion," making it sound as if that were because he planned to be making mad, passionate love to her within the hour. Shelly's smile was a bit pained, and again he frowned. "You *are* upset about something," he said.

"No, no," she insisted, and caressed his hand. Her look was tender, and he leaned forward to kiss her at her hairline. Her eyes closed.

Betsy wished with all her heart this was just a simple lunch. But it wasn't, and what she knew must be shared, despite the pain. But not just yet. She determinedly stuck to trivialities until their food came.

When it did, the tension rose in her breast again, and blocked any appetite. She moved her salad around in its bowl and said, "Ian, tell me how you came to do those amazing metal sculptures that are so different from the big beams you used to do," she said.

"Have you seen them?" he asked, surprised.

"I went to your website. That one of the angry child is very touching."

He swelled just a little. "Thank you." He took a bite of his sandwich and thought while he chewed, then swallowed and said,

"It's not easy to explain. I had some hunks and strips of metal in my studio, something I rescued from Sylvester Osman's studio."

"He's the artist you helped with a mortgage," said Betsy, with a little nod. "I thought you said all you rescued from his studio was an oxyacetylene welder."

"That's all that was in its original state," he said. "A little smoky, but a good scrubbing cleaned it off, and there was no other damage. This metal had been in the heart of the fire, and it changed the surface somehow."

"Put a patina on it," said Betsy. She smiled. "See how quickly I pick up the terminology?"

He smiled back. "Yes. He'd apparently been planning to make something using the metal, from the way he'd cut it up. But any plans or models he'd made were destroyed in the fire."

"You're a liar, Mr. Masterson," said Betsy quietly.

"I am?" His mouth stayed open, his bushy eyebrows rose, but his eyelids dropped to half mast.

She nodded and said, "I think they weren't just random strips of metal."

The eyebrows came down and met in a hairy frown. He said, "Yes, they were. I took them home, because the patina on them interested me. And they were mine now. Whatever I could find in the ashes was mine, because of the mortgage. The welder didn't pay half what Osman owed me — but as it turned out, the plates did. Because I got to fooling around with them and came up with the idea of those figures. It was as if — as if . . ." He stopped, looking from her to Shelly and back again. "Is that's what's wrong here?"

"Yes. You're not only a liar, Mr. Masterson, you're a thief. And something worse than that."

Shelly began to cry. "Oh, Ian, tell her it isn't true!"

"What isn't true? I don't understand, sweetheart!" But he betrayed himself by looking over at the other table. Mike and the police officer had put down their food and were paying close attention. Ian twisted around and saw that the counterman had vanished into the back. Alarmed now, he looked at Betsy. "What is this?"

"I am sorry, Ian. I wanted for Shelly's sake for this not to happen, but you're going to be arrested for the murder of Rob McFey."

He produced a patently false grin. "I thought we agreed that the viatical I bought from him wasn't any kind of a motive. Anyhow I wasn't in the park on Sunday, I told you that."

"You said you were there on Saturday," said Betsy, reaching into her purse. "And perhaps you were. But you were there Sunday, too. Look at this." She pulled out a photocopy of a sketch, a reduced version of the caricaturist's sketch given to Mike Malloy. Mike had brought it to her on his way to Sol's Deli. She unfolded it now and handed it to Ian. He looked it over and shrugged. "What?"

"It was done on Sunday — see the raindrops? It didn't rain on Saturday." They were indicated on the sketch by broken diagonal lines. "And in the bandshell, back row, second from the left."

Shelly leaned sideways for a look. She took a quick breath, but didn't say anything. The figure in back, second from the left, was a hippie, a tall, stocky man whose long hair was pulled back into a ponytail. Mostly hidden by the woman in front of him was a hand with a bandage on it. Ian put his bandaged hand into his lap.

"That's why there were no fingerprints on the knife," said Betsy, noting the movement.

Ian bit his bottom lip. "I didn't do it," he said in a low voice. He looked at Shelly. "I really didn't do it," he repeated.

Shelly said, "I don't think I believe you."

"Why not? This is ridiculous! Why would I kill Robbie? She doesn't know what she's saying! How can she? She's not even a private eye, much less a cop!"

Betsy said, "But I do know what I'm

saying. I don't think you went there with any intention of killing him, Ian. But you did — and I'm sure it wasn't necessary; I can't believe he really would have sent the little caricature of you."

Ian widened his eyes. "What caricature, the one of me setting my peacock tail on fire?" He snorted.

"No, this one." Betsy went into her purse again and this time came out with one of Rob McFey's little basswood animals. It was of the robber raccoon with the sack hanging down his back.

Ian stared at it. "Where did you get that?" he whispered.

"Skye had it, and showed it to Shelly. This is the raccoon you were so worried that Shelly had seen the first time you came into my shop, isn't it? I woke up this morning with a curious notion, and I phoned Deb Hart to ask about the slides Rob sent of his work. She still has them, and one of them includes this one. I'd seen it during the jury process, and Deb showed it to me again a couple of days ago. You see, it's not a burglar's cudgel sticking out of the raccoon's sack, it's a little arm with a fist at the end of it. We thought it was just a raccoon. They're a nuisance around here, they get into garbage cans and bird feeders and steal things off decks and patios. But all the other figures are people Rob knows. The lazy plumber possum, the weasel lawyer. So who was the raccoon thief? And why was there a fist sticking out of his sack of boodle?"

Ian did not answer. He was still staring at it, his interest fading into depression.

Betsy touched the tiny fist gently. "It's the arm of an angry child, from your metal sculpture. And here, look at the way he cut into the tail for the black bands, kind of emphasizing them. Like the way you do your hair, with three scrunchies."

"Well, so what? Yes, he made that, and yes, he said it was me, but it was a joke, because I got the metal I made it from out of the Osman fire. I didn't murder Robbie. That kid did it, they've got his fingerprints and everything."

"They found his fingerprints on the cash box, but not on the knife. There are no fingerprints at all on the knife."

"Yes, so see? You can't prove it was me."

"Someone told me he thinks maybe the murderer wore gloves. But I don't think he needed gloves, not when his hand was already bandaged."

Ian sighed and shook his head. "You're so wrong about this."

Shelly said, "Did you steal the little girl?"

He looked up at her, frowning. "I told you, I took the steel from the burned-down house. Robbie called it stealing, but it wasn't. They were mine, I had a mortgage."

"Yes," said Betsy. "But the steel plates were already assembled into that little girl. What about the crying woman and shouting man? Did you assemble *any* of those first pieces you sent to your gallery in Tucson? Or were they all stolen?"

"I tell you, I didn't steal them! I found the metal in the ashes of his place. Everything I found was mine."

Betsy nodded. "That's true. You could have kept the sculptures, or you could have sold them as the work of Sylvester Osman. But you said they were your work, that you were the artist who made them. And while the art world will forgive an artist anything else, they won't forgive that. You knew that. Rob McFey knew that."

"You're wrong," he said, but without strength. He looked at the raccoon, then at Shelly. "How come Skye had this piece?" he asked, trying for normalcy.

"You let her keep Coyne's caricature but you took the peacock from her. And you told her you were going to sell everything. She loved you, Ian, and she thought the raccoon was funny. She wanted it for herself — see how the face on this one sort of looks like you? Her father didn't explain the significance of it to her, that it was pointing to you as a thief of another artist's work."

Ian sat silent for a long while. Shelly took a breath to say something more, but Betsy put a hand on her knee under the table, and she kept still. Finally, Ian said in a low voice, "He told me he was going to send it to the Marvin. They had a big photograph of my angry child on the wall, they would have seen that raccoon and asked me about it. I can't duplicate Osman's work, though I tried. I even burned my studio down to get that patina. That worked, all right, but Osman's stuff isn't just the patina. He brought a passion to those pieces I can't duplicate. But you see, I have the name now, I have the fame, I could go back to doing my own work and they'd see I was just as good an artist as Osman. There was no harm done. See?" He turned to Shelly and repeated in a confident voice, "There was no harm done."

"Oh, Ian," murmured Shelly, and he immediately looked as bleak and hollow as his claim.

"How did Rob find out?" asked Betsy.

Ian grinned painfully. "I told him. We went out drinking to celebrate that damn lion and got really drunk. I wasn't sure the next day what I'd said, and I sure as hell hoped he wouldn't remember any of it. But then he produced that thieving raccoon. I laughed at it and said what's that about, and he said it was in memory of Osman, the poor bastard. I wouldn't have minded him keeping it around or even showing it to people who could never guess, but he said he was going to send it to Santa Fe with the other samples of his work. It was me that got him a chance at Marvin Gardens, and he was going to pay me back by ruining me. I came to the fair on Saturday and asked him not to send it, and he shrugged me off, saying he'd think about it. He'd been drinking and I thought it was the liquor talking. But he wasn't like the rest of us, he could drink all day and still be sharp. So I came back early Sunday morning and I told him, dammit, I couldn't have him sending it and I reached for it, but he grabbed it before I could. I was mad and scared and swung at him. He swung at me — he had that knife in his hand, and I got it away from him and — and I don't know exactly what happened. Next thing I knew he was on the ground and blood was pouring out of him. I ran out the back of the booth. I was wearing a dark brown shirt and pants and already wet from the rain so no one could see the blood on me. But this woman started looking at me funny, so I ducked into the band shell until she went away. I was halfway to my car when I realized I had the piece in my hand, which was a good thing, because I sure as hell wasn't going back for it. I burned it in my fireplace at home. Then damn it all, Skye told me he makes practice pieces even of those little things, and I was sick thinking there were other raccoons. We went to his apartment and I searched and searched and managed to get hold of a broken practice piece of it without Skye seeing me, and I thought I had everything."

He looked at Shelly, but couldn't bear her regard, so he looked at Betsy. "Now what? I assume those cops are over there for a reason."

"I'm afraid so," said Betsy. "You — you aren't going to make a fuss, are you?"

"In front of the one woman whose opinion I value above everything? No." He looked again at Shelly. "I am more ashamed of myself right now than I was the night after I killed Robbie, and that was a night in hell, I assure you."

"I suppose it must have been."

"Please don't turn your back on me."

"I . . . I don't know what I feel right now."

Mike Malloy's hand fell on Ian's shoulder, startling him. "I'm going to ask you to come with me now, Mr. Masterson," Malloy said. "You are under arrest for the murder of Robert McFey. You have a right to remain silent. Anything you say will be written down and may be produced against you in a court of law. You have a right to consult with an attorney before any questioning. If you want an attorney but can't afford one . . ." Ian shifted a bit at that and almost smiled. Malloy continued, "One will be provided for you at no cost. Do you understand these rights as I have explained them to you?"

"Yes, I do."

Mike lifted him to his feet by one arm, and the uniformed officer produced the handcuffs Mike used to fasten Ian's hands behind his back.

"Please . . ." Ian said to Shelly, but she turned her face away, and he, head down, went out the door with Mike and the uniform.

It was two weeks later. Shelly had come back to work after four days, saying she couldn't stand just staying at home. She was in the back, unpacking a pair of Prairie Scholar's Angels, models done for the shop to display. One was done in beads, and Betsy smiled to hear Shelly's exclamations of delight and envy. This was the first sign of pleasure she'd gotten from Shelly since the day Ian had been arrested.

Betsy was talking to Pat Maze, who had come to town for a needlework convention and stayed to visit friends. She came into the shop to show her collection of little Christmas stockings. One had a top of twin hearts done in bargello stitch, waves of color shading from maroon to pale pink. The rest of the stocking had a diaper pattern of diagonal lines, the diamond shapes formed by the lines filled with alternating rows of the asterisk-like stitch called the fancy cross, and a capital I. "It's called my heart's in Indiana," Pat was explaining. "But you can put an M for Minnesota."

"I haven't tried bargello stitch yet," said Betsy.

"People are surprised how easy it is," said Pat. "Look, I'm coming to Des Moines for CATS next year, and I'm teaching this pattern. Why don't you take the class, and if you like it, you can teach it. That's how easy it is. And of course, I hope you'll carry my patterns in your shop." She looked around. "It's a nice place."

"Thank you. I think I'll do that. Could I buy some of your patterns right now? I'd like to see if there's any interest."

"Sure." Pat sold Betsy two copies each of four patterns and left.

Shelly came out after Pat was gone and picked up one of the patterns. "Oh, I thought that was Pat! Isn't she nice? I took one of her classes a couple of years ago. She's a good teacher." She put the pattern down. "Can I talk to you about something?"

"All right."

But Shelly couldn't look at Betsy and say anything, so she turned away and spoke to a turner rack of overdyed silks. "I've been getting letters from Ian."

"Have you answered them?"

"No. But I want to. Am I being a fool? I really liked him — I more than liked him.

He says what he did was wicked — and he means stealing the Osman sculptures. He says what happened in Mr. McFey's booth that Sunday morning was an accident." She turned around. "Could that be true?" The hope in her eyes was indecent, and Betsy looked away.

"I can't answer that. I don't know."

"Oh, don't be Minnesotan now! I need a rude, flat-out opinion!"

Betsy turned back. "All right. At best, Ian Masterson is a greedy, immature thief who lost his temper in a very big way. At worst, he is a man so hungry for fame he'll steal to get it and murder to keep it. He saw those wonderful sculptures, and came to the same conclusion that Mickey Sinclair did about the money in the cash box: The rightful owner was dead, so whoever found it first could take it."

"He isn't like the Sinclair boy! How can you possibly say that?"

"He's worse than the Sinclair boy — he killed a man and was willing to let someone else take the rap for it. You asked for a rude opinion, and that's mine."

She saw the shock in Shelly's eyes and conceded, "Okay, in one regard he's a better person than Mickey: He says he's been living in hell and is ashamed of himself, which is more than Mickey will likely ever say. But that's not enough, Shelly; he killed a man who was his friend."

"He's not asking me to forgive him," said Shelly. "He just wants to know if he can keep writing to me."

"And he hopes someday you'll write him back, maybe come back under his spell. He doesn't deserve it, but if you want to play 'Stand by Your Man,' that's fine with me. In fact, if you do, you'll be the best thing that ever happened to Mr. Masterson, I don't care how rich or famous he was. Maybe prison will make him grow up — maybe it will coarsen him to where even you can't stand him. Maybe your standing by him will help prison reform him. But he's ruined as an artist, he'll never come back from the scandal. And it bites me no end that it's the theft of Osman's work, not the murder of Rob McFey, that has destroyed his reputation. Oh, and be reminded: Standing by him may injure your reputation as well. But here's something almost as important: Think what that child Skye, the daughter of his murder victim, will think of you for standing by Ian."

Shelly paled. "That was . . . not unfair. Not unfair." She pulled herself up to her full height. "Do you want me to quit my job here?"

Betsy blinked at her. "No, of course not. Why would I want you to quit?"

"You said . . . my reputation."

Betsy smiled. "It's your job as a school

teacher I'm concerned about."

"Oh. But you'll let me keep on here?"

"Certainly. Think of my reputation. Maybe your standing by Ian will counterbalance my penchant for sending people to prison. Come on, Shelly, how could you think otherwise?"

"Because . . . well, because . . . My God, I hadn't thought of Skye. She called yesterday and left a message. She wants to see me. What am I —"

"You'll tell her to come over, of course."

The door made its irritating *Bing!* announcement that a customer was coming in just as the phone rang. Betsy waved Shelly toward the door and picked up the phone. "Crewel World, Betsy speaking, how may I help you?"

Instructions for the Pattern

"CUTWORK"

Designed by Julie Norton and Denise Williams

Take this page to a copy shop, or scan it into your computer, and enlarge it to a suitable size. Tape the copy to a window and tape a piece of white cloth over the copy. Trace the pattern onto the cloth, using a soft pencil or some other marker that will wash out. If you will be using the cloth as a handkerchief or napkin, hem it. Using buttonhole stitch, stitch around all the edges of the leaves and flowers, paying particular attention to the outside edges and the lines surrounding spaces marked with a small x. Traditionally, cutwork is stitched with white thread on white fabric. Use small beads or French knots for the centers of the flowers. Cut out the segments marked with an x. The pattern may be cut out entirely and applied to a dress or blouse.